A Medieval Tale
First Lessons

Lina J. Potter

Translated by Elizabeth Adams

ISBN: 9781980565512

LitHunters, 2018

With thanks to:

I would like to offer my thanks to you dear reader for enjoying this adventure. If you like it then please leave a review and enjoy the rest of the series.

Contents

Chapter 10

Prelude

What does it mean to be happy?

Aliya stood on the train platform waiting for her parents. Her suitcase, full of presents for them, was pleasantly heavy in her hand. She didn't care that she'd had to work nights as a janitor in a supermarket in order to earn money to buy those presents. Any job was a good job, even if it didn't pay much.

For Aliya, happiness was going home to the small town where she grew up. That might not be enough for some people, but it was enough for her.

Aliya's father was an officer in the army, and her mother was a nurse. They had traveled from base to base, raised Aliya, and finally settled in the small town she called home. Aliya's mother, Tatiana, put her heart into her profession and taught her daughter to love it, as well. Aliya had chosen to go to medical school and was in her fifth year of training to be a surgeon specializing in abdominal surgery. When she finished, she planned to live and work at the military base where her father was posted. Her goal was to graduate and gain some experience before returning to her hometown. She liked it there. She also liked Alex, a handsome officer she was looking forward to spending the rest of her life with.

Aliya had a printout of her grades—all A's—folded in her purse, and she had just recently assisted with her first operation. According to the rules, she wasn't far enough along in her program to operate, but the surgeon kept a close eye on her, and the operation was a success. It was just a case of appendicitis, but she was proud of herself and couldn't wait to tell her parents.

She kept an anxious eye out for her father's old car, which soon enough came around the corner and parked. Her parents jumped out, and Aliya was hit with a wave of familiar joy. She was alive and healthy, and with the two people she loved best of all, and they were alive and healthy, too.

A quarter of an hour flew by before Vladimir was able to get his wife and daughter back in the car and turn the wheel toward home. Their overwhelming joy was interrupted halfway home when a large truck came roaring over a hill in the middle of their lane. Vladimir swung the wheel to avoid a collision and would have managed it if another driver hadn't stopped in the same spot on the shoulder to send a text just two hours before. That car left behind a large puddle of oil that sent their car skidding. It flipped several times before hitting a tree.

A last, despairing thought shot through Aliya's mind, Is this it? I don't want to die! I want to live! Then everything went dark.

With only the full moon for light, an elderly woman picked her way through the strangely quiet forest. She wore roughly made wooden shoes and carried a large basket.

In the moonlight, tree branches seemed like monstrous claws, and an owls' hooting filled her with blind fear. But the darkness did not dissuade her; she knew where she was going.

Finally, she reached a small hut in the center of a clearing. Cheery in the daytime but in the moonlight, the stream running by the hut became the river of the dead, and the garden seemed bare and empty. To the woman's eyes, the door to the hut looked like the jaws of a beast.

She took a step forward. There is no way back, she thought, scratching at the door.

Several minutes passed before it opened, and an old crone—like a fairytale witch—appeared in the doorway. Her gray hair fell uncombed around her shoulders, and a wart sat on her chin. Her once-white nightgown was dirty and patched. But it was her black eyes that distracted the old woman. They were bright, intelligent and surprisingly youthful, Like the eyes of a young girl, she thought.

"What do you want?"

The woman offered her the basket. "This is for you."

"I asked what you wanted." The crone made no move to take the basket. From out of nowhere, a large, white cat appeared at her feet, rubbing against her legs. It looked up at the woman with red eyes. In the wavering light from the hut, the cat seemed like an evil spirit that had come from hell to take her soul.

She did not retreat. "I want you to help My Lady."

"Help her? How?"

"You know all about it, Moraga. Lady Lilian has been in a bad way for three days now. Her childbed fever will take her to her grave. The doctor came and gave her a cleansing and let her blood, but the fever won't let go. I don't want her to die."

The old witch shrugged. "But what does your lady wish for?"

"She wants to die." The woman looked down. "I know she does, but I…"

The witch's face softened. "I understand. Even with all her faults, she's like a daughter to you. You love her. Let's see that basket."

"Yes. And this." As the woman took a purse from her belt, something in it jingled. "This is also for you."

"Good."

The witch didn't bother to look at her fee. She put her hand under the woman's chin and lifted her face so she could see her eyes.

"I will give you something—something strong. You will mix it with milk and give it to her to drink. Then, you'll need to sit by her bed and call her by name or call her by the name you used for her when she was small. Talk to her about anything, but keep talking. If she decides to live, she will come back to you."

"What if she doesn't?"

The corner of the witch's mouth twitched. "My remedy can bring a soul back into the body, but it won't work if the soul doesn't want to stay. Do you understand?"

The woman nodded.

"It all depends on you. If you get through to her, she'll come back. Otherwise, she'll be gone forever, and nothing will help."

The woman nodded again. "I will do it."

"Then wait here; I'll bring you the remedy."

The witch disappeared back into her hut, leaving the woman on the step. She was still afraid of the forest noises and the trees stretching out their claws to her, but she waited for the medicine, thinking of the walk back through the forest.

When I get home, I will do everything as the witch instructed. I don't want to lose my girl. I will call her name—Lilian, Lily, Baby. She'll come back to her old nanny. She just has to.

Chapter 1

Secrets and Lies

The first thing Aliya felt was pain.

And the second.

And the third.

Then she opened her eyes. The face hanging over her gave little cause for optimism. *She doesn't look like a nurse.* Aliya closed her eyes. She remembered the car flipping, the sound of her neck snapping. *I ought to be in the hospital,* she thought, knowing it would take at least a year of rehab to get back on her feet.

That means putting off my residency. She had been looking forward to it, especially since they had promised her a rotation in trauma. *I'm probably in the trauma department now—as a patient.*

She opened her eyes again. Why is there a dusty pink rag hanging over my head? And who is the lady with no teeth who keeps bending down over me? Is she asking me something?

"Has My Lady come around?"

The woman's breath was so vile that Aliya groaned and lost consciousness again.

෫ ◆ ౿

She felt a little better the second time she opened her eyes. She still hurt all over, but the pain was less. Aliya couldn't understand why her pelvis ached so badly after the car accident. She remembered hitting her head but nothing that would have caused injury to her lower half. *But who knows? Maybe I have a fractured pelvis. It hurts, for sure.*

The dirty pink rag was back above her head. The room stank of smoke and feces, but she didn't feel like fainting again…yet.

Aliya looked around the room, and what she saw made her doubt she was in her right mind. She must have hit her head so hard that she was hallucinating.

She lay on an enormous bed in the center of a large room that had to be at least as big as her parent's entire apartment. On one side of the room, a window showed her the forest beyond. On the other side, stood a massive set of wooden wardrobes, and in front of her bed, she saw a magnificent gilded door. Everything was pink. The walls were covered with fabric in a sickly pink color with huge gold flowers the size of cabbages. The curtains were a happy shade of pink. The wardrobes had been clumsily painted the same shade of pink with gold accents. The room was furnished with a writing table the color of a robin's breast with roses painted up the legs, as well as several armchairs, upholstered in the same fabric that was on the walls, and a couple of large vases full of live roses. Topping it all off— literally—was a dusty pink canopy, complete with gold bows hanging over the bed.

It's the perfect room for an unhinged Barbie doll. Aliya saw pink circles swimming in front of her eyes, but fainting wouldn't be so easy this time.

"My Lady!" The same face appeared again.

Aliya pulled together what strength she had left and breathed out a question. "Where am I?"

The words came out like "E… a… I?" It was a terrible attempt, but it was all she could manage.

Apparently, the nurse's aide *(Who else could she be?)* took that as permission to speak, and burst out, "My Lady, how glad I am that you've come around! You've been lying here three days. The healer came and said not to touch you. She said that your body would fight off death if it could. Otherwise, it would be your fate to follow your little one. Childbed fever has taken many women. We were afraid that the malady would get you, but we prayed hourly. With the Lord's help, you'll be back on your feet in no time. Would you like a sip of water?"

A giant cup made of a yellowish metal appeared under her nose. Could it be gold? Red stones glittered around the edge of the cup.

Aliya felt like a malfunctioning computer. Without thinking, she put her lips to the cold metal and took a sip. The water was delicious, and it was cold. *Tasty, clean water without a hint of chlorine.* It seemed to have been mixed with something like a cheap, boxed wine.

What is happening to me? Aliya was afraid to ask questions. As a doctor in training, she knew there were times that demanded action and times that required silence. Holding your tongue was always a good idea; she knew that for a fact. *You're never sorry for the things you don't say.*

Instead, she closed her eyes and frantically tried to think. Whatever else they have done to me, the gods have not deprived me of my ability to think.

She pushed to remember more of the accident. The truck was the last thing she saw. Her father yelled, then something hit her head, and her neck snapped. Then everything went black.

There was something in the darkness with me, but what was it? She didn't know. So, she began analyzing what she had learned from the nurse's assistant.

My Lady. She was obviously talking to Aliya, but ladies were all done away with in 1917, which was a mistake in Aliya's opinion. She would have to think about that later. For now, she was a Lady. *Where in the world do people still talk like that?* She had no idea.

She refocused. *You've been lying here three days.* After an accident like that, Aliya wouldn't be surprised if she'd been lying on her back in a coma for twenty years.

The healer had been there. What the hell kind of facility has healers instead of doctors and nurses? Even if I were in Africa, there would be Red Cross doctors, and this doesn't look like Africa. It's too cold, and the sky outside is gray. Healers aside, why did they wait for me to fight off my "malady" in the age of antibiotics? You just give your patient a mega-dose and watch the bacteria die off.

And what did the woman say about a little one? Did she mean a baby?
Aliya had only slept with Alex a few times over the holidays, and they had been extremely careful. She wanted to finish medical school, and he was expecting to be promoted to major, so they wouldn't get married until they reached those targets. Plus, she had had her period several times since then, right on schedule. *I would know if I were pregnant. So what "little one" is the woman talking about?*

However, if she'd given birth that would explain the severe pain around her pelvis. *But how is that possible?*

Aliya had two imaginable explanations for everything. The first was simple. She walked away from the accident, got married, got pregnant and gave birth, and now, because of the stress of postpartum fever and clinical death, she had forgotten everything since the accident and would have to start all over again.

There was a second explanation, but it seemed beyond belief… Her roommate at medical school was a Tolkien freak. She was into role-playing games and believed in parallel worlds, and her half of their room was littered with fantasy books and posters. Aliya knew how Ella would have explained these strange circumstances.

She would say I'm in a parallel world and have to find my way back. Aliyah shuddered at the thought. It defied all the logic instilled within her. And besides, if I am, indeed, in another world, I'll probably never find my way back! I'm much more likely to die a rapid death without antibiotics. Everything in this room is a potential germ factory—by the looks of it, the fancy cup I just drank out of has never been washed, and the old woman hasn't seen a bath in her lifetime.

In the end, Aliya decided not to say anything. That seemed the safest course of action. She remembered the Inquisition. *Those priests would have known exactly what to do with visitors from other worlds.* They'd test her to see if she was an associate of the devil, and that meant going for a swim with a heavy rock tied around her neck. If she managed not to drown, then she was guilty, and the devil had helped her. And if she did drown, they'd say, "Too bad, she must have been innocent. Let's pray for her soul and thank God for knowing best." *Fun times all around.*

What if this is all a bad dream? Aliya didn't want to drown or be burned at the stake, even in a dream—even as an act of faith. She didn't care what world she was in or what planet it was or what century. *Judging by the fact that there are no mirrors, it has to be no later than the 15th century.* She didn't care about anything but her health. She needed to sleep and get her strength back.

Sleep. Aliya gave a deep sigh and started counting sheep. She was asleep by the time the sixteenth sheep jumped the fence.

ജ◆ଔ

Aliya got her second shock when she woke again. After she opened her eyes, she drank some water and realized she needed to pee. Her trusty nurse, who stank worse than ever, pulled back the blanket and stuck some kind of medieval pot under her patient.

Aliya was about to protest until she caught sight of her body. *That. Is. Not. My. Body.* Her whole life, Aliya had had dark hair, olive skin, and gray eyes, and she'd never been over a size 8. *Which is a perfectly average size when you're five and a half feet tall.* But instead, lying on the sheet, which should have been washed a month ago, was a doughy, fair-skinned body that looked like it took a size 16 or more. The body's dirty nightgown had ridden up, and she saw that she was a natural blonde.

Aliya fainted dead away, but that didn't keep her from peeing in the pot.

ജ◆ଔ

When she opened her eyes again, the sun was up. She still felt awful. Her mouth was dry, and her head ached. She felt nauseous. And she preferred not to think about her perineum. If she had, in fact, given birth recently, the baby must have been a giant porcupine.

Someone was holding her hand and talking. "…Visa Hadson's ewe threw a two-headed lamb. The medicus, the same one who came to see you, went to look at it and said that he would stuff it and send it to the King's

Museum of Curiosities. By the way, he promised to check on you today. Oh, please don't die, my girl! Just don't leave me! I nursed you and carried you in my arms and raised you, and I raised your father, too! You're all he has, his only flesh and blood. And you're all I have. I know you want to go back to the earth as your mother did, but he won't survive without you. Your husband may be an earl, but he's a villain! Here his poor wife is on her deathbed after trying to give him a child, and he's back in the capital carousing with whores. I steeped a piece of gold in holy water for you so that you'd be even more beautiful after giving birth. Please get better, my precious angel! I can't stay here without you! Who would look out for me if you weren't here?"

The woman's words dissolved into unintelligible muttering.

Aliya didn't know anything about a Visa Hadson, but she assumed it was a person. She (or he) has a sheep, which makes her (or him) a person, right? The medicus (Is that a colleague? Why "medicus" instead of "doctor"?) is planning to stuff it and send it to the King's Museum of Curiosities, which makes no sense because if I'm still in Russia where I belong, there have always been tsars instead of kings.

"I raised you" (she must be a nanny or a wet nurse) "and I raised your father, too." Aliya was sure that her father had never had a nanny. He had grown up in an orphanage. "You want to go back to the earth as your mother did." But my mother is alive, and my father is just fine. At least, as far as she remembered after the accident.

In an instant, it all came together. She was in someone else's body in a completely different world. Apparently, I have a husband who is an earl and a royal jerk. Just what I need. So, my job was to give birth, and he doesn't care too much whether I live or not. He could find a new wife; earls are always in demand.

There wasn't much more she could deduce from what she had heard. Aliya made a decision. She could stay in bed as long as she liked, but judging from the sound of crying, there was at least one person in this world who loved her. If she got up, she could make this woman happy and perhaps learn some more about where she was.

Strangely enough, with that decision, her head was completely clear. Aliya opened her eyes and whispered, "Nanny."

That was enough. The old woman leaped from her stool like someone had poked her with a needle. She smiled with all eight of her teeth.

"Lily! My baby! How do you feel?"

Aliya dropped her eyelashes a bit. "It hurts. Talking hurts. Give me something to drink."

"Of course, right away, my dear," the woman began puttering around. "Right this minute, I'll mix you some water and wine. Or would you rather have milk? We have fresh milk from this morning."

"Just water," Aliya said. She felt like she hadn't eaten in a while, and milk might upset her empty stomach. Buttermilk would be just the thing, so she asked for some.

The woman smoothed the hair back from Aliya's face. "I'll start some buttermilk for you this very day! It will be ready tomorrow. For now, take a sip of this."

Aliya saw the gold cup with rubies flash in front of her eyes. She obediently drank the water with wine. Just a little, to keep it from going to her head. She looked up at the woman who handed it to her.

"Nanny, what happened to me? I can't remember. My mind is in a fog. Tell me what happened."

The woman looked away. "You're too weak still to hear the whole story."

I don't see how suspense will make me feel better, Aliya thought. Then she made a sad face. "Please tell me. Please."

She couldn't force a tear, but the woman was touched anyway. She looked down and said quietly, "You lost the baby. It was a boy."

It wasn't clear what kind of reaction she expected, but Aliya kept her eyes down and asked another question. "I see. What else?"

"You had childbed fever for three days. The medicus came and let your bad blood and gave you a cleansing remedy. Nothing helped."

Aliya's eyes flashed in anger. "Don't let that fool in here to see me again. I'll rip his legs off."

The nanny almost choked when she heard that. "But child, how can you say that? Your husband sent him all the way from Lavery when he heard you were unwell."

"Perhaps he hoped that idiot would do me in," Aliya grumbled.

"Whatever do you mean?" the nanny burst out. "Medicus Craybey is one of the best physicians in Lavery. Even the king has deigned to use his services."

"That's the king's problem. Why did I lose the baby?"

The nanny shrugged. "Medicus Craybey said that you fell on the stairs."

"Is that so?"

"We found you at the bottom of the stairs. There was a lot of blood. I was afraid you wouldn't make it." The nanny sniffled and hid her face in her apron.

"Not a chance of that," Aliya whispered to herself. The woman didn't hear her and continued to sniffle.

Aliya studied the woman. She was short and looked to be about sixty years old, with a tired but pleasant face. She had something like a little cap pinned to her hair. Aliya had only seen things like that in movies, but she was pretty sure that the sleazy fabric covering half the woman's hair was intended to be a cap.

Her dress was made of what looked like homespun fabric in a grayish-brown color. It was plain, without bows or ruffles. The apron was as dirty as the dress. She couldn't see what the woman had on her feet because the dress went all the way to the floor. *It must function like a prehistoric vacuum cleaner when she walks.*

Aliya sighed and spoke again, making her voice as sweet as possible, "Nanny, I need your help. I'm alive, and I want to get my health back. It's going to take a lot of effort."

The old woman dropped the apron from her face. Her gray eyes shone with fire, and Aliya realized that the woman loved her just as fiercely as her parents did back in her own world. This was a person who would do anything for her.

Anything at all. Whatever I ask for. A person like that is valuable. She could be useful.

Aliya kept her face neutral. She put on a small smile and said, "I want to try to stand up. I need to wash."

"How can you stand up, child? The medicus said that you should stay in bed another tennight!ⁱ"

"It's all right," Aliya gasped as she struggled to sit, ignoring the pain in her lower abdomen. "I can do it. And I really need to take a bath!"

"But washing is so unhealthy! That is what Father Vopler says."

"He's welcome to have all the lice he can handle," Aliya said, her patience wearing thin. When she saw the disappointment on the woman's face, she changed her tone to something between whining and begging. "Nanny, please help me."

The nanny *(it would be nice to know her name)* sighed and shook her head. "But Lily dear, it's so bad for you."

"Please!"

"Oh, all right. You lie here while I order some hot water. When I come back, I'll help you stand up."

Aliya nodded in agreement.

Thoughtfully, Aliya watched her leave. Then she began studying the room again. Unfortunately, all of the pink décor was still there. Looking closer this time, she began to suspect that the fabric on the walls was pretty expensive. Aliya was sure that the curtains would cost a fortune in her world. She had a friend who moonlighted as a seamstress and was always trying to teach Aliya about armsyces, darts, gussets, inserts, cross-stitch, machine embroidery and all the different kinds of seams. There was too much to remember, but Aliya could tell hand stitching from machine stitching, even at a distance.

She turned to study the furniture. The wardrobes were huge, pink monstrosities. And who thought it was a good idea to make a table out of heavy marble? It was impossible to move, and if it fell over it would put a hole in the floor. The chairs looked like they had been carved from whole pieces of pine.

One of the chairs looked more like a wooden chest that someone had nailed an uncomfortable back to before covering the whole thing in fabric—pink fabric, covered with ugly gold roses.

She hated this kind of stuff.

The pink canopy over her head needed to be shaken out before the dust completely obscured its gold roses.

Aliya plucked up her courage and looked down at her bed. The bedspread was an expensive brocade, but it was filthy—and pink. It was obviously handmade. The sheets were pink silk. They were dirty and stank. Aliya gritted her teeth and pulled the sheets to the side. She had to have a look at herself. She was dirty; she smelled bad; and she was covered in fat like a big, pink whale. Offhand, she figured she weighed 260-270 pounds. She almost cried; it was the worst reincarnation imaginable. She took a deep breath. *I can deal with this. I'll just watch what I eat and start exercising.*

The floorboards outside her door creaked. Aliya pulled the bedspread back over her body just as three men came in dragging a large metal washtub. When they let it down, it hit the floor with a boom that made Aliya jump. The men went out and returned ten minutes later with buckets of boiling water, which they poured into the washtub. After emptying three buckets of boiling water and three buckets of cold water, they put two more buckets of hot water on the floor by the tub. Aliya watched their preparations in surprise.

The youngest of the three men looked to be eighteen. The oldest of them was way past fifty. The third looked to be about thirty-five or forty, no more. All of them were wearing tunics and strange leggings that had once been white. The tunics were pink. *Of course.* The two older men had beards, and the youngest was working hard to grow out some hairs on his chin. Their heads were uncovered, but they had sprinkled them with some kind of powder. Their hair was tied back with dirty pink ribbons. On their feet, they wore felt shoes that had apparently been designed to make the wearer look dumpy.

They looked awful. She wondered if all the men in this world dressed like that.

Aliya noticed that none of their clothes had buttons. The tunics closed with ties. Her nanny's dress was the same way. She wondered if buttons had yet to be invented. If not, she would have to invent them and get the patent…if they had patents in this world. And if they didn't, she would find a partner and open a button-making workshop.

Stop. My mind is wandering too far. I need to stay in the here and now, at least until I've had my bath.

The men left, and her nanny came back to her bedside. "Let's get up, Lily, dear."

Aliya tried to stand. She almost groaned in pain. Every muscle and cell of her body was in agony. She gritted her teeth. She was used to standing for hours at a time and knew how to deal with pain.

Her nanny helped her up. It became clear that the woman intended to put her into the bath in her nightgown. Aliya stared at her. "Nanny, I won't wear this nightgown again. Help me take it off and have someone wash it. Then tell me if I have a clean one I can wear."

"You do, but Lily…"

"I'm begging you, Nanny! I feel so awful. Do you want me to trip on this nightgown and fall again?"

Her nanny was horrified. She helped Aliya get the disgusting sack over her head.

Aliya almost broke down in tears when she saw the rolls of fat on her body, but she kept it together.

"If only I had a mirror," she mumbled.

"You ordered one, remember? Let me help you, my pretty butterfly."

Aliya nodded. Her nanny led her to one of the wardrobes and opened the door. Aliya gasped. The wardrobe held a full-length mirror, which was just a sheet of polished metal, and Aliya could finally see what had happened to her.

She had to admit that she had her good points as well as her bad ones. While her legs, hips, and butt were very large, and her waist was obscured by four rolls of fat, she had small, high breasts and a long neck (even if it was partially hidden behind three chins). Her hands were elegant, and her legs were well proportioned. All she needed to do was lose about a hundred pounds.

Aliya was also pleased to see that she had a heavy braid of hair that fell almost to her knees instead of the rat's tail she was used to. *It must be all the organic food you eat in a place like this.* She studied her face and liked it. Large cheeks got in the way, but her eyes were big and green. Her nose wasn't hooked or turned up; it was just a plain, straight nose. Her ears were fine, too. Best of all, she didn't see any acne, warts or other spots on her smooth skin. Thank goodness, she didn't see any of the pits left by smallpox, either. There was just a small birthmark at the corner of her lip. Her teeth were all there, and she could tell that her wisdom teeth hadn't come in yet.

So, she had a good foundation, and everything else could be fixed. While she was getting in shape, she'd have time to assimilate. Aliya thought of herself as a pragmatist. She wouldn't try to change everything around her all at once. *Why bother, when all I really want is a convenient, easygoing lifestyle?*

She would start at the beginning by finding out what was going on in the outside world. Aliya turned to her nanny and flashed her a babyish smile.

"Come help me wash and tell me all the things that happened while I was ill."

The old woman smiled broadly. "Whatever you want, Lily."

The clever schemer hiding behind Lily's eyes grinned; she knew exactly what she wanted.

ꟷ♦ꟷ

"Anna! Sweetheart! Open the door!"

The man kept his voice down and glanced from side to side as if he was afraid of something. He didn't have to wait long. The door opened, and someone pulled him inside before the lock clicked shut.

"Have you lost your mind?"

The woman who posed the question had passionate, southern features, with dark hair falling in waves over her round shoulders, and a sensual, full figure, with an innocently round face. Her forehead was high, and her hair had been plucked according to the latest fashion so that it formed a triangle above her face. Her thin, arched eyebrows framed large, brown eyes, and she had a small nose and heart-shaped lips above a round chin with a dimple.

"What are you doing here? My father is here today!"

"He won't be singing you to sleep tonight, and I have my rights as your husband!"

The girl's face was tight with fear. "Be quiet! You'll get us both killed!"

"Maybe I'll save us. You're already sixteen, and you've been my wife for a year. Come here and stop stringing me along!" The man caught the girl by a lock of hair and pulled her to him. Anna cried out quietly, but he had no intention of stopping. He knew she liked a little bit of rough play.

ꟷ♦ꟷ

A short time later, they continued the conversation where they had left off, only this time they were in bed, and the sheets were crumpled.

"How much longer will we keep hiding?"

"Lons, you know my father is in charge of my fate until I turn eighteen. After that, I'll be free. There won't be any dowry, but at least we can announce our wedding. Just wait a little longer."

"Two years is a little longer? You want me to hide in the corner for two more years? Two more years of catching your every glance like it's a favor. Two more years…"

A soft hand covered his mouth. "My father controls my life. With just a word from him, I'd be sent to a convent for knowing you like this. He could have our marriage annulled. The Holy Throne already looks askance at him. You don't want to have your head on the block for seducing the king's daughter, do you?"

That subdued him.

"And I don't want to lose you. You're my husband. I love you. Everything will be fine. Just have patience."

"I see you're a teacher as well as an aristocrat."

"People will say that you took advantage of my youth and inexperience. Would it be so hard for you to stay away from me when His Majesty and his entourage are here? We can be together again after he leaves. I promise!"

Lons sighed. "Anna, love of my life, I never could refuse you. I promise. I'll wait a tennight. But tonight, you're mine!"

There was a predatory light in his eyes as he pulled the girl to him. Anna moaned and ran her fingers through his dark hair. Now, she knew for certain that he wouldn't be leaving until morning.

And she didn't want him to.

His Majesty, the King of Ativerna, Edward VIII, shuffled papers around on his desk. The life of a king was hard labor from dawn to dusk, dirty work for no gratitude or appreciation after he was gone. *Nobody thinks about the king when things are going well, but any problems always end up in the king's lap. He is, after all, the favorite of the gods. His Majesty.*

It could take a toll on a king's personality, and in the end, have the historians say, "King Edward was a tyrant and a despot." He wondered how the historians would fare if they had to do his job. Maybe they would behave like Radiant Ones[ii], but he doubted it.

King Edward was no tyrant or a despot either. He was almost unnaturally lucky for a king; he was loved and had friends.

ॐ◆ॐ

Thirty-six years before, Edward had married the Princess of Avesterra in an arranged marriage to further his country's diplomatic aims, but the day of his wedding was also the first time he laid eyes on Aloysius Earton's daughter, the sister of Jyce Earton. Jessamine was her brother's younger twin, born half an hour after him. She was charming, beautiful and intelligent and had everything the Princess of Avesterra lacked, but Edward knew he would have fallen in love with her regardless. Love at first sight really happens, he knew. *You see a person and realize that you're looking at your other half. Nothing else matters. That's true love.*

Jessamine had fallen in love with the young prince, too. She was crazy with love, and Edward's new wife never stood a chance. Her husband was calm and indifferent to her both day and night. His eyes often wandered to the dark-haired figure of Jessie. His gray eyes would find her blue eyes, and their hands would meet when they danced.

"Why are you a prince?" the blue eyes whispered.

"Why aren't you a princess? I would make you my queen, my goddess," the gray eyes answered.

The storm broke during a royal hunt. Jessamine's horse threw her and trotted back to rejoin the others. Several of the men spread out to look for her, but it was Edward who found her. They spent the night together in a woodsman's cabin. By morning, the prince had an official mistress.

It was an awful scandal. Princess Imogene of Avesterra screamed and cried. She threw dishes. She fainted. The old king shook his head in disappointment. Members of his court gossiped with the outraged members of the clergy.

Edward never hid his relationship with Jessie. The old earl and the old king disapproved but said nothing in public. The lovers did, however, have the support of Jessamine's brother.

Jyce, Viscount of Earton, adored his twin sister. If she needed the prince in order to be happy, then he figured she should have the prince. Edward knew that, in Jyce, he had gained a true friend. After all, they both loved Jessie.

ಬ◆ಞ

Two years into their marriage, the Princess of Avesterra gave birth to her first child. The following year, Jessie had a daughter. When Jessie was pregnant for the first time, it was Jyce who helped them decide what to do. He knew that he was impotent, a consequence of the edematous fever[iii] he had suffered as a young man. He would have no children of his own, but that was no reason to let the line of the Earls of Earton die out. It would be easy enough to marry some girl and send her away, supposedly to give birth, so that he could claim Jessie's daughter as his own. And when she bore the king a son, Jyce would announce the birth of his heir.

On the surface, everything was fine, but things were not quite so simple behind the doors of the family home. Jessie's mother decided that she could not live down the shame of her daughter's illicit affair and left to live in Earton, the ancestral estate. The earl, on the other hand, loved his daughter and, seeing that she couldn't live without Edward, found no reason to go against his son's plan. There was also the future to think of. By providing assistance now, he would gain the good graces of the future king, who would be sure to provide for all of his children, both legitimate and illegitimate. The Earton family would do well in the end.

Jyce's bride was chosen by a secret council. Alicia Weeks was no longer young, she wasn't much to look at, and she had little property, but she had a long list of illustrious ancestors and family pride to help her keep her head up. Jyce's offer of his hand was like a gift from heaven to her. She listened to the unique terms of the arrangement without batting an eyelash and put forward a term of her own: that she wouldn't actually have to give birth. Doctors had told her that her hips were too narrow. If Jyce could be satisfied by a life where they only saw each other on occasion, it was all right by her. They would each lead their own private lives without interference from the other. She was happy to claim Jessie's offspring as her own, and Jyce was welcome to take lovers as long as he did nothing to shame her publicly.

Jyce agreed to the bargain and never looked back. Over twenty years of married life, he "fathered" two children: first Amalia and then Jerrison, called Jess, five years later. Alicia had no interest in the children, but for propriety's sake, she appeared in public with them once a year so that she could be seen petting them, after which she went back to her own affairs.

She shone in high society, flirting, gossiping and behaving like any other lady at court with the assistance of her husband. Jyce was so pleased that his wife provided cover for Jessie's children and otherwise left him alone that he would have done anything for her. Alicia had all the money and social position she could possibly want.

Amalia and Jess lived with their "father" and a whole host of nannies. The house next door belonged to the king's official mistress, whom he visited eight times a tennight. During those years, Edward's wife, Princess Imogene, gave birth to another son, and two years later, she died of a fever.

After his wife's death, Edward asked for permission to marry Jessie; the old king just shrugged and gave his consent. So, Jessie married a prince and became a queen one year later when Edward ascended the throne. For the next twenty years, the royal family lived in peace and harmony and welcomed two more beautiful daughters.

Then, Jessamine died of a fever and was mourned by the king and the entire nation. The people had always loved their kind queen, and wandering minstrels composed songs about the romantic tale of Jessie and Edward.

There was, however, a dark side to the story. Edward's younger son with Imogene of Avesterra, Richard, adored his loving stepmother, who sang him songs and told him stories in an attempt to take the place of his dead mother. But his oldest son by the princess, Edmund, was an exact copy of his mother and had inherited her hatred of Jessie and the rest of the Earton family. He tried to avoid showing his true feelings in public, but his father knew.

The oldest son was first in line for the throne, and Edward would have liked to find a wife for Edmund when his son turned thirty, but Jessie's death was followed by a two-year period of mourning. Edmund seemed to be in no hurry, and his father never forced him to do anything. Sadly, a year and a half after Jessie's death, Jyce, Earl of Earton, and prince Edmund were found dead in Edmund's sitting room. Both had been poisoned, and questions abounded. Had Edmund tried to poison his father's oldest friend? Or had Jyce decided that it was too risky for his family and his sister's children to let Edmund come to power? Edward didn't want to know the truth. Jess took up Jyce's position as Earl, and a friend to the king and to Richard. Edward never told the boys that they were brothers, but they were best friends anyway.

ౠ◆ঙ

Richard, like his father, was a tall blonde with gray eyes, and Jess was a soldier. Just as his father, the Earl, had been a marshal under King Edward, Jess would serve someday under King Richard. If Jess was lucky, his son would serve under Richard's son.

That was, if he had a son. Jyce had already married his son off three times, the first time when the boy was eight. His bride-to-be was the daughter of the Earl of Errolston, but young Eliza died at the age of twelve, and Jyce found his son another wife. Magdalena Yerby, daughter of the Barron of

Yerby, died giving her young husband a daughter. After that, it became harder to find a wife for Jess. People were superstitious and felt he brought his wives bad luck.

Then August Broklend offered to help. He had a single daughter named Lilian. She was ten years younger than Jess, but that made no difference. She was old enough to have a child, and she had a nice dowry. Jess and Lilian were married, and the house of Broklend joined the house of Earton, greatly expanding their land holdings and giving Jess access to the Broklend family boatyards.

Lilian was August's only child, despite the fact that the old man had been married three times. He hadn't wanted to leave his boatyards to a woman, so he was pleased to have Jess for a son-in-law. Jess was not a born sailor, but he set out to learn the boatbuilding business from the ground up with August's help.

The king was proud of his son's ambition. Lilian, however, was another story. His Majesty saw her just once—at the wedding—and realized that his first wife, Imogene, could have been worse. At the very least, he could take her to bed without shuddering.

Lilian was dim-witted and overweight. The king couldn't think of any other way to put it. He quietly held out hope that she would die in childbirth or that Jess would find a lover, as he had found Jessie. His son had already seduced half of the women at court, and the king felt that the love of a good woman would settle him down. It was about time.

Ж

Speak of the devil… The king's musings were interrupted as the door to his chambers creaked.

"Is that you, Jess?"

"Yes." The man stepped from the shadows into the light.

Edward pointed to a chair. "So, you've returned."

"I have, Your Majesty. I am prepared to give all my attention to government affairs."

"Jess, I don't like it when you use that title with me."

"All right, Uncle Ed."

To the world, the Earl of Earton was the king's nephew by his second marriage, and the king preferred to hear his own son call him "Uncle Ed" instead of "Your Majesty."

The young man's face took on a roguish expression. The king shook his head. "Forget the government. I wish you'd pay some attention to your family."

"Government affairs happen to be my family affairs," the young man answered impudently.

"How wrong you are. The government's business concerns me alone," Edward grumbled. "Stop avoiding the subject. You should have given me at least a pair of nephews by now."

"One may be on the way." Jess sighed. Then his voice scaled up a notch. "I can't do it, Uncle! Just look at her. She's stupid, she throws fits all the time, and she's ugly! If you saw her in a dream, you'd die in your sleep. You wouldn't touch her with a barge pole!"

"No one's asking you to fall in love with her. Just give her a baby, that's all. You can cover her face with a handkerchief during the act if you like."

"Or hold a pillow over her face," Jess spit out. "I'm telling you; she's pregnant already."

"How many months?"

Jess thought for a minute. "About three months. Or four."

"Will you bring her to court after the birth?"

Jess made a face. "I'm sorry, Uncle, but I'd rather not."

"Think about it. You won't have to see her often, and…"

"No. She can stay in Earton, so I don't have to see her ever. I sent her a physician and some money. That's more than enough!"

Edward shook his head. He had given up trying to raise his son. The boy was already a man, and the king had problems of his own. "What other news is there?"

"I have some reports from the boatyard. We can build very good boats using the drawings we borrowed from Fereiry. The shipwrights want to build one as a trial to see how it turns out."

"And you agree with them?"

"Of course! August is curious to see the result, as well. I've brought the drawings to show you. Would you like to take a look?"

"I have some reports from the treasury to go over. Do you have any idea how much they stole this month?"

"I don't. I want to build the boat using my own money. It will have two decks, with—"

"Tell me about it later. Have you seen Richard?"

"Not yet. Should I?"

"Yes. I have decided it is time for him to marry. Keep an eye on him. Make sure he doesn't do anything scandalous in the meantime. Is that clear?"

Jess grinned. Edward's heart skipped a beat. *How he looks like his mother!*

"Of course, Uncle. I'll watch him. Who is he going to marry?"

"Marry? I don't know. There are two princesses that I know of who are the right age. It will be either Anna of Wellster or Lidia of Ivernea."

"But—"

"Both girls' families want to be chosen. The Wellsters have five other daughters, so they'd like to get rid of one. Anna is the right age, and my contacts tell me she is attractive."

"That's good. At least Richard wouldn't need a handkerchief in order to sleep with her. What about Lidia?"

"She's the only unmarried daughter in Ivernea. She's never been married or even engaged. They say she's plain as a wool sock[iv]."

"That bad?"

"Anna is certainly the more handsome of the two."

"Then why not choose Anna?"

"Beauty isn't everything. And I want Richard to have a choice; I was never allowed to choose."

"You made your choice later," Jess winked. "I think you did the right thing. My aunt was still beautiful at forty."

"Like I said, beauty isn't everything. Jessie was kind and intelligent. Those are much more important qualities in a wife."

Jess's face fell. Then he shook himself and smiled again. "I'm no king, so my wife can have as many children as she wants. I'll find kindness and intelligence somewhere else. They say Lady Wells has returned. She needs someone to console her after the death of her old, awful husband."

Edward shook his head. "How is your daughter?"

Jerrison's face lit up with a smile. "Miranda is sharp as a tack. Her teachers are pleased with her. But I can't take her with me."

"Send her to the country."

"To be with Lilian?"

"Do you have another choice? Send governesses and nannies with her. People you trust."

"I may have to do that."

"What if you send her to your sister?"

"There's no point trying. You should have seen how Miranda screamed and cried after her last visit. She refuses to see Amalia, and I haven't the slightest idea why."

"Fine. You'll figure out what to do with her. Give it some thought. Now, leave me those drawings and run off. Just don't let Richard get into trouble. Is that understood?"

"Yes, Your Majesty," Jess replied. He gave a military salute and disappeared out the door.

The king shook his head as he watched him go. *Good-for-nothing pup.* Nobody could claim that the young man was especially talented. He didn't win all his games of squares[v], he didn't command the best regiment in Ativerna, and he didn't get up extra early to get a jump on his affairs. He didn't have a hard body with muscles of steel under his courtly clothing, and he probably wasn't prepared to give his life for his country and his brother.

No, Jess was just a typical courtier. He liked to play with expensive toys and gilded weapons. He was just like all the rest of them. None the less, Edward thought that he and Jessie had made a wonderful child. *Perfect in every way.*

His Majesty sighed and turned back to the Treasury reports. He knew his duty.

☜◆☞

Lady Adelaide Wells was overjoyed. She kept it under wraps, of course; a lady was not supposed to be in high spirits just three months after her husband's passing—even if that husband was fifty-two years her senior and the bane of her existence, constantly blowing his nose, coughing, and sweating. Even if he was a source of daily torment, a widowed lady was supposed to mourn.

So, Adelaide mourned. She did a beautiful job of it. Other women were welcome to sob until the paint came off their faces. Adelaide would mourn in her own way, with just one diamond-like tear lingering in the corner of her eye. And she would have the most wonderful mourning clothes.

With her black hair and dark-brown eyes, green[vi] looked good on her, especially with the right powder and blush. She knew how to use makeup; she had suffered a bout of smallpox five years before and had learned to conceal the few scars remaining on her cheeks. They didn't mar her beauty in the least.

She was sure to find another husband, but she didn't want to find him right away. Society was permissive with young widows. They could get away with a lot, as long as they observed certain proprieties, and Adelaide was an expert. She had learned to be cautious at the tender age of fourteen.

೮೦ ◆ ೮8

"That's enough, Richard. Let's go. Camelia is putting on a fantastic show this evening."

Adelaide started when she heard the man's voice. She knew that she wasn't the type of woman that interested Richard, and she had heard that he would be marrying soon. She wouldn't waste her time or risk her reputation. She felt she was more attractive as a widow in mourning than as the prince's abandoned lover. The man walking next to Richard, however, aroused her serious interest. Adelaide noticed his broad shoulders, the cut and cloth of his tunic, and the expensive weapons he carried. This was a man worth her time.

He looks like he could do more than snore in bed, and he'd send me expensive gifts afterward. Adelaide was not feeling particularly wealthy on her own. Her husband had left her a sizeable sum, but a house in the capital, a carriage, expensive gowns and jewelry—it all added up. The stranger was just what she needed.

She went into action, unhooking the brooch from the light shawl she wore around her shoulders and letting it drop to the floor. The brooch, an aromatic sphere made just for such purposes, rolled obediently across the floor in just the right direction. This was the key moment. "I apologize, My Lord. My brooch!"

She fell to her knees to retrieve the golden sphere and looked up into the eyes of the man, who had also bent down to pick it up. She blushed deeply and looked him in the eye before dropping her lashes. Her silk shawl slid from her shoulders, revealing her full breasts in a low-cut décolleté.

The man was composed as he gave her one hand and carefully replaced the shawl with the other. As he took his hand from her shoulder, his fingers ran lightly over her breast. Adelaide knew this was a test. If she made the wrong move, the man would visit her bed, but he wouldn't stay, and she wanted him to stay.

She took a step back and blushed even brighter before lowering her eyes and whispering, "Thank you, My Lord. Forgive me, Your Highness." Then she got out of the room as fast as she could so that Richard could tell his friend all he knew about her.

She would use her time to find out more about the man. *Hunting season is open.* There was something exquisite about hunting while pretending to be the prey. The only thing that worried Adelaide was the thick wedding bracelet on the man's wrist. A wife, however, was less of an obstacle than a husband.

She needed to find out who he was right away.

Chapter 2

Growing and Learning

Despite her best intentions, Aliya remained in bed and in a trance the first ten days. And she had a cold.

In Ella's books, when characters found themselves in a parallel world, they just shrugged their shoulders and marched off to change it however they wanted. *They made it look easy.* Aliya didn't believe life worked that way. And she didn't really read Ella's fantasy books; she just flipped through them at night when she wanted to fall asleep. It helped. Now, however, she was sorry she hadn't read more about time travellers, *those unfortunate wretches*. If she had, she would at least know where to start.

As it was, she was clueless, and her inability to find a starting point left her in a dark depression. Besides, she couldn't stop worrying about lice and fleas. Somewhere, she had read that French women used to use gold tweezers to catch fleas; just the thought made her nauseous. So, her only demands were hot water for a bath every day and a daily change of sheets. Close inspections of her hair revealed no insects; that was good news.

Aliya wanted to stay in bed as long as she could. She usually didn't allow herself to fall to pieces like this, but her body hurt like nothing she had experienced before. Just getting out of bed to take a bath was an ordeal; her muscles shook, sweat stood out on her skin, and she felt dizzy. She was in the wrong world in the wrong body, and those two things came with side effects—muscle spasms, for example, or sudden fits of hysterical crying. Common sense told her that there was nothing to cry about, but the tears just streamed down her face.

She had strange nightmares… in bright colors… about a little girl.

She sat at a table while an oddly familiar woman pleaded with her.

"Eat a spoonful for Mama, eat a spoonful for Papa."

"I don't want to!" she complained. "Leave me alone, Nanny!"

Porridge and spoon fly off the table, but, instead of boxing her ears like Aliya would have been tempted to do, the nanny picks her up and continues to plead with her. "Lily, my dear, my angel…"

Then the picture changes.

Grown-up Lilian is watching a dream as if it were a movie on television. She sees the same girl at five, at seven, at ten… She throws tantrums, tries on new dresses, argues, demands something, hits a servant in the face, screams at a tired old man.

Somehow, Aliya knew that the old man is Lilian's father. The dream was unpleasant, but Aliya couldn't turn it off. Then the picture changed, swimming up out of a dark pool of memories.

"Daughter, the Earl of Earton has asked for your hand in marriage."

"The earl?"

"Yes. I have decided to give my consent."

"Didn't it occur to you to ask my opinion? Is he old and horrible?"

"The earl is young and very handsome."

That doesn't stop her; she yells and throws something that looks like a vase. Her father holds firm. The picture changed again.

An engagement party. She saw a handsome young man with long, dark hair, bright blue eyes, and a hard, muscular body… She also saw distaste in his eyes. He bent down to hand her a bouquet of flowers. He said something to her. Her heart is racing so fast she's afraid he can hear it.

Is this really my husband? To have and to hold, for better and for worse…

The young man's lips touched her plump hand. Her cheeks grew suspiciously warm. But his eyes remained cold and unemotional. He just didn't care about any of this. He was indifferent, and that scared her.

She was also scared of the wedding night. When the time came, she blew out all the candles. Her young husband stubbed his toe on a piece of furniture and cursed. Then he lights a candle.

"Please don't," she begged him.

"Why? Do you think being in the dark will give me feelings for you?"

She froze. Her husband went on, his tone lethal. "I'm not attracted to you in the least, but I have to have an heir. Your job is to lie still and keep your mouth shut. Maybe that way, I won't feel so nauseous."

She couldn't remember what came next. She just remembered the humiliation… and the sharp pain between her legs that she felt after each visit from her husband.

She was like a second-rate purebred mare—not a person, not a lover, not even a wife.

She was just a vessel he would use to obtain an heir.

Icy, black despair rolled over her.

At first, Aliya didn't understand what the dreams were. Then it hit her. Her mind was her own, but she still had Lilian's memories, knowledge, habits, reflexes… Two people had merged into one. Aliya was the stronger of the two, and she was used to assimilating large amounts of information, so she simply assimilated Lilian Earton's memory.

It was the memory of an unhappy young woman who simply wanted a family and children and to be loved by her husband, but was met with cold contempt instead.

On the tenth night, Aliya dreamed about her accident in shocking clarity. She heard the crunch and saw the column of flames rising into the sky from the wreckage. Then, she saw her parents. Her father was wearing his dress uniform, and her mother was young and beautiful. They looked at her with reproach, displeased with her. Aliya was upset, wondering what she had done.

Then she understood. They hadn't raised her to just give up and die; they wanted more for her. They were dead, but she was alive.

She was finally truly convinced that she could do this. The woman who had gotten in bed the night before had been confused, trying to figure out what had happened to her and where she was, but the woman who woke up in the morning was decisive. She put her feet firmly on the floor and launched a mission to change her life.

ༀ◆ༀ

Aliya began by studying her new world. At night, she wandered through the house to discover where everything was, hiding whenever she heard servants near. In the early morning, she slept and watched Lilian Earton's dreams. She had fewer of them now, and they had lost their bright colors and drifted away from her, just like Lilian was drifting away. In the evening, Aliya listened to her nanny, Martha, tell stories.

Through her wanderings, Aliya learned that Earton Castle was built in the shape of a letter H lying on its back. The center bar of the H was the largest part of the castle. The first floor had an enormous hall, a ballroom, a smaller hall and a dining room. The upper right end of the castle held a library, the earl's study, a music room for the ladies, and a game room for when the weather was bad. This part of the castle was obviously for guests and had a door that led to a porch overlooking the garden.

The kitchen was on the lower right end of the castle. On the first floor were the rooms where the servants did their work, as well as the entrance to the cellar and storerooms, where valuables, such as fabric and furniture, were kept. The servants' bedrooms were on the second floor.

The lower left arm was divided into a portrait gallery, a knight's hall and armory on the first floor, and rooms for guests on the first and second floors. The upper left arm of the castle belonged entirely to the family. The castle's four arms were only connected through its center, with gorgeous, massive wooden staircases leading to the second floor of each arm.

The whole place needed a good cleaning, in her opinion. The curtains hadn't been washed in ages, there was dust everywhere, and spiders had taken over all the quiet corners. *So what if the ceilings are fifteen feet high? Haven't they invented ladders yet?* She would have to see about that.

Several centuries' worth of soot had accumulated on those high ceilings, and there were rooms in the castle where the corners smelled suspiciously of urine. *Do they not make it to the toilet in time, or do they just not care? What an aristocratic pigsty*!

When Aliya finally found the actual privy, she almost vomited. She located it by following the smell, which was strong enough to knock out a fly. She opened the door and saw a room with a hole in the floor. No running water, no nothing. Whatever went into the hole ran through a stone pipe into a ditch outside. Aliya decided she would have to do something about that, too.

She noticed that most of the doors in the castle were unlocked and that the few locks being used were primitive. The lock on the door leading to the storerooms was an ancient hunk of metal, but after studying it, Aliya figured any ten-year-old with the nerve could open it using a pen. The only danger was the lock's weight; if you dropped it on your foot, you'd need crutches the rest of your life.

She wasn't interested in the storerooms behind the locked door; she wanted to find the library. Aliya had always valued a good education, and she would need to know how to write and count according to local custom in order to avoid being taken advantage of. She had things to accomplish, so she was relieved when she finally found what she sought.

Her relief didn't last long. She reached for a book and gasped in horror. She reached for a second book, and then a third. They were all manuscripts written on parchment. She opened as many books as she could; first on one shelf, then the next, as far up as she could reach. A stash of unused parchment got her hopes up, but they fell again when she found a goose feather dipped in ink. One more item hit her to-do list: *find a blacksmith and get some pens made.*

The best thing she discovered in the library was that she could read the local language. She was as slow as a first-grader, but she could read. That was important.

The next book she laid her hands on had an intriguing title: "A Detailed Description of the Lands, People and Customs of the World, Made by the Humble Kalerius of Ativerna." *That sounds useful.* She hoped the book wasn't a work of fiction, like *Gulliver's Travels.* And she hoped Lilian's brain was capable of reading a whole book.

Aliya could tell that her host didn't like to study. Lilian preferred embroidering with gold thread. Taking a deep breath, Aliya set the geography book aside. She would read it later. She also slipped a few pieces of parchment into the book, but not too many, so that no one would notice.

Further digging on the same shelf failed to turn up anything else useful, but Aliya decided she had enough for now. The book would teach her things she couldn't find out from her nanny's stories. She would make this new brain of hers work harder than it ever had before. After spending so much time in close study of Lilian Earton's lazy, half-empty mind, Aliya decided that she couldn't really blame the woman's husband for staying away.

There was no sign that the woman had ever read anything—books, newspapers, or even letters. She knew some prayers by heart, but that was it. *I wonder how her husband stays awake when she talks to him.*

She stopped. The unfairness of the situation was obvious. Lilian never had a chance to get even a basic education. Family and custom kept her at home working on her embroidery, so it was no surprise if people found her boring. From her nanny's conversation, Aliya knew that the Earl felt that way; he stayed well away from his ancestral home and his wife. Aliya felt her hands clench into fists. She didn't care if that Earl husband of hers held all the titles in the kingdom; he'd need a dentist after she got in a room with him. And then she'd divorce him.

But for the time being, she had work to do.

The stove in Aliya's room was always fired up, keeping the room hot as a greenhouse. She decided that pieces of coal would make better writing tools than feathers that always needed sharpening. *Note to self: invent pencil.*

Aliya lived like that for two weeks. The book she had found turned out to be a treasure chest of information. Good old Kalerius gave a thorough run-down of all the countries in her new world and described the people who lived in them. Some of it was probably lies, but she was grateful to at least have the geography under her belt.

It became clear that her fears were justified; this world was stuck in the Middle Ages. They hadn't even invented gunpowder. Aliya knew that gunpowder was made of sulfur, charcoal, and potassium nitrate. She also knew how to prepare nitroglycerine, but she decided to keep that information to herself. *A little less civilization would mean a much healthier planet; that's a fact.* In her previous life, Aliya had read somewhere that technology should never be allowed to outrun morality. Otherwise, the clock will strike Armageddon, and both God and the Devil will turn tail and run.

Reading further in her new geography book, Aliya realized that glass was so expensive that no one had ever tried making mirrors out of it. They didn't even have tools for cutting glass properly. She smiled to herself. Not all progress led to war and destruction, and not all inventions could be used for murder. She would have to be careful what she shared with this world. She couldn't do everything for them, but she did have medicine on her side. They didn't have surgeons in her new world, and without her help, it might be another five hundred (or more) years before they learned how to operate on the human body.

She read on. Wars were fought the old-fashioned way, with bows and arrows and catapults. Soldiers were wounded by the cartload, and most of them died, even if their wounds could have been treated easily on Earth. That was sad, but it meant that a good doctor would always be popular. Aliya didn't plan to stick with the Earl of Earton long, so it was nice to know that she could earn money treating patients.

Industry was non-existent, and most people were subsistence farmers. She liked that because it meant that there were no factories or pollution. When people traveled by sea, they used sailboats. When they traveled by land, they rode horses. They had wagons and carriages, judging by the drawings in her book, but Aliya thought they looked like coffins on wheels. *Shock absorbers? Not invented yet.* There wasn't much she could do about that. Medical school was great for learning how to stitch people up, but Aliya wasn't even sure what shock absorbers should look like.

Backwardness wasn't always a good thing. There were no factories, but there were also no schools. Most people were illiterate. Aliya decided to work on opening schools for the children of Earton—or at least preschools that would teach them to read and count. Her schools would run in the winter since the farm families would need their children to help in the fields in the summer. Those same farm families, she read, had to spend two out of every ten days working in their lord's fields.

House servants were a different caste. Aliya's castle had eight of them. Martha was both her nanny and her servant, and apparently, she had served Lilian since she was born. Martha loved her like a daughter, and Aliya appreciated her for it. The three housemaids, Mary, Sara, and Ilona, bustled around cleaning all day, but the castle never seemed to get any cleaner. There were three manservants, Jean, Peter, and Alex, and three grooms who lived in the stables. One of them—Jacques—was a brother of Jean. The other two were Claus and Rene.

Then, there was the cook, Tara. She was the estate Comptroller's wife, and she made awful food. Her husband's name was Etor. It seemed like a small crew for such a big castle and estate. Aliya would reform how the estate was run once she got her bearings. For the time being, she stuck to her reading.

Kalerius, the geographer, hadn't thought to put a map in his book, but Aliya was able to deduce some important facts from the text. The mainland (of which there was only one because this particular world was flat) was made up of eight nations.

Ativerna was where Aliya now lived. She felt almost patriotic about it. Her nearest neighbors were Wellster and Ivernea. Avesterra was next to Ivernea, and Elvana shared borders with Wellster and Avesterra. There were no elves in Elvana, as far as she could tell. Darcom bordered on Avesterra and Elvana. Not far from the shores of Ativerna, was the island nation of Virma. Aliya thought the people of Virma sounded like Vikings from back home. The local climate was interesting. Virma bore the brunt of the cold, but even in Ativerna, they had a long, four-month winter and a short summer. Wellster and Ivernea had slightly better weather. Elvana and Avesterra were the warmest countries. Aliya wondered why. The weather left the soil poor.

At the far end of the large continent, was the Vari Desert, which was governed by the Vari Khanganat. The Vari people were nomads since nothing grew in the desert.

Kalerius had never visited the eighth nation, which was on the other side of a steep mountain range. He simply stated that Elvana was bordered to its west by high mountains. There were rumors, he wrote, of people living beyond the mountains, but most rumors were lies *Kalerius would know*. He also hinted that there might be a large island somewhere past the Vari Desert, but the details were sketchy. Aliya longed for some satellite images.

❧◆❧

Once she finished the book on geography, Aliya visited the library again and chose some religious literature. *I need to know what these people believe.* The huge book, bound in a red velvet cover and entitled, *The Book of Radiance*, turned out to be very much like the Bible. Aliya wondered at that for a while but then decided that people who don't want to believe that their fate is in their own hands come up with tales of a kind, heavenly father who hands out candy and spankings, depending on what you've done. *That's no surprise. Nobody wants to admit to their own mistakes, so they say that they've been punished by God for their sins.* The tales in the *Book of Radiance* reminded Aliya of the Old Testament, with an avenging God and his eternal antagonist. The god was called Aldonai, and his opponent was Maldonaya. Maldonaya happened to be female. *Of course. Women are always the source of evil, right?*

In this world, women held a position somewhere between horses and cows. Aristocratic women were slightly better off. They were still treated like property, but they were allowed to handle their own lands and servants. That suited Aliya just fine.

There were just four things a woman could be (five at most): daughter, wife, mother, widow, and slut. That was it. There were no other roles for them—no free and independent women, no feminism, no self-sufficiency. If you didn't like it, you could be branded a witch and executed. Witches existed, but they weren't respected. Aliya ran across a couple of stories about how people dealt with witches, who were thought to be servants of Maldonaya and were summarily drowned or burned at the stake.

She particularly enjoyed the story about how women were ruled to be humans. One prophet was having a trouble with his wife, so he complained to Aldonai about her stupidity and evil temper. He asked Aldonai if it would be possible to categorize women as animals. *Rats, perhaps?* Aldonai thought for a while and answered, "Have patience, my son. If we categorize women as animals, then you and all the other men will be guilty of bestiality. You would be born from animals and live in sin with animals, and there would be chaos and disorder in the world." The prophet shut his mouth, and women were allowed to remain human. Aliya rolled her eyes. *What a mental asylum.*[vii]

Aliya felt she had mastered the fundamentals of their religion. She now knew not to make the sign of the cross, but to trace a circle—the sign of the Sun—in front of her face and then touch her lips and forehead. She memorized the local prayers and read all the biographies of saints that she could find in the library.

Knowledge was the best weapon in any fight, Aliya knew, and she knew herself. There was no way she would sit at home and work on embroidery. She wanted to bring new inventions to this world, if only for her own convenience. Doing so would put her on the wrong side of accepted female behavior, so she had to be prepared.

If the priest said, "My child, women do not do these things. Are you perchance a witch?" she could reply, "Father, have you forgotten that Saint Marilda healed people with laying on of hands? Saint Yevgrastia traveled. Saint Ridalina preached in brothels. So, refrain from your rebukes, for I have been touched by the Holy Spirit. If you don't believe me, I can call down the heaviest of the spirits to fall on your head. Then you'll really see radiance!"

There was one other thing Aliya loved about the stories of the saints' lives—they were written on weighty parchment scrolls. She could easily use the reverse side to practice writing. She knew that it would be a while before she was ready to go out into the world, and she wanted to copy down what she already knew about medicine before she began forgetting things.

She didn't want to start writing yet—there was a lot of other more pressing work to do—but she made note of where the scrolls were. She would rather have a good text on pharmacology than the life of Saint Ridalina. Her new world had saintly fools on every corner, but it would be a long while before they discovered anticholinergics.

She would write out all the muscles and nerves and make a detailed drawing of the human skeleton. *Anatomy alone will take up so much paper.* Aliya sighed. *We know so much, and yet so little.*

She also knew—and could probably copy out from memory—all of the classic novels, from Gogol to Dostoyevsky, but there was no paper for her to do it on. She would have given anything for a piece of paper—even toilet paper or maybe some leaves. Aliya was grateful for her profession as never before. *All those lawyers, economists, and sales managers do well for themselves in our world, but how would they like it here, where half the people can't even read? More than half! I bet ninety percent of them sign their name with an X. Fights are decided by who has the heavier fist or the sharper knife. They probably think that double-entry bookkeeping means that your estate Comptroller is a thief.*

Now that she thought about it, her estate Comptroller probably was a thief.

Aliya continued studying the castle at night. She stayed inside for practical reasons. *I don't want to run into a guard dog in the yard.* She needed to lose some weight, but getting bitten by the castle guard dog was not how she planned to do it.

In her nocturnal walks through the castle, she decided that all the servants were on the take. Everything was too old and run-down. True, there was little reason for Lily to use large sections of the castle—she never had guests, so she only used six of the many rooms—but according to Martha's stories…

I'll deal with the crooked servants later.

ଽ◆ଔ

Food was another problem. Aliya wasn't just hungry, she wanted to eat everything in sight. Her new body had lost weight during its illness and demanded food. During her illness, she had been given chicken broth, red wine and something like toast, which wasn't bad at all. Once she got out of bed, however, the food seemed to Aliya like something Ivan the Terrible might have had on his table: roasted hare's kidneys, head of pike with garlic and other modest dishes. On her first day out of bed, her breakfast was brought in on a tray. She counted at least ten eggs that had been hardboiled, chopped and mixed with what looked like wine. There were two types of porridge: oatmeal with mushrooms and wheat porridge with berries. Off to the side, lay a piece of ham that looked like it weighed at least a pound, and a piece of cheese the same size. There was a large loaf of wheat bread, accompanied by at least a half-pound each of butter, honey and jam, all in dishes the size of large plates. She was expected to wash all of this down with beer, wine or cider.

Her stomach grumbled happily. Aliya grumbled not so happily. "What is all of this?"

"Your breakfast, My Lady."

There's no way I can eat all of this! Or can I? In her previous life, Aliya would have needed a week to plow through the food on the table, and she would have shared with friends. She wrinkled her nose at the eggs in wine, but her stomach was raring and ready to go.

She felt nauseous just looking at the unsalted sheep's milk cheese, but her hand reached out with a spoon to scoop out a chunk of it.

The drinks on the table made her teeth clench shut, but her fingers held onto the pitcher of wine. *What if I'm an alcoholic in this life? That's the last thing I need.*

Aliya pushed away everything but the two dishes of porridge. "Martha, I only want porridge for breakfast from now on. Nothing else."

"But Lily, you'll starve like that."

"It's not up for discussion."

It was obvious Martha heard the steel in Aliya's voice. She nodded in assent.

Aliya did the same at lunch. Of the twelve dishes offered to her, she kept just two. Soup and a meat of some kind. Nothing heavy and nothing fried. She was just as strict at dinner. She instructed the cook to serve her only vegetables—any kind of vegetable—but no meat, cheese or bread. Wine was off the table, but they could leave the cider.

I'll teach you to make fruit juice and wash the pots before you use them, but until then, I'll stick to cider. The alcohol kills bacteria, so there's less chance of dying of dysentery. Based on what she knew of healers in her new world, Aliya suspected that there was no treatment for something like dysentery.

ಖ◆ಣ

She was fed up with her forced isolation but prevented by irrational fear from going outside. She argued with herself and called herself a coward, but nothing helped. She was afraid that as soon as she left the castle grounds, she'd be recognized for what she was: a woman from another world. The people would cry, "Seize the witch!" or something just as bad. So, she put off going outside. *I can study this world perfectly well using books.* Then reality crash-landed on her.

Martha scratched timidly at the door, slipped into the room and announced, "Lily, dear, Doctor Craybey is here to see you."

"So what?" Aliya had told her Nanny never to let him near her again, and she had no intention of getting out of bed, but she decided she couldn't send him away.

"He can't examine you like that! You need to get dressed."

Aliya stayed right where she was. She was comfortable in bed, and she also had a book hidden under her blanket. She couldn't get up without exposing her source of knowledge.

"Nanny, when I was sick, did I get dressed for doctor visits?"

"No, my dear."

"So let him in. He's already seen it all."

Unable to argue, Martha went out. Aliya quickly hid the book under her bed. Judging by the quantity of dust, it had been twenty years since anyone even looked under the bed, and it would be another twenty before they peeked under there again. It seemed like a safe hiding place.

She was nervous about talking to the doctor. He couldn't know much about real medicine, but he wouldn't be a complete fool, either. This would be harder than talking to Martha, who was so happy to have her favorite little girl back that she ignored the strange things she said and did.

Aliya pulled the piglet-pink blanket up to her chin. The door flew open. *Jerk. Didn't even knock.*

Medicus Craybey presented himself to Aliya-Lilian in an outfit of tight brown pants, a carrot-colored tunic, and a short brown cape. His high boots were made of pale blue leather and were filthy, and he had a large bag strung over one shoulder. Aliya concluded that this was the typical male garb for that world. She glanced at the doctor's long hair. It was pulled back in a ponytail, tied with an orange ribbon and sprinkled liberally with something that looked like powder. Some of the powder had fallen on the man's shoulders. *So much for local fashion.*

"Good day, Countess," he greeted her.

"Good day," Aliya nodded.

She did not extend her hand to be kissed; he could stay right where he was. She wondered if he would climb up on her bed in those dirty boots to do the exam.

"How do you feel?"

"Fine." Aliya wanted to send him packing, but she exercised self-control.

"Do you have any pain? Bleeding? Sharp or burning sensations? Has the fever returned?"

"No, it hasn't."

Aliya tried to stay calm and keep her replies brief. This was her first test. If the doctor noticed anything strange about her…

But Craybey *(Is that his first name or his last name?)* gave a broad grin. "I'm very pleased. I knew your body could defeat the illness. I simply followed my teacher's instructions by letting out the bad blood and giving you cleansing treatments. You'll be fine. I always knew that my teacher was a source of wisdom."

Aliya's eyes were opened. Under all the power and show of importance, she saw a kid who was just twenty or twenty-five years old—a loser like many of the guys she went to school with.

"Do you mean your teacher told you to treat miscarriage by letting a woman's blood and then giving her emetics and enemas?" She spoke quietly to keep from screaming. Her self-control had abandoned her. It was the satisfied smile on the kid's face that did her in.

"But you're alive! I did everything correctly. If…"

Poof!

A pillow hit him in the face and landed on the floor. Another pillow followed, but it hit the foot of the bed and exploded, covering the doctor in a cloud of feathers.

"If you come back here, I'll have them set the dogs on you! Get out, fool!" Aliya had forgotten all about being cautious and keeping a low profile. *To hell with it all! I'll bury this idiot!*

By the time Martha came running in, Aliya had regained her calm demeanor.

"Take that away," she said, pointing at the feather-covered doctor. "Don't let him in here again."

Martha didn't bother arguing. She simply dragged the doctor out of the room. Ten minutes later, two snickering servant girls came in to clean up the feathers.

Aliya gave them a cannibalistic smile. Still riding high on her bad mood, she issued more orders: wash the windows, take down the curtains and the bed canopy and wash them, dust the shelves and under the bed.

The girls followed her orders to the letter. For a while, she sat back and watched them. She decided that the time had come to get up and go outside. Her nanny didn't see anything too outrageous in her behavior, and the servant girls obeyed her.

But since her heart was still racing from the doctor's visit and it looked to be about five in the evening, judging by the sun, and she believed mornings were the best time to start important projects (except for Monday morning), Aliya decided to start her new life the next day.

For the moment, she would put the book back and think about where to begin.

৪০ ◆ ৫৪

Anna Wellster went to the mirror. She fixed her hair and checked the folds of her dress where it stretched across her chest.

"Wait a moment, my dear." Her elderly lady's maid pinned up a lock of hair and pushed her toward the door. "Your father won't want to wait."

Anna shivered, but she wasted no time. She feared and hated her father, and for a good reason. He was Gardwig the Twelfth, his Majesty the King of Wellster. Gardwig had ruled for over a decade and was known for his hot temper, cruelty and shrewd opportunism. He'd been married seven times and had no intention of stopping there. The Holy Throne disapproved of divorce, but they had to bend the rules for Gardwig. If a priest had ever dared to inform him that divorce went against God's law, Gardwig would have answered, "As king, I am no less than a god. I have my own laws." Any priest who tried to excommunicate him would have found himself facing a death sentence.

Gardwig won all the fights he started and most of the ones he didn't. Other countries criticized him freely, but at home in Wellster, they tried not to annoy him. As a rule, people didn't want to die just so they could present a list of their complaints to Aldonai.

In the end, Gardwig married, divorced and executed his wives whenever he saw fit. He paid his soldiers on time so they would remain loyal, and the simple folk were proud of his powerful image without caring much what he did. They were too busy planting and harvesting their crops.

Anna's mother was his second wife. She had been executed. He divorced his first wife because she was too old, but he executed his second wife for cheating on him. Despite that, he recognized Anna as his lawful daughter and sent her into the country to be educated. He divorced his third wife for giving birth to too many girls. Anna had four sisters who were raised alongside her. None of them could stand the others.

Gardwig's fourth wife died in childbirth along with the child. It was a girl, so Gardwig didn't feel too bad. His fifth wife was caught cheating and put to death before he could get her pregnant. The sixth tried for two years to give the king an heir. In the end, she threw herself at the king's feet and begged for a divorce. If she couldn't give him a son, she felt it would be a sin to deprive him of the love he deserved and the kingdom of its heir. Gardwig met her halfway, and they put the petition to the Holy Throne in her name just to keep things interesting. The religious leaders grumbled a bit, but they felt sorry for the poor woman and finally approved the divorce.

Gardwig's seventh wife proved once and for all that seven is a lucky number. Mila of Shelt, the quiet, gray-eyed daughter of a baron, with a long, thick braid of dark hair, loved her tyrant husband sincerely. She surrounded the aging Gardwig with loving care, making sure that he ate well and gave him two sons. To top it off, she was pregnant again. Gardwig seemed to enjoy his last marriage with no thought of divorce or execution.

Anna was sure of one thing—if her father learned of her dalliance with her teacher, he would have her put to death, and even Mila wouldn't be able to dissuade him.

ଚ୦◆ଙ୩

Anna knocked at the door and waited before going in. His Majesty was sitting by the fireplace with a glass of wine and a plate of food. His faithful jester was on the rug in front of him. Anna had never seen her father without his jester, a small man with extremely intelligent eyes and a wrinkled face.

"Your Majesty," Anna curtsied.

"Come on in. No need to sweep the floor." He nodded at a bench by his feet. She sat down on it—bringing her down to the jester's level—and kept her eyes on the floor.

"Look me in the face." Her father's hard fingers pushed her chin up. Anna fought the desire to close her eyes. "She's not bad at all, is she Harvey?"

"She has nice breasts."

"Men like breasts."

"You can't keep a man with nothing but that."

"Who knows? Richard is just a boy. He may fall for it."

Richard? Who is Richard? Thoughts fluttered like frightened birds in Anna's head. Gardwig must have noticed, for he explained, "Richard of Ativerna. He's coming here with his ambassador. His father wants to marry him off, and you're the right age. You're not bad. You look like your mother; she was dark like you."

Gardwig had a thick mane of golden hair and gray eyes, but Anna had dark hair and eyes like her mother, whom she had only seen in portraits.

"As long as she's not a fool. Have you gotten mixed up with anyone?" The jester's voice was calm, but he glared at her.

Anna flushed. She knew that this man could have her killed, but she was angry. Almost without thinking, she burst out, "Who needs me without a penny of a dowry? I have to alter my own dresses!"

"Idiot!" Gardwig spat out, his eyes flashing. "Do you think that coins and rags make up your dowry?"

Anna recoiled. She slipped from the bench and fell on the floor, but Gardwig continued to thunder away at her. "You are a princess! You may even be queen someday! Your dowry isn't dresses. Its connections, land, and treaties! If Richard takes a liking to you, you'll be the one handing out dresses and jewelry to others. Ativerna is wealthy, and I need Edward as an ally. Richard will be my ally after him. If you marry him, I won't forget you. You can have the province of Bali as your dowry."

Anna smoothed her skirt and sat back down under the jester's mocking eyes. In a calmer voice, she asked, "Your Majesty, am I supposed to charm him?"

"Yes. After he comes here, he's going to Ivernea. You're the first one he's going to see, and your job is to be the only one he thinks of."

Anna nodded. She saw visions of balls, diamonds, and knights in armor, and above all, she saw herself with an elegant crown on her head—the crown of a princess, the future queen.

Oh, hell! Why did I get mixed up with Lons?

Gardwig looked at her for a minute and then nodded. "Go calm down. Speak to Mila tomorrow. She'll fit you with dresses that will make you shine. I'll tell her. You may go."

Anna managed to curtsey again and left the room.

Once she had gone, the king's jester shook his head and said, "I don't know about this. She's selfish and stupid."

"Just like her mother."

"Do we have anyone else we can use?"

"No. The next oldest is just twelve. This one is sixteen. Edward wants his son married in the next year or two."

"True. And there's Lidia in Ivernea."

"She's plain as can be. Eighteen years old and thinks about nothing but books—an old maid."

"Mila was over twenty, wasn't she?"

"She was a widow; I got lucky with her."

The jester nodded. He didn't have the least respect for Gardwig's wife, but he valued her. He saw how she loved the king and did her best to care for him. She was like a little hen on her nest, but she was just what the aging king needed. She wasn't vengeful or sly. All she wanted was a home and children, and she gave birth to boys, which was a good thing. Gardwig would have lost his mind without the boys.

"Fine. If you think he'll go for that snotty little girl, then I'll have a talk with her. Will you permit it?"

"When have I ever told you not to do something?"

Few people knew that the jester and the king had been raised by the same nurse. They were childhood friends who considered themselves brothers. The violent, capricious Gardwig loved no one in the world like he loved his brother, and his brother worked hard to deserve that trust. *Why is he a jester? Why not? He needed a day job when he wasn't busy stirring up intrigue.*

🞜◆🞜

Anna danced back to her room.

A princess! She would finally be treated like a real princess! And if she played her cards right, she would be queen someday.

She knew that she was beautiful and intelligent. She was educated, as well, thanks to Lons' hard work. She grimaced at the thought of him. *Maldonaya take him, why didn't I wait a few years? Because I always have to have what I want right away. Money, dancing, love, life!*

Lons was poor as a church mouse so he couldn't give her money and dancing, but in love… Anna shivered when she thought of Lons' hands, his lips, his body. Suddenly, she froze. She was already married; that was a big problem. One thing was clear: she could never tell her father the truth.

🞜◆🞜

Jess Earton—true earl, handsome devil, and warrior to boot—looked down at his sobbing child. He was lost as to what to do.

"Precious, don't cry. Sweetheart…"

The little girl cried even harder.

"Miranda Catherine Earton, stop the bawling this instant!"

It didn't help. In between blowing her nose and sobbing, the girl managed to say, "You're leaving me here, abandoning me."

Jess passed his hand through his hair. He adored his daughter. The six-year-old knew it and had him wrapped around her little finger. He had no choice, though. He couldn't take her with him. He would be busy with work, balls, tournaments, and intrigue. *How can I take a child with me if I don't even know where I'll be sleeping at night?*

When he suggested she stay with Lilian, Miranda became hysterical. It sounded like she might be choking. Jess was afraid, so he gave in. "Sweetie, you just have to stay at Earton over the winter. I'll come get you in the spring, all right?"

He didn't mention that at that moment, it was only the end of summer. Miranda kept crying, anyway. It took a long time to calm her down.

While he held her, in his mind, he composed a letter to Lilian. He had no love for his wife and considered her stupid and unpredictable, but he knew she wouldn't hurt the girl. His letter would warn her and maybe even frighten her a little. In the meantime, he tried to soothe his daughter.

Chapter 3

Threats and Promises

It was around noon when Martha came in, and Aliya was doing squats in the middle of the room. She had just started, but she was already sweaty, and her knees ached.

"What in the world are you doing, Lily?" her nanny gasped.

Aliya grinned at her. "Nanny, dear, order a bath for me and find something for me to wear. It's time to get out of bed!"

"Lily, the doctor said…"

"He'd better keep his distance from me if he wants to stay healthy. Nanny, I'll lose my mind if I stay in bed another day. I've been self-absorbed for too long. How about that bath?"

Martha shook her head but didn't argue. She left without saying a word.

ဆ◆ၛ

By the time she returned, Aliya had completed twenty squats, twenty lunges, forty jumping-jacks and thirty sit-ups. In her previous life, a routine like that would have been easy, but in this body, it was another story. She felt like she'd been hauling bags of cement all day.

Her plan was to repeat the exercise routine three times a day for three days. After that, she would increase the intensity of the routine every three days. It would be hard, but she knew she could do hard.

After her bath, she opened the curtain and followed her nanny into the closet, where she had never been before. After all, she had been hiding out in a roomy nightgown since she woke up. When she saw the inside of the closet, she burst out with "Holy fukalite!"

She had picked up that phrase in medical school. It got the job done and had the added benefit of being safe to say in case there was a professor in the room. If anyone had asked, Aliya would have explained that fukalite was a mineral made up of calcium, oxygen, and silicon.

Aliya couldn't think of anything else to say. Her closet was a room the size of her bedroom back home, and it was full of the most luxurious, beautifully made dresses—silk, brocade, lace, satin, velvet.

And all of them—down to the very last one—were pink and gold. It was enough to make a saint swear.

Aliya looked around the room and pointed at the plainest of the dresses. She silently resolved to find a dressmaker to remove all the gold bows and ribbons from the rest of the garments. She could do it herself, but she didn't think she could keep her sanity in the process.

Aliya knew how to sew, knit and embroider, and she even knew how to work with beads. She was fairly good at crafts, but she had no intention of wasting her time on things like that. There were too many other more important things for her to do in this new world.

The simplest of the dresses was modest, with a high neckline and three rows of gold ruffles around the hem. To Aliya's surprise, the fabric was plain linen.

All would have been well, but Martha informed her that she would need three crinolines underneath the dress. "But Lily, you can't go out without crinolines! The priest would call you a loose woman!"

She would also have to wear cotton pants with a slit in a very interesting location, an undershirt covered with cheap lace that ended up poking out through the slit in her pants, and yet another undershirt made of something that looked like cambric.

Aliya refused the thick wool stockings her nanny offered and slipped her bare feet into shoes made of soft, pink leather. *At least the shoes are bearable.* They tied with ribbons, and since she had taken up dance many years ago, she knew she would get used to them. A mere two hours later, Aliya was ready to go out. She felt like a big, pink cabbage…or a Brussel sprout. *Oh hell, nobody's looking anyway!*

The doors to her room swung open and ushered Aliya into the dark, dusty hallway. At that moment, Aliya decided to start the way her mother always started when they moved into a new place: with a big, spring-cleaning. She would have the castle cleaned from top to bottom, and during the process, she would learn the faces of everyone who worked there and teach them how she wanted them to do their jobs. She was in charge of this place—at least while her husband was away—and she intended to be the boss. The knowledge she had picked up while reading in bed would come in handy.

ॐ ◆ ℭ

Aliya threw open the door to the kitchen and smiled sweetly at the servants sitting around the table. The four women and seven men were having a terrific time drinking wine out of large glasses, laughing, and gossiping. She had seen three of the men before when they brought in her tub and hot water. The others were strangers.

All of them were up to no good, of that much she was sure. Aliya knew just how much work was needed to clean a small apartment; in a castle this size, there shouldn't be time to sit around telling jokes. One of the men had his hands all over the knees of the woman sitting next to him. Aliya wondered if she was responsible for paying for family leave when her servant girls got pregnant. She would have to find out.

Aliya took a deep breath and barked, "You idle, good-for-nothing, time-wasting freeloaders! Did you think I was too fancy to come down here? You were wrong!"

She scanned the servants' faces. The oldest woman was probably the cook. The only man dressed in a color other than pink (he was wearing blue) was most likely the Comptroller. She could tell by the young girls' faces that they were chambermaids. The girl whose knee had a man's hand on it was blushing. If she got any redder, her cap would burst into flames. The three young men with hay in their hair and a barnyard stench about them must be the grooms. The others were house servants.

Aliya was sorry she didn't know any of their names, but she wouldn't let that stop her. She could get to know them while giving them an earful.

59

"You've let things go while I was ill, but I'm back on my feet, and I don't like what I see. This place is covered with dirt, dust and spider webs. We have enough spiders in here to start selling silk. Now, you three grooms, get up!"

The boys leaped to their feet.

"You're lucky to still have your jobs for today. By tomorrow, I want the stables to shine. Haul out the manure, get rid of the spider webs and brush down all the horses. I'll check your work tomorrow, and if you don't do it right, you'll be cleaning each horse's ass with your own gossiping tongue. Now get out of here!"

She turned to the cook. "My dear, I don't like your kitchen for the same reasons. The pots aren't washed, the tables are covered with crumbs, and you let the servants hang out in here drinking my wine and doing God knows what else." She turned back to the servants. "And you there, with the pie-face. Get your lecherous hand off that girl's knee before I rip it off along with your head."

The man's name was Jean, and the girl of "easy virtue," was Mary. He blushed and snatched his hand away. Aliya sneered at him and looked back at the object of his affections, "Honey," she said in a poisonously sweet voice, "you and the cook will be busy in the kitchen today. You have until this evening to get the dishes sparkling and clean out the ovens. And you," she pointed at another servant girl, "will clean out the fireplaces in the whole house. I want them all clean as a whistle, just like the conscience of our Comptroller here."

Judging by how the Comptroller twitched when she said that, his conscience was none too clean. Aliya decided to leave him for dessert.

She turned back to the cook. "I will not let you turn my home into a brothel." She hit all the right notes like she meant it. "If I ever see something like this again, you'll be out of a job." She looked back at the floor. "Sweep out this straw and make the floor shine. Don't bother making lunch today, and just make something simple for dinner. I don't want any more of these twelve-course meals."

She turned to two chambermaids, "You two, grab your buckets and rags and follow me. You'll be cleaning all the rooms in the castle, starting with my room. And you can re-clean everything you supposedly cleaned yesterday. I've seen how lazy you are. We'll need one man to go with us. You'll be bringing water from the well for these ladies to clean with. Heat it here in the kitchen in the largest pot."

"Get some firewood!" the cook shouted at the man.

"Go get it yourself," Aliya replied. "It won't kill you. Otherwise, you're out of here tomorrow morning."

"My Lady," she heard someone say in a timid voice. It was the Comptroller. He had been sitting quietly through Aliya's tirade but felt he had to say something when his wife was threatened. "Your husband instructed me that during his absence…"

Aliya turned to face him. She was a large woman now, and she intended to use her size to good effect. "Did you interrupt me?" Her voice slithered like a snake through the leaves. *If I bite you, there isn't enough anti-venom in this whole world to save you!*

"Since you are the Comptroller," she continued, "you can give me a detailed explanation of how the estate has sunk to this level. I have been too lenient with you, and my husband does not have time to watch your every move. I want to see you in the office. Bring all your reports for the past year—everything you've bought and sold, crops, supplies, everything. Is that clear?"

The Comptroller swallowed nervously and said nothing, which was smart. One wrong word from him and Aliya would have hit him over the head with a pot—not in anger, just to teach him a lesson.

She was the boss, and her word was the law. Anyone who had a problem with that or voiced doubt about her authority would have his head handed to him…instantly. So, the Comptroller was wise to keep his mouth shut. *Even thieves have an instinct for self-preservation.*

Aliya suddenly realized she had a big problem. She didn't know the prices for anything or how much she was paying the servants. Martha couldn't be much help—she had served Lilian her whole life and was almost a member of the family. She had never had a family of her own.

"Nanny, dear, are there any people in the village who aren't local? People who have traveled?"

Martha rubbed her forehead and replied that there was one woman named Emma Mattie who fit that description. She was the widow of the former Comptroller of the estate. She was from the city and knew a bit about life.

Aliya rubbed her hands together. That was exactly the person she needed. If the woman had been married to the estate Comptroller, then she couldn't be a fool. *Or could she? It was too early to say.*

"Nanny, how can I invite her to come talk with me?"

Martha thought for a moment and offered to run into the village. Aliya pondered the idea and decided to risk it. "Nanny, the servants can do the cleaning without us. Why don't I go into the village with you to see the Widow Mattie?"

"But Lily, why would you—" Martha began to object out of habit, but Aliya stopped her with a raised hand.

"I just need to. Let's go."

"Should I order the carriage?"

Martha left, and Aliya glanced around at the servants again. She wondered if she should say a few words before she left. *Of course, I should!*

"If any of you suppose that I'll forget what I've told you to do and that you can go back to your little games while I'm gone, be warned. I'll fire you without severance pay in a heartbeat." She realized that she was talking over their heads and corrected her error. "In other words, I'll lock you all in the stable! And I'll whip you for laziness! Is that clear?"

She really did sound like a commander. Aliya laughed to herself. *I'll teach you to clean your boots in the evenings and put them on quick in the mornings.*

She found it interesting that not a one of them seemed to think her behavior was strange.

Martha touched her elbow. Before she left, Aliya informed the servants that she would have them cleaning the floors with their tongues if they didn't hurry up.

ৰু◆ଓ

Outside the front door, stood a piglet-pink carriage with gold trim. It was a rectangular wooden box on wheels, with nothing even reminiscent of shock absorbers. The windows were covered with something that looked like parchment and framed with pink curtains. *That makes sense. If they don't have a good way to make glass, they won't waste it on carriage windows.*

The four horses looked so tired that Aliya felt truly sorry for them. She loved horses and decided to give each of them a professional exam. Her discoveries were alarming.

"Why doesn't this horse have proper shoes?"

Two of the horses were each missing one horseshoe, the third had an abscess on its neck, and the fourth was breathing hard like it had a cold.

The groom, who was also the coachman, mumbled something about a hard life and some bad weather. Aliya measured him with a steely gaze. "Where is the nearest blacksmith?"

It turned out that the blacksmith worked in the village. They didn't have one at the castle. *One more errand to run.* She also wanted to buy herbs so she could put together some basic remedies. She wondered if there were any healers in the village.

With a sigh, Aliya turned to climb into the carriage. That was easier said than done. The carriage sat on wheels as high as her waist, and she couldn't lift her leg high enough to get in. Martha ran over carrying a stool. Somehow, Aliya shoved her body into the carriage, almost leaving her dress hanging on the door.

I absolutely have to get in shape.

Martha wanted to ride up front with the coachman, but Aliya waved her into the carriage. Her nanny was afraid to sit on the pink and gold velvet seat, but Aliya pulled her down.

"Stop being silly, Nanny."

"It isn't fitting for me…"

"Don't be ridiculous. You're closer to me than anyone else in this world, so I say it's fitting."

Martha grumbled something about undeserved honors, but Aliya just threw an arm around her neck and kissed her cheek. "Nanny, you mean more to me than my own mother."

හ ◆ ෆ

For the first time ever, Aliya left the bounds of her castle and took in the sights of the surrounding countryside. There was plenty to see. If she had had a choice, she wouldn't take this earldom for free. She wouldn't take it even if they paid her. From the outside, Earton Castle looked worse than it did inside. Its stone walls were crooked and losing chunks of mortar. The moat was dry, and the bridge looked like it would fall apart if anyone tried to raise it.

What if there was a war? What if the castle was attacked by enemies or bandits? How exactly is this castle supposed to protect them? She doubted she now lived in a nation of pacifists. There was no army to speak of, no telephones, and the 911 dispatcher hadn't been invented yet. She was on her own. She would have to clean the inside of the castle and then reinforce its defenses outside.

But how? I have no idea, but I'll start somewhere and see where it takes me. Aliya smiled inwardly. There was no reason to upset Martha with her new plans yet.

Since shock absorbers hadn't been invented yet, Aliya felt every bump in the road, which was not much of a road to start with, even by Russian standards.

People say that Russia doesn't have roads, it just has trails. Earton doesn't have roads or trails. It has wheel ruts. Some of the wheel ruts are deeper than others, but none of them rise to the status of a trail.

Aliya stuck her head out the window for some fresh air and promised herself that she would invent some kind of open carriage. She saw fields, pastures, and forests, but best of all, she saw a river. According to Martha's stories, Earton Castle stood about a mile from a wide river with lots of fish in it. Aliya had her heart set on salting, drying and smoking lots of fish. She knew a million ways to do it. *Even plain old carp can be a dish for a king if you know what to do with it!*

It took them three hours to bounce, rattle and skid their way into the village, which gave her enough time to recall everything she ever knew about farming. She remembered something about three-field rotation, but she would need to find out what the local soil was like and what tools were available for working it.

Aliya wasn't afraid to get dirty. As a military brat, she had spent her whole life moving from one base to another. Wherever they ended up, her mother had always started a garden. Tatiana liked growing her own fresh produce, and the economic hardships of *perestroika* had convinced her that gardening was a wise use of time. She raised her daughter with the same beliefs. As a result, Aliya could study the lunar calendar in a garden almanac and not think she was reading Chinese. *Where do I get a garden almanac around here? And what if their moon is different? What grains do they grow?*

Aliya could have written a thick book on making dinner out of next to nothing, conserving fruits and vegetables for the winter, and producing your own spirits at home. Her mother had always made such aromatic liqueurs using herbs and berries that even the generals had looked forward to trying.

What else do I know? Chemistry. She knew plenty about chemistry, including its various applications. She wouldn't have made it in medical school without organic, inorganic and general chemistry. Aliya could draw Mendeleev's periodic table from memory. The problem was that she didn't have any real-life experience with chemistry. Her medical school's lab didn't have many samples, and as a result, she couldn't tell sulfur from old bird droppings. *No big deal. I'll figure that out as I go along.*

Aliya knew almost nothing about farm animals. She could ride a horse, milk a cow or a goat and even shear a sheep, but she had no idea how to actually take care of animals. She had "helped" her grandmother with farm chores during summer vacation, but medicine had always interested her more than agriculture.

Aliya had dreamed of becoming a doctor her whole life. She devoured the books her mother gave her on the topic, including books on folk healing using herbs. All of it was interesting. Aliya and her mother re-read those books on folk healing in later years, when pharmacy shelves were empty, and it was hard to obtain actual medications. In those years, her mother expressed a lot of anger at the government. She was a nurse and people were sick, but there were no drugs to treat them with. *I'll treat people here with whatever I can find!*

Raspberry could be used to reduce a fever, and coffee raised blood pressure, especially if it was strong. Aloe juice could clear up a runny nose and reduce inflammation in the throat, making it a great cold remedy instead of store-bought nasal spray. Aloe wouldn't dry the nasal passages or have any other side effects. Sage and Iceland moss were both good for a cough. Aliya's mother had known plenty about medicinal herbs. She could prepare cough syrups, mustard plasters and lots of other useful things. Aliya could, too. As a child, her favorite game was to go to work with her mother and watch her examine patients while paging through thick medical reference books and asking questions. It was a game she and her mother had never tired of.

Studying pharmacology in medical school had expanded her knowledge, but Aliya never forgot those folk remedies. When she was at home, she and her mother always collected bark, herbs, and berries in the woods. And Aliya helped out in the family garden.

She took stock of what she could do: she was a decent surgeon and knew pharmacology better than anyone in her class, and she had a good head on her shoulders and golden hands. *What else?*

When she was in her own body, Aliya was an excellent athlete. She could also shoot straight and drive anything with wheels. Neither of those skills would help her now. She'd never handled a bow and arrow, and the only vehicles in her new world were pulled by horses and oxen.

There were two physical skills that might be useful. Like all children, Aliya had enjoyed playing with knives. She could throw them with decent accuracy and had other knife skills, as well. She was a surgeon, after all. It was a terrifying profession, cutting into living people every day.

Her second advantage was her army training. Hand-to-hand combat was a dangerous skill if used properly by a person in peak physical fitness. *But what if your body isn't in shape at all?* She felt more like a sofa cushion at the moment.

Aliya could have screamed in frustration, but she had no choice. All she could do was up the intensity of her exercise routine, knowing it would take a while before her new body started to show any changes. She could hurt herself if she rushed things.

On the seat next to her, Martha was still mumbling about something. Aliya leaned over to listen. The old woman was relieved that Earton was an out-of-the-way estate. It was a twenty-day trip to the nearest city, and over fifty days to the capital.

Aliya hoped that meant she wouldn't see much of her dear husband. The less he came nosing around, the better. She had no love for a man she'd never seen, and in fact, she would have been happy to arrange an "accident" for him—something along the lines of "I was minding my own business peeling potatoes with an antique dagger when my husband slipped and fell on it fifteen times." *How else could I feel about him?* He had married an unhappy, overweight girl just so he could get ahead in the world and then sent her away to live on an estate that was literally in the middle of nowhere.

If that wasn't enough, the "inseminator" just turned up once a year to spend three nights with his wife (when she was most likely to conceive) and then raced back to the capital. *What a prick! But they're all like that in these times.*

Aliya pricked up her ears as Martha griped quietly about the area. She hadn't found a map in the library, and she wanted to know where exactly she lived in this world. She knew Earton was in the sticks, bordered on the north by the Earta River, which was wide but not used much by boats. From what she could tell from Martha's grumblings, the Baron of Donter had his lands on the other side of the river, and the lands around Earton weren't very hospitable—cliffs and swamps to the south and east and, on the west, a pine forest that ran down to the sea. Even the sea had few boats—it was too shallow, and there were dangerous reefs. The family seat didn't have much going for it.

Aliya had no idea how she was supposed to live there. It was also a mystery to her why no one went down to the sea. They could at least have had a few fishing villages on the shore. She just didn't know enough about her new home yet.

She needed a business plan, and, for the first time ever, Aliya was sorry she hadn't studied economics. She could be sitting on a gold mine for all she knew. *Okay, I can figure this all out.*

She suspected that she could do what she wanted in Earton as long as she didn't go too far; there was basically no one there to stop her. She was the wife of the Earl of Earton—or an extension of him. Women weren't supposed to have their own ideas, so her will was his will. She would just have to know when to stop, and she had learned that lesson well in medical school. *A doctor who doesn't know when to stop can kill a patient.*

Aliya decided that when she got back to the castle, she would write out what she knew, summarize it, and draft an action plan for the next few months. With those thoughts in mind, she saw that they had arrived.

Chapter 4

Determination and Discovery
One word described the village: poverty.

There was a dirty 'street' down the middle of the village, where a crowd of skinny children stood around with frightened, hungry faces like stray dogs. Their eyes asked, *Is this new person going to kick me?* All of them wore gray shirts that came down to their knees more or less, and their dirty hair was cut short on both the boys and the girls. The dogs were as dirty as the children, and their ribs stuck out. The village was surrounded by the forest, and the houses were just huts.

Aliya started to get angry. *People shouldn't be living like this!* But here they were, and they'd been living this way a long time. They were surviving somehow, but their poverty was her fault. Well, it was actually the former Countess' fault, but the new countess was going to do something about it.

After looking around, Aliya got back in the carriage. Her eyes shone with such fire that Martha choked on her words mid-sentence.

"Who do I talk to here? Is there a village elder? Who's in charge of the village?"

"They're all out in the fields," Martha shrugged. "They won't be back until evening. If you want to talk to someone, there's just Old Mattie."

"Old Mattie?"

"I told you. Her husband was the Comptroller before this one. When Irk died, the master sent us Etor. Don't you remember? Your husband said—"

Aliya stopped her. "Of course, I remember all of that. I was just thinking of something clsc. Let's go." She wondered how old the woman was if everyone called her Old Mattie.

Martha stuck her head out the window and told the coachman to turn left while Aliya pondered the social rules that might govern paying of visits. She didn't think she could just walk in and say, "Hi, I live over that way in the castle. Have some flowers. I need your help." But if she didn't come up with anything better, that was exactly what she would do.

Her musings were interrupted by a child's cry. Aliya turned to see what had happened, and Martha called for the carriage to stop. Aliya threw open the door and managed to crawl out. *Life is ten times harder when you weigh over two hundred and seventy pounds.*

The children had been running around in the street, jostling each other and playing games. A carriage was something new, so they were excited. One of the children climbed up on a fence to get a better look and fell. He would have been fine, but his leg hit a sharp piece of wood that left a jagged wound. His friends saw the blood and started to scream and cry. All of this happened just a few feet away from Aliya.

Her reflexes kicked in, and she forgot about everything else—her new body, how she ended up in this new world. She knelt in the dirt by the wounded boy not as Countess Lilian Earton, brainless fool, but as Aliya Skorolenok, one of the best students at the Ryazan Medical School. Her ungainly body and the medieval conditions around her meant nothing. She was facing a person who needed help, and that was all that mattered.

Her voice was soft and calming as she spoke, "Don't worry, he's going to be fine. I can see that your friend is a brave boy, and he doesn't need to cry about a little scrape like this. It will heal over, and the scar will look good on him, won't it?"

She kept talking in a soft voice and carefully pulled the boy's hands away from the wound. At first glance, it was nothing serious. The bone wasn't broken, and no arteries had been touched. The skin was broken, and a muscle was hurt. She just needed to stitch it up and be sure to disinfect it.

"My Lady?" It was her faithful Martha. The coachman stood awkwardly nearby.

Aliya looked up at him. "You there. What's your name—Jacques?"

"Jean."

"Whatever. Take this child and carry him, let me see…"

"To my house," a friendly, deep voice interjected.

Aliya turned. "Who are you?"

"Emma Mattie, My Lady."

Aliya nodded. "Jean, take the boy to Emma's house. Hurry up. Emma, I need the finest needle you have and some silk thread. You can rip four or five of them off my dress. I'll also need strong wine, hot water, and clean rags. Can you get me those things?"

Emma nodded.

ౠ◆ಔ

Aliya worked fast and confidently. After drinking a cup of strong wine, the boy was almost asleep. She washed his leg, stitched it up, and applied a bandage. It was all done quickly and neatly.

Her professors would have been proud. Less than an hour after his mishap, the child was asleep on a bench in the corner under a warm blanket. Emma promised to keep an eye on him until his parents returned from the fields. Aliya promised to come back every day to check his leg. She would have preferred to take him back to the castle, but she didn't know where she would put him, and she wasn't sure where her rights as Countess ended. Martha was already shocked by what she had seen.

As was Emma. An attractive woman about fifty years-old with bright, intelligent brown eyes, and streaks of gray in her dark hair, but her posture was straight and youthful. She was dressed as if she had known better times, but even now, her clothes were clean enough, if plain and gray. Aliya watched the woman for a few minutes, unsure how to begin, before deciding to just jump in.

"I was on my way to see you, Emma."

The widow Mattie was obviously taken aback. Aliya gave her friendliest smile. "I know my arrival here was unexpected. Let me explain. Would you rather sit outside in my carriage or here in the house? Please don't worry. I came because I heard good things about you."

"What exactly?"

Aliya saw that the woman was smart. She nodded. "Plenty. You were married to the former Comptroller. When he was in charge, the estate was run properly. Doesn't it hurt you to see everything your husband worked for going to waste?"

She saw that she had hit a nerve. With the help of two women, I'm going to make a life for myself in this new world.

She told Emma Mattie the story she had cooked up: that after she lost her baby, she couldn't keep living as she had before. For a start, she wanted to bring order to the estate, since she suspected her Comptroller was stealing. Then she would turn her attention to the villages of Earton. What Aliya learned from Emma was worth the long drive.

There were three types of coin in Ativerna. Gold crowns and silver scepters, which were named for the symbols stamped on them, and simple copper coins. One gold coin was equal to twenty silver coins, and each silver coin was equal to fifty copper coins. A chambermaid was paid twenty copper coins a month. A soldier earned one silver. A bag of turnips cost three coppers. Five coppers would buy a pile of firewood.

The Comptroller was supposed to make sure that the peasants worked the Earl's fields, but he went beyond that and charged them ten silver coins per village, to be paid each month. The peasants scrimped and saved to pay the tax, but the Comptroller turned around and cheated the Earl by skimming off the top for himself. He padded all the estate's bills and put the difference in his own pocket, and he often claimed to have bought something for the estate that could never be found in any of the storerooms.

Jess Earton might not notice, but Aliya felt bound to do something to help these people now that she was in their world. She might have gone easy on the Comptroller if Emma had not added that he taxed some families by taking their daughters and selling them to the slave traders whose ships sailed down the coast.

And because the fewer witnesses, the better, he had sent all the castle guards and some of the servants home, despite the fact that the castle was already short-staffed with just ten of each. They were told that they wouldn't be paid any longer, so they could find other jobs or go sit at home. Whenever the Earl showed up, the Comptroller told him that the guards were patrolling the coast or staking out robbers in the villages. He was a professional liar, and it never entered the Earl's mind to inspect his villages and talk to people when he could be out hunting.

Once she had the whole story, Aliya was enraged. If she had been in her own body, she knew what she would have done—make the man cry until he gave all the money back. In this new body, though, she couldn't do anything at all. Except... An evil smile crossed her lips.

"How many strong young men are there in the village?" she asked Emma. "Or maybe some of the old castle guards still live around here?"

Emma frowned and thought for a while. Then she told Aliya that there were about fifty men between the ages of twenty and forty living in the village. Two of them had served as guards at the castle. The entire population of the village numbered about three hundred.

Aliya couldn't wait. "How can I find them?"

"There are three places they'd be: the fields, the forest, or down at the river."

"I don't want to go hunting around in the forest. Should I go out to the fields or send someone to call them in? I need about ten men; the sooner, the better."

Emma studied the Countess' face and gave a slow smile. *Has the time really come?*

A minute later, they had found some boys outside and promised them sweets in exchange for an errand. The children ran off in all directions to find their fathers and older brothers. Meanwhile, Aliya sat with Emma and listened to more of her stories. She couldn't stop clenching her fists in anger.

The villagers had few animals left. They were forced to sell their crops for next to nothing, and they were worried about making it through the winter. Each winter, the village lost several dozen members. Old people stopped eating so the children would get enough. Instead, they ate bark, acorns, and even grass.

And all the while Lilian Earton has been eating ten-course dinners! Aliya was ashamed to have Emma's eyes on her. All that kept her from dying of shame was the knowledge that none of this was actually her fault. It may have been Lilian's body, but it was Aliya's mind. Aliya knew she had been given a second chance—both for herself and for the silly Countess.

♦

It took at least an hour for the first group of five men to show up. Martha informed her of their arrival.

Aliya sized them up. They didn't look ready to set the world on fire. Their dirty gray clothes were patched and darned, and their shoes were wooden clogs. Their beards and hair were trimmed short. Most importantly for Aliya, their eyes telegraphed a message in giant letters: *What does this woman want?*

Aliya took the bull by the horns without waiting for them to speak. "Do you want to make some money?"

It took the men all of twenty seconds to think over her offer. Then the message in their eyes changed: *Silver coin!*

Aliya smiled. "As Countess of Earton, I am reassembling the castle's guard. I guarantee each of you three silver coins a month, as well as clothing and food while you serve. You can take extra food home with you. If you want to join up, take whatever weapons you have and follow me back to Earton Castle. We'll sign a contract, and you'll get your first payment."

"What do we need weapons for?" asked a young man with suspiciously familiar brown eyes.

Aliya grinned. "We're going to convince the Comptroller to let go of some money."

"You mean, kill him?"

"Just convince him."

Aliya, Emma, and the young man all had the same fire in their eyes. Sometimes, it takes a sharp blade to convince a man to part with his money.

"How about an ax?"

"Let me see it."

Aliya examined the weapon and nodded. "This will do for now. We'll get you a better weapon later. There must be some weapons left in the castle. He can't have taken them all!"

Judging by the looks on the men's faces, they knew exactly what she wanted and didn't mind doing it.

ଞ◆ଔ

Aliya didn't get home until late evening. She was mad as a hornet, tired, and hungry, but she decided she wouldn't eat until she had finished cleaning out the corruption in her household.

The castle was quiet. She smelled burned porridge and saw dirty streaks on the floor. She snorted and headed for the kitchen. Her instincts were correct. All the servants, the Comptroller, and his wife were sitting in the kitchen. They didn't look as cheerful as they had that morning.

Aliya sailed right in. "I see you're having a nice break. Is the stable sparkling clean, or does it look as bad as the castle? If you gentlemen, and I can't remember all your names, threw some straw on the floors and thought that was good enough, then I'm here to disappoint you. You'll wish you'd never seen that straw when I'm done whipping you. Is that clear?"

Judging by the color of the grooms' faces, they understood her perfectly. Aliya smiled and added a few more expressions she had picked up from her days as an army brat. She had read somewhere that what was called foul language actually used to be magical incantations, and that would explain the magical effect her words had on the grooms, who jumped up and ran off to finish their jobs.

She turned her bright eyes to the chambermaids, who didn't even wait for her to speak before flying from the room. Last, she turned to the Comptroller with a friendly grin that bared her teeth. "I think it's time for the two of us to have a chat."

Etor's face went pale. He swallowed. Then he followed her from the kitchen.

Aliya already knew where his office was. She sat down at his desk and smiled at him again.

"Well? Let's see your reports."

"But My Lady, why would you—"

"The reports!" she growled. Her tone was so convincing that Etor gave in and opened the chest where he kept his books. Aliya suspected that it wasn't just her voice that won him over. The four young men who had come in with her—two of Emma's sons, the village elder's son, and the older brother of the boy she had stitched up, all of whom held axes in their long arms—played their role as well, as they eyed the Comptroller.

It had taken her all day to find the men she needed, agree on payment with them, get transportation back to the castle for them, and have the blacksmith fix her horses' shoes. She was looking at more long hours back in the village the next day. Aliya was too tired to be angry at that point in the evening, but she still had plenty of choice words left in her vocabulary.

However, when the Comptroller laid six big books on the table in front of her, even her favorite swear words left her.

"Tell me what this book is."

"It's a list of revenue."

"What about this one?"

"Expenses."

Aliya thumbed through the books, which were nothing but columns of numbers. "Wonderful. Now, I want you to stand over here next to me and read down each column with me—how much the estate made and on what. Give me some paper and a quill. While you read out loud, I'm going to take notes and do some adding. Then we'll look at expenses."

She had hit just the right tone with him. She could have waded through the accounts on her own, but it would have taken twice as long. Time was money, and Aliya didn't want to waste either.

Etor did his best to weasel out of the position he was in. He wheedled and pleaded and tried to confuse her with complicated terms and irrelevant information, but he was out of luck. Aliya had been raised on 21st-century television news channels, the champion liars of all time; Etor never stood a chance. Once she wrote everything out, added it up and made some comparisons, the truth was clear.

The estate Comptroller had been ripping her off. He was stealing excessively, stupidly, and far above his pay grade. She had three options, the way she saw it: she could fire him, drag him into court, or have him whipped. A man couldn't walk very far after a hundred lashes, and he couldn't very well complain to the King while holding his head in one hand. She could do whatever she wanted with the Comptroller.

On second thought, it was her husband who could do whatever he wanted. Aliya wasn't sure exactly where her authority ended, so she decided to be creative. Turning to Etor, she suggested that he return three-quarters of what he'd stolen and take the remaining one-quarter to tide him over while he looked for another job. If he didn't like that option, he could always have his head chopped off, and Aliya would hold his wife's feet to the fire to find out where he kept all his money.

Etor's opening offer was one hundred gold coins. When she countered by threatening to hang him on the spot, that amount doubled. Aliya had no intention of letting him go easily. Hold a genie over a hot frying pan, and he will give you ten times more wishes. Etor quickly doubled his offer again. After lengthy negotiations (the young men did all the negotiating, with Aliya telling them where to hit him), he doubled it once again.

In the end, Aliya got about eight hundred gold coins out of him. She had a strong suspicion that this was only half of what he had stolen, but it was plenty for what she intended to do.

She should have had him disemboweled, or at least drag him in front of a judge. Execution was too good for him, but she didn't think she could hand down a death sentence, even if she had the authority.

Etor sensed her changing mood. He crawled in front of her and whined like a puppy, nearly licking her shoes, and begged to be allowed to care for his small children and elderly parents. Aliya knew he was lying and that she would lose face by letting him go. *On the other hand*, she thought, *no one in this world respects me anyway*. She wouldn't tell anyone that she'd let him go, and she suspected that she could make the village men hold their tongues, as well.

There was always more than one way to shear a sheep. Instead of a judge and public hanging (where she suspected she'd make a fool of herself), she asked Emma's son to ride through all the villages and tell people that the Comptroller had been thrown out and would be leaving Earton in the morning with his wife. If Emma's son didn't wish to go on this errand, he could send boys to carry the news.

Then she caught the young man's eye and, smiling broadly, added, "Let the people sell him a horse if they think he deserves it."

The young man gave a wolfish grin that made Aliya shiver. She wouldn't use her own hands, but the Comptroller would get what he had coming to him. *Let the people you robbed be your judges.*

ಋ◆ಛ

Morning came early the next day. She had left the curtains open on purpose, and the sun's first rays made it impossible to sleep. Lilian Earton's body protested, and its sore muscles whined, but Aliya was ruthless.

Time to get up! Don't like it? That's your problem. I've got exercises to do. Squats, push-ups, sit-ups, jumping jacks, lunges.

She grabbed the first dress she saw in the closet. Aliya decided she would ask Martha to sew her a couple of simple dresses for every day. She would have preferred to wear nothing but an undershirt, which in 21st-century terms, was a plain shift dress that went to her ankles, but people would be shocked. She did, however, refuse the myriad petticoats and cotton pants as too much fabric for one woman to wear.

Martha appeared after Aliya had already managed to pull a dress over her head and was swearing at whoever decided that women's clothes should lace up the back. Without the bulky underclothes, Aliya no longer felt so huge.

"Good morning, Lily. How did you sleep?"

"Wonderful, Nanny. Could you help me with this?"

"But why were you doing it alone? I always help you." Aliya barely listened as her nanny went off on her favorite topic. "It doesn't fit for a lady… I can do everything for you… You shouldn't have to lift a finger…"

Good grief! Next thing I know, Martha will try to help me on and off the toilet.

She interrupted the old woman with a question. "Nanny, has Etor left?"

"Yes, he and his wife left as soon as it got light."

Aliya smirked to herself. "Did the people sell him a horse?"

"The boys from the village came back to see them off. I believe they knocked him around a little bit before they let him go."

"I hope it was more than a little bit."

"Lily!"

"He had it coming. But that's enough of that. Back to cleaning. I won't live in this sty!"

"Lily, surely you exaggerate?"

"Can't you see it? This place is knee-deep in dirt everywhere I look! We've got some hard work ahead of us. At least ten days. Shall we get started?"

"But what about your breakfast?"

"I thought I fired the cook."

"You did, but you can always order…"

"None of that. Isn't Emma here yet? I'll send a carriage for her."

"Lily! You want to send your carriage for a peasant woman?"

"So what?"

"Even the doctor has never ridden in your carriage."

"Emma is much more intelligent than the doctor. I hope she found the people I asked her for."

The day before, Aliya had asked Emma to find two dozen women for the dirty job of cleaning the castle properly. She had no money for real repairs yet, but even a good cleaning would help.

"Who around here knows how to cook?" Aliya was perfectly capable of cooking for herself, but she didn't know how to use a wood-burning stove, and she was afraid she would look silly trying to learn.

"I suppose anyone can…"

"Perfect. Then have one of the girls cook something simple."

"But…"

"I don't want any more fancy breakfasts with eight different dishes. Just a big pot of buckwheat with meat, and maybe some bread and cheese. Is that clear?"

"Lily, I don't think…"

"I can live on porridge. It won't kill me. Nanny, please just do as I ask. And have all the servants who are still here wait for me downstairs in the kitchen."

Martha nodded and hurried from the room.

Aliya sighed. She opened the wardrobe and looked at herself in the polished metal mirror again.

"What do you say, Lilian Earton? We aren't from around here, but we can shape this place up. I hope. Are you scared? Just take a deep breath and hold on. Nobody dies twice, right?"

Her reflection shook all three of its chins. It was not happy.

Aliya laughed out loud when she thought about what she had just said. She'd already died once. She wondered if it were possible that she had become immortal. In any case, she wasn't Aliya. She was Lily—Lilian, the Countess of Earton.

Anyone who doesn't like my new ways will get a mop upside the head!

8o ♦ ෆ

The woman who went downstairs was in a good mood and feeling sure of herself; the inexperienced girl left farther in the past. Her servants met her with foreboding, but the young men she had hired the day before were pleased with the turn of events thus far—especially the estate Comptroller's ouster.

"That's just the start," Lilian said to herself, grinning.

"More cleaning today," she said briefly. "The grooms get another day to finish the stable. The horses are in terrible condition, and so are the carriages. If you let things get that bad again, I'll have you all whipped. Get going! Breakfast will be later, once I see that you know how to do something other than eat."

One of the grooms opened his mouth to say something, but Lilian brought her fist down on the table. The table groaned. *Sometimes, being a large woman comes in handy.*

"Quiet! Do as I say! All of you, march!"

The grooms obeyed in silence. Aliya slowly let her breath out. When she turned around, she almost fell over Emma's son. He had been standing behind her the whole time without saying a word, but his eyes spoke clearly. She sighed. Apparently, she wasn't as convincing as she had hoped. She realized she needed her own guards. It was the Middle Ages, and people would only listen to her if they thought they could get something out of her or if she had proper firepower. Sad but true.

Lilian turned to the chambermaids. "Ladies, let's see your hands." The girls stared at her, but obediently held out their hands for inspection.

Their hands looked good. There wasn't a single callous among them. *These girls have been hired to clean, but they're sitting around eating and drinking at my expense without doing any work in return!*

Aliya knew how much hard work went into cleaning even a small medical office. She and her mother had often suffered from cracked skin caused by harsh cleaners. Her chambermaids' hands looked like they had never touched a floor, much less washed it.

Aliya's eyes flashed. "You listen to me; there will be no breakfast today. Mary and Ilona, take the sheets you stripped off the beds yesterday and go wash them. If I see a single spot on them when you're done, I'll have you whipped alongside the grooms. Sarah, go help Martha in the kitchen. Make enough food for about twenty people. Just buckwheat with beef, nothing else. Jean, Peter and Claus, you follow me."

She started in the library. The drapes came down, and the furniture was moved out so that the chambermaid could clean the entire floor. Servants with huge rags wiped the dust and dirt off of everything in the room. Jean climbed up a dangerous-looking contraption that he called a ladder to sweep the spider webs off the twelve-foot-high ceilings. Aliya emptied out desk drawers while she watched them work and issued orders. It was no easy feat to keep three full-grown men working on the task. As soon as she took her eyes off them, one would start daydreaming about his lady friend, Mary, the second would accidentally knock the moldings off the ceiling, and the third would begin tossing books as if they were bricks. She was lucky to stop him before he ruined any of them.

They don't scare me. I've done harder jobs!

ഉ◆ഇ

Anna slowly combed out her hair. Things were going well so far. Mila had made her try on dresses all day, which, when she thought about it, was a good thing. *If I want to catch a big fish, I need to use good bait. Help me, Aldonai.*

The door creaked.

"Lons! Have you lost your mind?"

The man slipped into the room. He took the comb from her hands and began to run it through her thick hair.

"You know I lost my mind over you a long time ago."

"I told you not to come near me while my father's here."

Lons put down the comb and pressed his lips against the back of her head. "Anna, I can't live without you. You're my whole life."

"This is interesting. Have you two known each other long?" the voice slashed the lovers like a whip. Anna would have screamed, but she clapped her hand over her mouth in time. Lons turned. The King's Jester stood in the doorway holding a crossbow, and the arrow was pointed straight at Anna's husband.

"I can't hear you."

To Lons' credit, he didn't fall on his knees. "I've loved Anna for a long time. She is my wife in God's eyes."

"How sweet. Who heard your vows?"

"The priest here at the castle."

"Father Linder?"

"No, Father Zemin."

"I see. The one that died this spring?"

Anna nodded. There was something of her father in her, so she knew what was coming.

"Then tell him he made a mistake." The bow twanged. If Lons hadn't made a dodge for the window, he would have been dead on the floor. As it was, the arrow, grazed his right side. An instant later the paper covering the window tore, and Lons disappeared into the night.

Anna pressed her hand to her mouth as hard as she could. The Jester noticed. He took a flask from his pocket and held it out to her. "Drink this."

She shook her head, but he insisted. She took a sip, and then another.

"It isn't poison. It's just strong wine. Drink."

Obediently, Anna swallowed some more of the heady drink. A warm, liquid flame ran through her body. She coughed but stayed standing.

"Good girl. I'm glad you know enough to stay quiet."

Anna nodded. She didn't know what this little man in bright clothes wanted, but she knew she'd have to go along with it, whatever it was. If he let a word slip, she'd be up on the scaffold in no time. Gardwig didn't play games. People called him the Lion of Wellster and, like a lion, he didn't care who he ripped into.

"Now talk. Who was that?"

"My teacher."

"I always said that education is no good for girls. Breasts are enough. How long have you been with him?"

"Two years."

"Fool. Do you have children with him?"

"N-no."

"That's bad. Are you barren?"

Anna shook her head. "Lons always brought a potion with him."

"I see."

"He wanted to ask Father for my hand."

The Jester sneered. He knew what the king would say about giving his daughter to a teacher who, although he was a member of the nobility, had no estate of his own.[viii] *Just hilarious!*

"Here's what's going to happen. Tomorrow, I'll let everyone know that he stole some jewels and ran off. We will keep the story simple."

Anna stared at the Jester. She was feeling the effects of the wine. "And you won't…"

"No, I won't. Hurting you isn't in my interests. If you keep your mouth shut, I will, too. Gardwig doesn't need a scandal right now, but he does need a closer friendship with Edward. I don't want to catch you with anyone else. Is that clear?"

She nodded. "Why would I bother with trifles when I can have a crown?"

"I see there's hope for you…and a little of your father in you."

Anna nodded again. "I won't say anything. But what about Lons?"

"Other than you and the priest, does anyone know?"

"No, just the priest."

"Did he write down your marriage anywhere?"

"No. Lons asked him not to."

"He probably paid him not to. Fine. He tried to win you, but you'll be the winner in the end. Let me do some investigating. If there are no records of the marriage, then just hold your tongue. Even if they threaten to cut you in pieces, just hold your tongue. You're a young girl, as innocent as a daughter of Aldonai."

Anna nodded. "Gardwig will show me no mercy if he finds out."

"You just remember that." The Jester patted her cheek. "Now, go to bed. You'll be wiser in the morning."

Anna nodded. She reached around to unlace her bodice and never even noticed when the terrible man left her bedroom. He just disappeared.

Lons was gone, too. From now on, she would have to be extremely cautious. *If only this Richard person would marry me!*

The strong wine did its job, and Anna fell asleep. She dreamed of balls, jewels, and a host of suitors crowding around her. Each of them had one of two faces: Lons or the King's Jester.

ༀ◆ༀ

Lily looked around the drawing room with a sense of accomplishment. She thought of herself as Lilian more often these days, and she felt no alienation from the name. *What a difference a week could make!* Everything pink in the whole castle was gone, except for Lilian's dresses. All of the pink fabric had been carefully taken down from the walls. Lily would have given it all away—she was starting to feel like a Spanish bull at the sight of pink—but Emma tactfully reminded her, "Countess, this fabric cost an enormous sum of money!"

Lily had no idea how much the fabric wall coverings cost, but she decided to find out where in her new homeland they made fabric. She carefully dropped a few hints, and Emma immediately picked up on what she wanted. The Widow Mattie was by no means simple. It turned out that silk (Lily was shocked to find that her walls had been covered with it) was only made in Elvana, on the border with the Vari Khanganat. She deduced that her father must have bought the pink fabric for her. It was a costly present. As the owner of several boatyards, he was a wealthy man and could afford such luxuries.

With a firm hand, Lily gave three square yards of the silk to the three women who had worked the hardest. The others received copper coins. She could tell that none of them had expected such generosity from her. Emma did not approve—she knew the servants would have been happy to receive their pay in groceries—but the job was done.

Once the silk came down, it revealed handsome oak panels. They darkened the room, but Lilian told the servants to dust and wax them. Once they were polished, they looked much better. Under the thick layer of straw on the floor, she found ancient stone tiles that looked like they could be marble. They would look better after a cleaning, as well. The room was dark, but anything was better than the awful pink and gold.

Everything Lilian laid eyes on needed to be washed or dusted, and she ran around the castle giving orders. In the ballroom, she had them open the windows, dust, and toss out any dead mice they found. She ordered the guest bedrooms dusted and then kept closed for the time being. She wasn't expecting guests, anyway.

In the formal hall, the game room, and the ladies sitting room, Lilian ordered the servants to take down all the pink fabric. Then she had them wash everything in the house, even the 'privy'. That done, she had them build an outhouse behind the castle. It was a standard army-style outhouse, with two doors marked M and W and three seats behind each. She informed the staff that anyone found answering the call of nature in the castle instead of the outhouse would be whipped as an example to the others.

She had to make good on her word the very same day when she caught Peter urinating on an oak wall with carved panels. Instead of raising the roof right then, she just slipped around the corner as quietly as she could manage at her current size and went off to see her guards. They had been pleased to return to work at the castle, so when Lilian nodded at Peter and ordered ten lashes, no one argued with her. When no one was looking, she whispered to one of the guards that they shouldn't break his skin. She wasn't being merciful; she just didn't want to have to treat him. Lily didn't want to go down to the stable yard to watch the whipping, but she knew she had to. Everyone needed to know that this particular woman always did what she said she would. Otherwise, she'd never make any progress.

She needed people to follow her orders. For now, she could lean on her title, her husband's shadow on the horizon, and a small band of young men with strong arms and axes. Lily had only been able to locate two members of the castle's old guard. The others had left the area looking for wars where they could hire on as mercenaries to feed their families. These two old-timers drilled the new guards whenever they had time, but they knew as well as Lily that it was just a drop in the ocean. And she needed every drop of help she could get.

"Countess…"

"Yes, Emma?"

Lily turned and smiled. She couldn't have made it without the woman before her. Emma was an expert at issuing commands, dressing down servants and throwing fits when necessary. Lily could do all those things, but she decided it would be better to have someone do it for her.

Emma enjoyed the work, and Lily had time to write. She kept an eye on progress in the castle and swore at the servants when absolutely necessary, but she spent most of her time in the library writing out notes with a quill pen that splattered ink everywhere. She wrote out everything she remembered about medicine because she knew that if she didn't use her knowledge, she was in danger of forgetting it.

❧◆☙

After two days spent writing, she took a day off to go see the blacksmith. The handsome young man was built like a large bookshelf. After about five minutes of drawing on the ground with a stick, he said he could make her several of the new metal quills she wanted, but he warned her that he wasn't used to doing such fine work and begged her not to have him executed if something wasn't quite right. Aliya thought for a moment and nodded. She would give him a chance. If he couldn't do it, she would find someone else who could.

A metal quill would be an improvement over a goose feather, and there would be demand for it. She also wanted to develop a non-spill inkwell, still primitive, but useful for merchants, sailors, and other travelers. The blacksmith understood and promised to make a prototype once he finished the quills. He could make plenty of inkwells; it wouldn't be difficult. Lillian smiled. She needed money to improve the estate, and while goose-feather pens looked pretty, they were awful to write with. She hoped if she patented her metal quills, she could really make some money.

✿

"Countess, Father Vopler is here to see you."

Shoot! The priest must have heard of Etor's departure and come to see what was going on. If I know anything about the church, he isn't just here to look. He'll expect to go away with something.

Priests were no fools. In order to serve the church, a man had to be well educated for his time, with solid theological underpinnings and the ability to use psychological pressure, even bordering on hypnosis, to imperceptibly get information out of his flock.

It's game over.

She would have to keep the interview brief, or he would see through her. To the peasants, she was just a countess with a gigantic attitude. Emma may have guessed at more, but a priest was a different matter. *What do I do?* She needed to scare him, but not too bad, and without making him mad; he could come in useful later.

"Fine. Have him wait and give him something to eat."

"We have boiled vegetables, Countess. We also have buckwheat with meat and black bread, as you ordered…"

"Then give him that," Lily snorted. There was a gleeful twinkle in Emma's eyes. Everyone in the castle was on the same diet. Lily had even given the keys to the food storeroom to Martha. Her stomach thought it was a bottomless barrel, so she wanted to keep temptation at bay.

"Will you be changing clothes, My Lady?"

Lily sighed. She suspected that Emma was much more intelligent than she let on, and she probably had some ideas about her Lady's strange behavior. But advantage was stronger than curiosity. As long as people felt that they were better off with the new Lily, they would support her.

She couldn't afford to alienate this priest, however, or cause him to suspect that there was something strange about her. Medieval religion was a powerful force.

I have to humor him, but I won't give him any money. Not a chance! Lily believed that priests were like gypsies—once given a handout they would never leave.

"Call Martha or one of the girls to help me get ready." She sighed and headed for her closet to choose her most ridiculous dress.

It took about half an hour to put on everything she was supposed to wear. Lily was so nervous that she argued with the servant girl and stomped her foot. *It shouldn't take this long to change clothes and leave my room!*

What's my plan? I have to get rid of him and make him never want to come back here. What do men hate most of all? Tears and argument. It doesn't matter what year it is—a loud, highly strung woman is a force to be reckoned with.

Looking like a gilded wedding cake, Lilian sailed into the drawing room and locked eyes with Father Vopler.

ꟹ♦ꟹ

He was an average male. Not bad, but not much to look at, either. His face had simple, serious features; he was well-built, and his hands looked downright aristocratic. *Is he the son of a nobleman who graduated from university and was sent to serve the church in the sticks?*

Lilian Earton's memory refused to be called up. She had never cared for trifling things like the village priest. After all, he wasn't edible.

Thankfully, Lily's body did its part automatically, lowering itself onto one knee and making the sign of Aldonai with the right hand.

"Give me your blessing, Father."

The priest slowly rose from his chair and put a hand on her head. "I bless you, child of light."

Lilian shuddered. Does he ever wash his hands?

Their greeting complete, both landed in the nearest chair, Lily heavily and the priest with more elegance. They looked at the table. There wasn't much to be happy about. The silver dishes held buckwheat with meat, slices of black bread, and a pile of sheep's milk cheese. The soup tureen was full of steamed vegetables.

Aliya considered it a perfectly acceptable lunch, but the priest was obviously dismayed.

"My child, I have heard strange rumors…"

Lily sighed. Her large eyes filled with tears. "Father, it was such a tragedy. Such a loss!" As soon as she remembered her parents, it was like a dam had opened, and tears ran down her face.

Lily told him about the awful estate Comptroller who had abandoned her, about the loss of her baby, about her husband who had left her without money, and about anything else she could think of short of a failed turnip crop. After ten minutes of this, the priest was bored. After twenty minutes, he looked depressed. Lily had no intention of letting him go that easily.

No, sir. You're going to sit here with me until you make yourself forget the road to my house. Even if I invite you back, you won't come. Lilian Earton might not have excelled at many things, but she knew how to throw a fit. Aliya used that talent in her own interests. All she had to do was start whining about her lonely life as an abandoned wife, and the rest of it came naturally. Lily didn't let the priest stand up, much less eat anything. She made a good show of sobbing. He tried to help her up, but she just slid to the floor and lay there holding onto the hem of his cassock (she considered using it to wipe her nose). Finally, the priest could take no more of her howling and crying, so he called for the servants.

Emma came in so quickly that she must have been listening at the door. She bustled around Lily, saying something along the lines of "Good Lord, look at how you've upset My Lady." Martha and Mary added to the confusion in the room, and the priest hurriedly made his exit.

As soon as his green cassock disappeared, Lilian stood up, dusted herself off and sent Mary out of the room to get some water for her to wash her face.

"Martha, stop jumping around me. Go see to things in the kitchen. Emma, dear, send someone to the village to see how the blacksmith is doing. We have so much to do, and we aren't making enough progress."

Emma looked her in the eye. "My Lady, you wanted to be finished by the autumn fair."

"I hope to do so." To herself, she thought, That priest had better stay away. I'm not ready for him yet.

೮◆ಐ

"The fair, My Lady!"

"The autumn fair!"

Grain, animals, food of all kinds… In years past, Etor had been in charge of preparing for the autumn festival, but alas, he was no more. In fact, Lily learned that the peasants had found the bodies of Etor and his wife just after they left. Apparently, the wolves had gotten them. No money was recovered, of course.

After consulting with Emma, Lily decided to go to the fair in person. It would be held in Altver, a ten-day ride from the castle. Boats would carry goods from all over to the river port, and merchants would drive wagons overland to get there, as well.

The market at the fair was the place to buy anything and everything—from farm animals, grain and firewood to clothing, dishes, and jewelry. In addition to a traveling theater with minstrels and jesters, a wide variety of pickpockets and other thieves would also be in attendance.

After much consideration, Lily called together the elders of all the villages. She had a task for them.

৪০◆ଓଃ

They met in her office. *It's actually my husband's office, but I'm assuming we have community property, right?* Lily sat in the only chair. Five more stools were brought in for the elders. She had wanted to organize a roundtable, but Emma had tactfully vetoed the idea, saying she shouldn't put herself on the same level as the peasants. It was no use arguing.

Emma chose the food and drink, setting out five tankards of ale and a plate of bread and ham. Simple fare was good enough, and the men were glad to see it. Lily studied them discreetly. All five were enormous. *Who said people used to be smaller?* She was no down feather herself, but these men were huge. The largest two had broad shoulders and stomachs that rivaled Lilian's. The other three were smaller overall, but she could see they were all muscle and bone, without an ounce of fat on them.

Ian Leig, Art Virdas, Erk Grismo, Sherl Ferney, and Fred Darcy. She had to find common ground with these five men or die trying. She could have ordered them to do what she wanted, but she wanted them to feel that it was to their own advantage to help her. *If they know they'll benefit from my plan, they'll forgive me my strange habits.* She was a stranger in this world, and she needed the help of people who were born here. Her role would be to manage, provide financing and learn.

The men were in no hurry to eat the food set out for them. No one spoke, so Lily jumped right in. "Good afternoon. I wanted to see you because our affairs are in a bad state."

Their five faces became thoughtful. They obviously expected nothing good of her. She smiled as kindly as she could, like a friendly snake. *A new commander always starts with a good dressing-down, just to get his men hopping. Then he shows them how useless they are without him.*

"I understand that there are approximately twelve hundred people living in all of our villages. For convenience, let's say fifteen hundred, including all the women, children and old people."

The elders said nothing. Lily continued. "You have around three hundred people in High Wold, Ian. Art has two hundred in Appleton. Erk has three hundred in Riverton. Sherl has a hundred and fifty in Fiur, and Fred has about three hundred in Runstaf. Of the women, children and elderly, how many will survive the winter?"

The question cut like a knife. The men looked away from the Countess' bright green eyes.

"I see. How many died last winter?"

"I'd say about a hundred people," Ian rumbled. "This year, it will be no less than that. The little ones will die of hunger. They go first when the women's milk dries up. The men don't know where to get feed for the animals. If they feed them grain, they won't have anything to plant come spring. But if they slaughter the animals, they'll lose everything they have."

Lily's ears turned red, but she couldn't turn back now. None of this was her fault, and she was going to put a stop to it.

"So what have you elders been doing about it? You are supposed to protect your villages. Why didn't you come to the Earl or to me? I see you'd rather keep your heads down and say nothing and watch your children die of starvation, is that it?" Lily's voice rose to a scream. She remembered Perestroika like it was yesterday, watching her mother measure out the buckwheat from her father's rations to make sure it would last until the next distribution. She always ate less to make sure that Aliya got a little extra.

Countess Lilian Earton leaned over the table and glared at her guests. "You said nothing and waited. So, you'll just have to wait a while longer. Now, listen to me. We'll start with the soil. We can't afford to lose the soil, can we?"

It took Lilian ten minutes to explain the three-field rotation system. The elders began to glance around at each other. They realized that they weren't about to be executed, but Lilian's anger had gotten their attention. They could tell that she was restraining herself by force of will as she talked to them. Her restraint scared them. *Anyone can yell, but it takes a true master to show restraint.*

Finally, Sherl spoke up. "We don't have enough grain for that."

"True. We'll buy grain at the fair. If we're choosing between wheat and rye, I suggest wheat. We'll divide the land into two parts: one for wheat and the other for oats and barley. Next year, we'll clear more fields and plant them with wheat. This year's wheat fields will grow oats and barley, and the fields where we had oats and barley this year will be left to rest. We'll plant grass, and pasture the animals on them. The fields need to rotate like that every year. If we're able to buy extra seed, we'll find a place to plant it."

"We are low on oats," Art sighed. "And we sold all our fruit to merchants for next to nothing just so that blood-sucker wouldn't take our daughters. I have three of my own, and two sons."

Lily sighed. "We'll buy grain at the fair. And we'll buy cattle. Good cattle, not those skinny cows you keep."

"How are we going to feed them? On prayers?"

"You're right about that. We'll have to buy feed this year. Next year, we'll have our own grain stores. And I'm canceling your taxes and your fieldwork obligations this year, but only for this year. I'll collect after the next harvest—one-tenth of the whole harvest. Next year, we will turn my fields that you've been working into pasture for the cattle and let it rest. Let's talk about the fruit trees. Emma says that most of the orchards are in Appleton; is that right Art?"

"Yes."

"Who takes care of them?"

"We all take turns."

"And seven nannies let the baby drown. Here's what you do. Choose two families to oversee each orchard. Make that three families. Tell them to do a good job, or I'll have them whipped. If the trees do well and the fruits are harvested carefully at the right time, I'll pay them a silver coin each month. At the end of every month, I will inspect the orchards and pay them. Will that take care of the orchards?"

Art nodded; of course, it would.

"The same goes for all the other orchards by Fiur and Riverton. Next item. I plan to buy several cows for each village. I'd like to get some bulls, as well. Do you have anywhere to keep them?"

The men glanced at each other.

"I see. You will fix up your cow sheds and insulate them against the cold. I'll come out later to inspect. I won't give you the cows if you're just going to let them freeze or get eaten by wolves. The same goes for your goat sheds. I want to see at least a hundred goats in each village. Fix up the henhouses while you're at it." The men nodded.

"Next item. I want to have fish ponds dug in Riverton next year. We'll use the ponds that are already there. They just need to be cleaned out before we put fish in. Carp will do well. And each village should have about thirty pigs. That's just to get through the winter so that no one slaughters any cows. We want to keep the cows and goats for breeding and milk. You can keep a few pigs for breeding and eat the rest. When we buy grain, we'll get enough for seed and for feed." Again she paused to see that they understood.

"Good. We won't have any trouble on the way to market, but we'll come back as a caravan for security."

Fred, who had been silent so far, spoke up. "My Lady, what about the cost?"

Lily nodded. "A cow costs around eight silver coins. A pig costs three. That's for a good, young sow. We'll see when we get there, but it might do better to get shoats and feed them. I'm not sure, yet. We'll have to do the math. All I can do now is estimate. We'll see the actual prices when we get there."

Based on her estimates, Lily thought she had just enough money, barely. And she had some ideas about where to get more. She had found some of Lilian Earton's old letters and was working on forging her signature. She would write to her husband and tell him that if he didn't send her some money, then she would come to live with him in the city. *That should make him feel generous.*

The blacksmith had already given Lilian her inkwells. If they sold, that would bring in a little money. They looked good, but they were too simple, and she didn't have enough of them to turn a profit before others started to copy them. Large-scale manufacturing didn't exist, and she had no idea where to start to get a patent.

Then there were her dresses. The fair was the perfect place to sell them. They were all expensive silk, with gold embroidery and pearls. Better yet, each of them had enough material in it to sell for the price of three dresses. Lily decided to take her jewels with her, too. If she ran out of money, she could always hock or sell them. With babies in danger of starvation, she couldn't care less about her fancy jewelry. She'd buy herself something nice next year if the estate turned a profit. Farming required investment if she wanted to see a harvest, so Lily was prepared to spend some serious cash. What worried her was how to get all the purchases back home safely.

At least a ten days' trip—that was nothing to sneeze at. And it was only ten days if they went at a good pace on horseback. *How many miles is that? Oh right, they haven't invented miles yet. Or meridians, either! It will take longer if we're driving cattle. How many herders will I need to drive a herd of cows? I need people to feed the animals and guard them, too. I bet everyone between here and the fair would like to get their hands on some free cows. And there's so much that needs to be done here before we bring all those animals back.* She decided to leave the organizational issues to the elders: who, how, what, and how much. If they wanted to benefit from her goodwill, they would use their hands and heads to get the work done. In the process, she would see who the hardest-working was.

The cows weren't really a gift—they would eventually have to pay her back. When she made this clear, the men lost some of their enthusiasm and starting hinting about their hungry children. Lily kept her temper in check but explained in a sweet voice that if anyone lost a child to hunger that year, she would blame the father for being stupid, lazy, or greedy. She didn't need men like that in her villages and wouldn't be surprised if they ended up as crow feed. If they were looking for a handout, Lily told them, they had the wrong countess. She was barely making her own ends meet, but she'd be glad to help anyone who wanted to invest sweat equity in fences and a cow shed in order to keep one of the cows she would buy.

It was evening by the time the meeting broke up. Before they left, the men suggested what looked like a good plan. Instead of driving the cows overland all the way back from the fair, they could take them up the Earta River most of the way and then make the rest of the trip as a caravan. It would still be dangerous, but less so.

Lily wasn't sure. Where would they get that many boats? And if the Earta was safe for navigation, why weren't there any villages along it?

The elders explained that their villages were already small, so they didn't want their young men to be tempted to run off down the river to the big city. They also worried about defending themselves from river pirates. After all, peasants weren't allowed to own serious weapons.

Lily didn't believe they were completely unarmed, but she decided to check out the selection of weapons for sale at the fair. If necessary, she could have them make slingshots. Even a child could use one, and nobody—even a pirate—wants to catch a rock to the head.

We're ready. Well, almost. I still have to learn to ride a horse.

Chapter 5

Pain and Gain

On her first day in the saddle, Lily managed to bruise everything below the belt. She finished the job on the second day, bruising everything she hadn't already landed on. Still, she was glad to have a horse that could carry her. The handsome draft horse went by the name Chestnut and was equally happy to see Lily and the piece of salted bread she brought him.

It took skill to ride a horse. Aliya had those skills, but Lilian didn't, and all of her body memories belonged to Lilian. Even wearing three pairs of pants—silk, wool, and leather—she suffered from a sore butt and ripped seams.

At least she wasn't trying to ride a side saddle. They had tried to convince her to use one, but Lily put her foot down. She would have a regular saddle and wear pants covered by a skirt with slits cut in it to cover her legs and allow her to sit more or less comfortably. The skirt wasn't hard to sew, and she had plenty of pink fabric to choose from.

What was it with Lilian and the color pink?

She didn't expect her skirt to stay fresh and pink for long. Horses sweat, and after a day's work, they don't smell like roses. She knew by the end of the day, she would smell about as bad as the horse, and there wouldn't be anywhere to take a bath. Lily was afraid to stop at any more inns along the way to the fair. The one time she had set foot in an inn, the odor hit her in the face so hard that she stood on the porch retching. *Even the city morgue didn't smell that bad! Just dead bodies and formaldehyde.* The inn had smelled of rotgut, rotten meat, and unwashed bodies, like a dumpster and a homeless camp all in one small space.

Lily ordered the servants to buy food in the villages. They would be camping out in the fresh air. She didn't care if her meat was tough from roasting over a fire. With a full set of molars, she had no complaints about Lilian's teeth.

That reminds me, I need to look for a toothbrush and tooth powder at the fair. What else do I need? Soap. It isn't hard to make soap, and I can use local ingredients. Something to scrub with. Do loofahs grow here? Would some other plant work? Maybe I can grow something.

They bought bread and soft, yellow cheese in the villages. Lily was nervous about eating the bread. She knew that if the grain hadn't been stored properly, rye bread could be contaminated with spores of a dangerous fungus that could cause hallucinations or even seizures. That was why she had told the peasants to grow wheat. She knew that poorly stored rye was a hazard, but she didn't know the right way to store it.

Lily wanted to bang her head against a wall; there was so much she didn't know. She realized that her education was sorely lacking. *What are kids learning in school? They certainly aren't taught how to survive in the wild. People in our times don't know how to make shelter, start a fire without matches, tell edible mushrooms from poisonous ones, grow wheat, or work with a horse... They want to "put religion back in schools," but who the devil needs that? Basic survival skills would be a better use of kids' time.* Lily figured she didn't need help dealing with God. She needed help making simple things like paper, ink, and salt...

There were no comforts in her new world. It was pure stubbornness and a will to survive that got her back in the saddle every day. She had to grit her teeth and keep moving forward. Nobody cared that she was tired. So, she held on. After a while, the peasants stopped looking at her with contempt and distrust. Now, they only distrusted her. She saddled her horse without help, climbed into the saddle every day, and rode without complaining.

There were just five men with her on the trip; the elders Art Virdas and Sherl Ferney came along to consult with her on what to buy, and Jean Corey, Rem Veras, and Tres Mattie provided security. Jean had once been captain of the castle guards, and he kept the other young men on their toes. Lilian sighed. In her previous life, she could have kept up with them all day, even with a heavy pack on her back. Now, she couldn't even do her exercises for fear the men would see her. She was afraid of being found out—very afraid.

There were other fears to consider, as well. Her former Comptroller had traded with pirates. With their source of slaves out of the way, will the pirates get pushy? How can I defend my lands from them?

The estate was basically defenseless. Anyone could walk right in and take whatever they wanted. Lily didn't like that. She was responsible for five villages in a world teeming with bandits, wolves, and bears. People in the 20th century hunted wolves from the safety of helicopters, but in this world, you had to climb a tree and shoot arrows. There were too many wolves and not enough arrows. Threats could come from the river or the sea, as well.

She needed an armed militia. She had watched the guards training at the castle and tried not to laugh. In her old life, she could have flipped all those heroes like turtles. They were slow, and she could see their moves before they made them. When they practiced sword fighting, none of them thought to trip their opponents. *Is that some ancient code of honor? Dead men aren't interested in honor!*

Lily needed real warriors—hardened wolves, not barking dogs. She would use the guards she had for now, but she knew they would be useless against real fighters. On the other hand, she suspected that a real militia would cost her more than an iron bridge. Professionals don't graze on grass.

⁞◆ 

By the fourth day of the trip, the men pitied her as she wheezed and groaned her way into the saddle. After another two days, they started to respect her. They could see she was having a hard time riding, but that didn't stop her. Nothing would stop her; that earned their respect.

When they finally came within sight of Altver fortress, Lily almost rolled off her horse laughing.

Is this what they call a fortress? I've seen churches taller than this!

The fortress consisted of a stone wall that was three or four times as high as a man is tall. The corner towers were slightly higher, and the total area was just enough to fit two of Lily's castles. It was enough room to hide people—without any comfort—during a siege.

The fair was already in full swing at the foot of the walls.

"I wonder where I can spend the night," Lily mumbled.

Art heard her. "I was here year before last. There's a nice inn called The Pig and Dog. The keeper rents rooms, but they aren't cheap."

"Are they full of fleas and bedbugs?" Lily asked suspiciously.

"No." Art knew how she felt about insects and permitted himself a smile. "The keeper's wife is a Virman. They have to clean their houses out ten times a day. Their god makes them do it."

"I like that god!" Lily exclaimed.

Art made the sign of Aldonai. "My Lady, don't talk that way where others could hear you. Our priest can't stand other religions. He says they were all invented by Maldonaya!"

"I promise I won't. But I do like clean habits. Tell me about Virmans."

"Virmans? But don't you already know, My Lady?"

Lily's eyes grew sharp. "Next you'll be asking me what I learned in school! Mind your own business, elder!" Of course, she knew some things, but not enough by a long shot.

Art looked down. Peasants knew better than to answer a question with a question. "Virma is an island not far from the shore of Ativerna. The Virmans are sailors. They do a little trading and a little pirating. They aren't bad people, and they're good at music, but mainly they live by the sword. Their land is poor, so they can't farm, but goats and sheep do well there. They make shawls out of goats' down that they bring to the fair to sell. Those shawls are so fine that you can pull one through a gold ring!

Lily nodded. "If we have any money left over we'll look at getting some shawls as gifts. Let's go."

ଆ◆ଔ

Lons Avels had spent several days hiding out in the coalman's hut deep in the forest. He hadn't seen this coming. The youngest son of a landless noble, Lons received a decent education at the monastery. He wasn't cut out to be a monk, though; he loved a life of drinking, dancing, and pretty women. The monks knew he would never join their ranks, so as long as his father paid for his schooling, they left him alone. Then fortune seemed to smile on him. Father Julius found him an ideal job. He was to teach the princesses to read. He was euphoric as he traveled to the castle.

His dream came crashing to the ground as soon as he arrived. The castle was falling apart, and his salary was tiny. He had thought the princesses lived at court, but Gardwig had little use for his daughters. He wanted them to be literate, but otherwise, he had no intention of wasting the treasury's money on them.

The princesses all slept in a single room, wore each other's handed-down dresses and sniffled and sneezed through the winter because the castle was impossible to heat and always frozen like a cube of ice by morning.

Food was another problem. The princesses were expected to be extremely pious, so they observed three twenty-day fasts and nine three-day fasts each year. The fasts were strict, with only grains and vegetables allowed. Even worse, the entire household was supposed to practice piety along with the princesses.

Lons quickly learned to make quiet purchases of fish or meat and keep them in a cold corner. Otherwise, he wouldn't have survived. He was a grown man and couldn't live on vegetables, and he couldn't be seen going out hunting during a fast.

With a pitiful salary and little in the way of material support from his family, Lons soon grew bored, so he embarked on an affair with a dairymaid from the village and otherwise devoted his time to teaching the princesses. Anna was the most interesting of the group. She was the oldest, bright and intelligent, with a thirst for life. She was like a black diamond surrounded by white quartz, all glittering and shining. When Lons arrived at the castle, she was just eleven or twelve, but her eyes were far from childish—the eyes of a grown woman angry at the whole world. *What did she have to be angry about? And why did Anna fall in love with him, a man living close to poverty and with few prospects for the future?*

He taught her, and she learned. She seemed like a grown woman already. She was small, but she was a woman. There were smiles and glances between them from the very outset. She was thirteen when she bled for the first time and wrote him her first love letter. More letters followed, and they turned into looks, touches, and hints.

Anna was hunting like an experienced woman. *Where had she learned the skills?* Lons was no match for her. No, he stood firm for half a year and tried not to notice her. He even burned her letters. In the end, he gave up.

She knew what she wanted, and there was nothing he could do to turn her off. Their romance burst into flame as if Maldonaya had blessed it (or at least spit into the fire). Lons completely lost his head over her eyes, her lips, and her body. She couldn't get enough of him, and he felt the same. He didn't want to be her lover; he wanted to be her husband. So, he struck a deal with the priest. The papers confirming their marriage and a little bit of gold were hidden outside the castle.

Lons hadn't expected to have to run, but the situation snuck up on him. So, he found himself, sad and unfortunate, pondering his next move. His options did not look good. He could go back to the castle, but after the scene with the Jester, he was worried about ending up on the scaffold or having an 'accident' somewhere in one of the castle's darker corners.

They wouldn't hurt Anna—that much he knew for sure. Gardwig didn't want a scandal. *He wanted to marry her off!* Lons ground his teeth. "I won't allow it! She's mine!"

On the other hand, what am I going to do—go holler outside her window? He could slink off and never see his Anna again, but Lons couldn't make up his mind to do that. As usually happens, fate made the decision for him. The door of the hut creaked. Lons was reaching for his weapon—an old knife on the table—when he was struck by a blow to the jaw that knocked him against the wall.

The young giant who delivered the blow nodded. "The coalman was right. He's still here."

Strong hands picked him up. Through a haze—after a blow like that he expected to be spitting out teeth for three days—he felt a rope tighten around his wrists. Then they dragged him off.

Will they kill me? Probably. Farewell, Anna…

ഇ♦ങ

The Pig and Dog was fairly clean, and the floors were covered with straw that, while not fresh, was not rotten. The tables were clean enough to sit at, and she could touch the cup and plate without feeling disgusted.

Lily liked the looks of the innkeeper. Tall and hearty, with blond hair and blue eyes, he reminded Lily of a Viking.

"Is the keeper a Virman, too?"

"You bet. He bought this inn about twenty years ago, and he's done real well for himself," Art answered.

The food was good. They were served large pieces of roasted goat, a hot soup made of something like beans, goat cheese, soft rye bread, and a savory drink served in clay cups that reminded her of mead. Judging by the taste, it was no more than five-percent alcohol. Barely more than water.

Lily noted that she would need to distill something like moonshine for medical uses. As far as she could tell, the strongest drink they had was something called "iced" wine. This was wine made from grapes that had been frozen to remove a portion of the water, making it a little stronger than regular wine. *It tastes like juice, but I'll be glad for a glass of it after this trip!*

Lily frowned as she bit down on a chunk of goat meat. The trip was doing her good. Her dresses already felt looser, but she had a long way to go. And she needed to do strength training to avoid baggy skin.

Is this hard? Does it hurt? Too bad. I just have to grit my teeth and keep going. My parents are gone, but I'm alive. Somebody must really want me to be in this world. And I owe Lilian Earton something, too. She's dead, and I'm living on in her body. I want to live a life that I can be proud of.

She had other, more far-reaching goals, as well…

I don't want to just plant crops and build houses. I want to do my best to prevent this world from repeating the mistakes I saw in my world so that technological progress doesn't outstrip moral and ethical progress. First, I have to invent paper and promote literacy. Then I'll write a bunch of books. And I'll need a travel-size set of lead weights to keep my hopes from getting too high…

♊ ♦ ♋

"Innkeeper, bring more wine!" Leif hollered and banged his fist on the table, even though the innkeeper was already hurrying toward the Virmans' table. They were his countrymen, at any rate.

Leif was feeling rotten inside. His people called it "cat scratches" when a man's soul was ripped up, but Leif was sure the cats had already dug a deep moat around his heart. He only knew of one way out—to drown the cats in cheap wine. He couldn't afford expensive wine, or even something decent.

It all started back in Virma… a small, rocky and inhospitable island at first sight, but it was his home. When Leif closed his eyes, he could see the steel-gray waves hitting the shore and the seagulls spreading their wings against the low sky. The home he had been forced to leave was in Erkvig. It had a low, sloping roof, and the fireplace in the room where he was born—and where all his ancestors had been born and died—was charred black with soot.

In his mind's eye, he saw the thick column of smoke rising into the sky and blotting all of it out. The Virman moaned softly. He didn't hear himself, and he didn't notice how Ingrid glanced worriedly at her friend, or how the innkeeper turned pale, knowing if the table of Virmans took to drinking to drown their sorrows, it would be the end of him. They could pull the whole place down and leave a pile of burning woodchips.

Leif knew the fire he had left behind, and he knew he would never go back.

Ingrid put her small hands on his shoulders. "Leif…" The Virman smiled and turned to his beloved. He had no idea how that smile changed his face. Instead of a seasoned cutthroat, he looked like a young man in love with a queen, or a goddess. The innkeeper had reason to hope that the day might end without a fight.

Ꭿ♦Ꮳ

Virma is a small island inhabited by large clans. Most of the time they get along fine and intermarry, but sometimes they get involved in feuds. The Erkvig and Torsveg families were sworn enemies. Leif had killed two Torsvegs, and he knew who was responsible for his brother's death. He had wanted to get another one of them in revenge, but he had missed his chance.

The Virmans put away their swords one day a year, on the day set aside for Fleina, the goddess of love and fertility. On that day, no one risked spilling even a drop of human blood. They propitiated their goddess by dancing, jumping over fires, and partying all night. Anyone who failed to celebrate the day properly would be struck by infertility. If the goddess turned away from a Virman, his love would bear no fruit. Such was her power.

On that very day, the oldest of the Erkvigs and the youngest of the Torsvegs met their deaths.

Everyone was making merry. Young people were burning bonfires on the beach and having a great time. Leif had just returned from a campaign and was staying with a friend. He was not one for games and merrymaking on the beach. He just wasn't interested. His mother often reminded him that it was time for him to wed, but he felt like an old sea-wolf who didn't want to be chained down. His friend talked him into going, however, and it just so happened that Ingrid ran away from her nannies and her brothers to see what was happening there.

Leif saw her leap over one of the bonfires in a storm of golden sparks. Just at that moment, Fleina smiled at him. The young woman in the simple dress seemed so beautiful to him that his heart beat faster than it ever had before.

"Who is she?" he asked his friend in a gruff voice. He didn't know, so Leif decided to approach her.

No Virman was willing to risk the wrath of Fleina. Everyone needed someone to love, and it was in Fleina's power to bestow that love. As his legs carried him past the bonfire, Leif was worried that Fleina would punish him for avoiding the festivities in previous years, but the girl did not look away. She stood there and looked him in the face, and he saw something strange in her eyes. He had wondered, *Embarrassment? Confusion? Or was it…*

Leif would not have been surprised if she had cried out and run away. He had never been handsome in his youth, and he was nothing to look at now. He knew that the sea and the wind had turned his skin brown, and that his nose was broken in two places, and that he had old scars crisscrossing his cheek and chin. Even so, the girl looked him straight in the face. She didn't move away when he got closer. Instead, she smiled and held out a hand.

"I'm Ingrid. Who are you?"

"Leif."

"Leif." The way she repeated his name made it sound like music. "I've never seen you before, Leif."

That night they became husband and wife—on the one night of the year that young people were allowed to exchange vows in front of the priest, standing by the bonfire that burned to honor Fleina. Such vows were valid in Virma, as honorable as wedding bracelets in Ativerna. Neither dowry nor parental permission was required.

Young people didn't even have to give their family names. All the priest asked was their first names as he joined their hands over the sacrificial fire and poured a few drops of blood into the flames. Perhaps the priest was under the control of the fertility goddess, who wanted to reconcile the two feuding families. *Humans are still humans, however, and they often prefer to make war instead of love.*

They were discovered at dawn. No one was really looking for them. Gunnor Torsveg had just thought it would be a good idea to burn his enemy's ship, but when he got to the beach, he was surprised to discover his own sister sleeping on its deck in the arms of his sworn enemy.

Unfortunately, Leif didn't have time to think through what was happening. He always slept lightly, and that night, he lay awake holding his beloved, who had fallen asleep in his arms. She was his woman.

When a rowboat bumped into the side of his ship, Leif carefully set Ingrid down and reached over to where he kept his knives. There were eight of them; he figured that would be enough. He waited to see what would happen. Gunnor climbed aboard with a bucket of tar and froze when he saw his sister. That gave Leif time to throw his knives. One hit Gunnor, and one hit his friend as he climbed onto the boat. Leif tossed their bodies overboard and covered his beloved with a fur blanket. She was still asleep, and he didn't want to disturb these moments of peace. A few hours later, his men began to return to the ship and told their leader that Henrik Torsveg was looking for his daughter, Ingrid, who hadn't returned from the merrymaking on the beach the night before. Suddenly, the Virman began to suspect that he had given his vow to the daughter of his worst enemy.

When asked, the woman simply nodded. "I was a Torsveg, but now I'm yours. You can keep me or kill me as you like. I won't argue. I'd rather die now than have to live without you."

"Did you know who I was?"

"No. My father never told me much. I always thought that Erkvigs were wild animals. I was stupid."

Leif could tell she wasn't lying, not for a second. She kept her loving eyes on him the entire time they spoke. *It was love!* Then she trustingly handed him his knives, knowing that he might stick one of them through her throat.

Leif put his knives away, but one thing became clear to him: he couldn't live in the same country as the Torsvegs. If he stayed, there would be war. His father, mother, and brothers would never forgive him for marrying the daughter of their oldest enemy. And the Torsvegs would never forgive him for the death of Gunnor and for taking Ingrid. They would look for revenge. Leif was not afraid of fighting, but...

He decided his best move would be to tell his parents everything and then leave the island for a while. His father was understanding. He approved of killing Gunnor. Then he studied Ingrid, who was pale but stood straight as an arrow.

He smiled. "Fine. We'll continue our talk away from the women's ears. Let your mother meet her new daughter-in-law."

Leif's father had no objections to his plan. Leif left his family everything he brought home from his last campaign, taking only the bare necessities back to the boat. He and his men could always procure what they needed. *The sea takes care of Virmans.*

Thirty men joined him on his boat. They were his band. Ingrid was accompanied by nine other women who didn't want to spend several years apart from their husbands. There were twelve children on board, as well. There was room in the hold for them all.

All would have gone well, but once they were at sea, they encountered Henrik's ship. It had a red shield mounted on the bow, facing outward.[ix]

They engaged in battle. Ingrid begged Leif not to fight her father, and she tried to call to her father that she was Leif's wife now, but her attempts were in vain. Henrik shot the first arrow at his daughter, hoping to kill her. If Leif hadn't thrown his shield in front of her in time, she would have fallen dead. He dragged her to the deck and handed her to one of his men, who put her in the hold with the other women. The battle raged on.

It was not like a normal battle, where one group of men fought another. This battle was all about Leif. He lost control when he saw the arrow aimed at Ingrid. That was unforgivable. The demon in him awoke, and Leif gave an order that he never regretted: "Shoot with fire!"

Leif won the battle because of a new weapon he had paid dearly for at the market. No one knew what the steppe warriors put in their fire missiles, but the liquid in them would burn even in water. Just five missiles did the job. Henrik's boat caught fire like a struck match. The men on his boat were on fire, too. All Leif's men had to do was finish them off with arrows and spears.

Some men would have said that there was no honor in such a fight. Leif did not care. His job was to keep his men alive and to protect his wife. When he thought of the danger to his wife, it seemed to him that Henrik had not suffered enough.

His men were alive, but Ingrid mourned for her father for three days. For the first time in his life, Leif felt helpless. But with time, all sorrows pass, and Ingrid came around. One night, while he was standing watch at the tiller, she came to him and rested her cheek on his shoulder.

"Forgive me."

"For what? It is your job to forgive me. I know he was your father, but I had no choice. We would all be dead if I hadn't fought as I did."

"I know. I love you."

"I love you, too. Don't leave me. Please."

"Never."

"Never…"

And then they found themselves in Ativerna, which was where their real problems started. No one at the port of Altver was glad to see them; Virmans generally meant trouble. But Leif had to find a place to spend the winter with his crew and a way to feed them.

He had some money, but it wouldn't last long. It would be dangerous to try to waylay ships and rob them while living in Ativerna, where piracy was not a way of life as it was in Virma. He would be away from home for several years and had no desire for trouble.

Leif and Ingrid stopped at The Pig and Dog on a whim. Ingrid had wanted to refresh her stores of herbal remedies, so Leif took her to the fair. After making their purchases, they stopped to eat at the inn. That was a mistake.

When an insolent young man at another table started trying to attract Ingrid's attention, Leif groaned inwardly. Ingrid was everything to him. Fleina had made her as flawless as the sun, and he knew that suitors would have taken her house by storm if her parents hadn't hidden her. Now that she had been noticed, he would have to raise anchor and leave the port. Even such a drastic measure might not help. If his new enemy tried to sail after him, he had only two of the fire missiles left. They wouldn't be enough…

And then, out of nowhere, Leif was rescued by a large woman in a pink dress.

Chapter 6

Truth and Trust

"What's all that noise about?"

Lily was distracted from her problems by the sounds of a fight about to break out. She looked around the inn. Art and her guards were seated at a table. Sherl was at the bar talking to the innkeeper about getting rooms for the night. *Where was the noise coming from?*

When she saw the two men, Lily gasped and put her hands to her face. One was a typical Virman: tall, blonde, and powerfully built. Lily raised her eyebrows when she caught sight of the fair-haired woman hiding behind him. She was strikingly beautiful and had a perfect figure. The tall Virman had a friend with him. They were faced by three angry 'rich boys'.

No matter what year it is or what world you're in, Lily thought. The children of rich parents are all the same. Like fungus and tapeworms. They look the same, walk the same, and their butts have never been whipped. That's a shame. Who let those fools think they could do whatever they wanted?

"That's the Baron's son," Lily heard someone say. Apparently, the young man was well known for causing trouble and providing free entertainment wherever he went. *I see. He's the Baron's son. And a rude little prick, to boot.*

"Who's that with him?"

"His buddies. They're nobility, too, you see."

Lily snorted. Of course, they were nobility. She focused on what the young men were saying.

"You're just a puppy," the Virman growled. Lily agreed with him.

The Baron's son shot back, "You, serf, had better leave that whore with us and be on your way. She'll catch up with you later if she wants to, but I doubt she will. She looks like she'll enjoy being with real men. So get lost. This is no place for the likes of you."

Lily watched as the Virman put his hand on his sword. Then she looked at the Baron's son and the lovely young woman, who was pale as a sheet.

Then she looked around the inn and counted quickly. *Who else is in here? Any city guards?*

Two tables away, she saw a couple of men in red and blue capes.

"Are those city guards?" she asked Art.

"I think so, My Lady."

It was obvious that no fight had started yet, and the three rich boys were still alive because of the presence of the city guards. They were also the reason the locals were getting out of hand. Two men, even Virmans, had no chance against the three rich boys and the city guards. *What would happen to the girl? What on Earth am I sitting here for? She can't be a day over sixteen, and she's scared to death. If I don't put a stop to this, someone's going to throw a punch, and then they'll all drag this place down around our ears. They look like professional brawlers.*

She stood up from her table.

"My Lady, where are you going?" Art asked.

Lily put a hand on his shoulder. "I'll explain later."

She picked up a pitcher and a bowl of soup and headed toward where the fight was brewing.

"You belong in a pigsty," the baron's son finished his speech.

Lily aimed.

Fire!

The soup hit all three of the young men, and the bowl split in half against the head of one of them. He yelped and landed on the floor. The baron's son and his remaining friend turned to look at Lily and received a pitcher of wine for their trouble.

"Cool off, idiots," Lily told them icily. "How dare you behave like this in the presence of the Countess of Earton?"

She knew what she looked like to them. Her clothes were dirty from traveling, but they were expensive. Her face was aristocratic. She was wearing costly emerald earrings, a ring stamped with a crown, and a gold wedding bracelet set with emeralds. And she really was a Countess, which meant she had the advantage—although she would have dealt just fine with those fools in her own world, even without a title.

The young men's faces turned red. Lily continued her tirade before any of them could speak. "If my son behaved like you, I would have him whipped. Get out of this inn and don't come back until you can drink ale without turning into stupid beasts. Otherwise, I'll have these Virmans throw you out. I'm sure they will obey the Countess of Earton, who simply wishes to rest after a long journey."

A massive hand descended on Lily's shoulder. "With pleasure. Would you like me to remove them, My Lady?" asked a low voice. It sounded like the string of a bow.

Lily thought for a second. She didn't have to turn around. She knew the hand belonged to one of the Virmans. "Gentlemen, you have two choices. Either you pick up your trash," she pointed a finger at the third young man who had expressed interest in the girl, "and get out of here, or I'll have these Virmans drag you out by your necks. Which do you prefer?"

Without turning her head, she could feel the presence of the Virmans behind her. The two rich boys realized that no one was going to step up for them and that the Virmans would be glad to bounce them right out of the inn. After some dirty looks, they picked up their friend and headed for the door. At the doorway, the Baron's son turned around and spat out, "I swear…"

Lily reached behind her.

"…you will…"

She caught hold of a clay cup.

"…pay for…"

Bam! The cup shattered against the wall right above his head. Humiliated and insulted, he leaped away from the wall. One leg slipped out from under him, and he fell right on his rear. The crowd hooted. Red-faced, the Baron's son jumped up and ran out.

Lily smiled with pleasure. She had changed the story entirely on her own. Some people in the inn might have said the rich boys had merely expressed a polite interest in getting to know the Virman girl better, and the Virmans suddenly jumped up and drew their swords. That story wouldn't have ended well for the Virmans.

But with her involvement, the story was recast in a different light: a noblewoman was resting after a long trip when a group of three young jerks started to pick a fight with some strangers. Annoyed by the ruckus, the noblewoman threw a pitcher at them. When they refused to quiet down, she asked the Virmans to enforce some peace and quiet. Told that way, the Virmans had nothing to do with it. They were just following the Countess' orders, which was entirely reasonable behavior. She wasn't a nobody in that land.

She decided to take one more step to reinforce her version of the story. "Innkeeper, please see that no one else bothers me with such scandalous behavior. And pour everyone a glass of wine with the compliments of the Countess of Earton."

The crowd sounded happy. Behind Lily, someone coughed.

"My Lady."

Lily turned and saw the Virman who had started it all. She looked him over. Arnold Schwarzenegger wouldn't mess with this guy. He could flatten an opponent, roll him up and eat him for breakfast.

The Virman was at least six inches taller than Lily. The muscles in his arms and neck bulged, and he had some evil-looking scars on his face, but his blue eyes were lively and intelligent. *He may be a killer and a pirate, but he's nobody's fool.*

Lily shot him a friendly smile. "Lilian, Countess of Earton."

"Leif Torvaldson, from the Erkvig clan."

"Pleased to meet you. I trust you won't have any more trouble with those young pups."

"I don't believe we will."

"If they show up again, you can count on my assistance. I can't stand spoiled brats. I'll be leaving town in a few days, though, so if I were you, I wouldn't stick around too long."

"I'll take your advice, My Lady."

"Countess of Earton. You can find me here; I'll be staying at this inn."

Leif nodded. Then he took his girl by the hand, and they left.

Lily was highly annoyed with herself. She had just encountered two real warriors, but she hadn't found the courage to offer to hire them. Even if they had taken her up on the offer, it wouldn't have worked out. Men like that would only serve someone they respected, and she hadn't earned anyone's respect yet.

To hell with it!

Lily smiled around at the room and headed back to her table.

৪০ ◆ ଓଃ

Children are terrible creatures—just awful. The two minders traveling with little Miranda Catherine Earton had their own business to attend to in Earton, but they had been sent with the girl to watch over her health and instruct her and entertain her along the way.

Instead, the little monster always behaved so abominably that even the most stellar nannies and governesses would have wanted to stick her head down the outhouse hole by evening. She was a crybaby who found fault with everything.

The weather was too cold—she needed a blanket! Then it was too hot. Have the horses go faster! She felt motion-sick. Slow the carriage down! I'm hungry! Stop the carriage! Where's my favorite doll?

And on and on, all day… By evening, the entire group in the carriage was worn out. The girl was upset about leaving her father, so she decided to exercise what little power she had. After all, she was the daughter of the Earl, and as such, was not allowed to be punished. Her father had warned the two teachers traveling with her that if his daughter complained about them, they could lose their heads, thereby taking away their only source of control over the little tyrant.

To be fair, Miranda was never mean. She just complained all the time, and she had no intention of learning anything. Her teachers were terrified of the day they would have to report on her progress to the Count. And then there was the Countess…

What was a poor teacher to do?

These two men knew exactly what to do. They had their orders, and they knew who their masters were. They would perform their tasks to perfection. The rest of the entourage existed in a state of daily misery, however, which made the brat's shouting and tears especially hard on the nerves. They couldn't arrive at Earton soon enough.

Maldonaya take these backwoods!

❧ ◆ ☙

The Honorable Darius Avermal, the future Baron of Avermal (if his father ever passed away) raced out of the inn in a fury.

Why did the Countess take the side of those filthy pirates? The evening had been going so well…

Darius, Thomas, and Saul had wandered around the fair for a while. They ate some sweetcorn, drank some ale, and decided to continue their evening somewhere inside. They chose The Pig and Dog, where they drank a little more and sat for a while.

And then it happened. They noticed the Virman girl right away; it would have been impossible not to notice someone so beautiful. Darius' eyes ran over her golden hair, big brown eyes, and full, pink lips. *The outline of her figure! I bet I could fit my hands around that waist!*

He expected her to be flattered by the attention of such highly-placed gentlemen. *Why wouldn't she be?* There were three of them, so she should be three times as flattered.

After all, he was young and handsome and knew how to talk to women. *The servant girls in my father's house all like me, don't they?* His friends were pretty good looking, too. And if the girl pleased them, they would give her a couple of silver coins for her troubles. It was a generous, noble offer no matter how you looked at it.

But the Virmans turned out to be rude and ill-mannered.

Instead of being overjoyed and heading out to the haystack with them, the girl whispered something to her husband. They didn't care that he was her husband. *Good grief, we weren't looking to marry her!* Then she sheltered behind the immensely broad back of the man, while he glowered at them darkly. Darius and his friends were not afraid. If they called for the city guards, the Virmans would spend the night in jail, while the girl would spend it in bed with them. So, they didn't back down. *Why should we?* They were at home in their own city. The Virmans should be grateful that they were allowed to sit in a room with decent people. *Monsters!* Especially the chief. Anyone who ran into him in a dark alley would hand over his wallet without being asked. He definitely needed to be arrested.

Where did the fat lady come from? The young men didn't notice her at first because they were engrossed in their conflict with the Virmans. They only noticed that there was a crazy woman in the room when they got hit with the soup and wine.

They believed without a doubt that she was the Countess. Only a noblewoman could get away with behaving like that. But why did she defend the Virmans? She took the side of a couple of pirates without even trying to understand our position. And she shamed us in front of everyone!

Darius was enraged as he flew out of the inn. First, they would take Saul home, and then they would see about the Virmans. He would get revenge on them, as long as they didn't slip away in their ship the next day. And don't think you can get away with pirating around here. They would protect you back in Virma, but here you're a nobody with no name.

Darius' plan was to drag Saul home and then stop by the guards' barracks. He knew they would take orders from him. He couldn't tell them to fire on the Virmans' ship in the port; that would be too dangerous. Merchant ships could be damaged. But if the Virmans weren't in another alehouse…maybe he could catch the big one with the pretty wife. Remembering her gorgeous figure, Darius smacked his lips together.

You won't get away from me, darling. You'll be mine…

His wounded pride demanded that he get even with the Virmans, and the sooner, the better.

ဆ◆ဇ

The Lady Adelaide Wells was pleased with herself and life in general. She was young and beautiful and traveling with Estate's delegation to Wellster and then to Ivernea. Her prospects looked good. The red roses, accompanied by a note, that stood on the window sill brightened her eye and her heart. She had caught Jess Earton.

He sent her flowers the day after he first saw her. Adelaide, or Adele as her friends lovingly called her, thought for a moment and sent them back as if to say, "You're very charming, but I'm in mourning, you see…"

He sent even more flowers the next day. They continued to arrive each day. Then she started running into him at court. Adelaide shivered at the memory. No, there would be nothing like that. She wasn't free to do what she wanted. Jess Earton was too good a catch; handsome, spoiled, and accustomed to the attention of women. If he got what he wanted too soon, he'd forget all about her in short order. So, whenever she saw him, Adelaide blushed and lowered her eyes and whispered that she couldn't allow him to court her because her sorrow was too deep. It was hopeless; she was still suffering greatly from the loss of her husband.

Jess paid attention to her. He stroked her hand in its silk glove and told her not to bury herself alive. Adelaide let her head drop even lower as if to say "Don't trifle with a poor widow. You're leaving soon, anyway…"

Adelaide never knew how Jess managed to obtain an invitation for her. Once she knew she was going, she kept her servants busy with preparations for three days. *She absolutely had to look like a queen!* Jess Earton wouldn't be able to look at anyone but her. *Who cares that he's married! A wife isn't a wall—she can move over.*

"Adele?"

Adele gritted her teeth. *Not now!* Then she gave a lovely, glittering smile. "Alex! I'm so happy to see you!"

The man smiled. He pulled her close and kissed her cheek. "How are things going with the Earl of Earton?"

"You know I'm traveling with the delegation."

"I do. But don't rush to give in to him. Play with your prey, first." The two exchanged a look of understanding.

Alex was her husband's nephew. Against all odds, he got along beautifully with his uncle's young wife. The first time they met, they were drawn to each other as if by a powerful magnet. Their friendship continued in the drawing room, in the stables, and on picnics. Adele's elderly husband never suspected their affair. To cover for herself, Adele always complained to him that Alex was a lazy freeloader and a groveling toady. Alex, in turn, whispered to his uncle that his wife was corrupt and venal, a woman of loose morals. Her husband was certain that they couldn't stand each other.

The old nobleman never worried about a thing, including his financial affairs. *Old fool!* When he died, it turned out that Adelaide's inheritance would only be enough for about three years of humble country living. The lovers wouldn't settle for that. They sold what they could, pawned the rest, and headed off to conquer the capital. After all, they were both young and good-looking, and Adele had a title after her name.

Reality turned out to be more complicated. Their money drained away three times faster than they had hoped, and Adele had yet to find a lover who was well-placed at court. She could always marry another old man. She even looked into several options, but she dreaded going through with it again. Jess Earton was a gift from the heavens.

"I'll be very careful. I'm not sure what to do about his wife."

"She lives out in the country. Don't worry about her. I'll take care of her."

"How do you plan to do that?"

"Don't worry about it. Wives are mortals like the rest of us."

Adelaide made the sign of Aldonai. Alex shook his head. "Don't worry about it. You just tame your prey. We need him. Just don't forget about me once you're his lawful wife."

Adelaide smiled. "I doubt that Jess Earton can hold a candle to you in bed."

"Don't try to find out just yet. Remember, you're a good woman. You've never been with anyone but your husband, and only on special holidays."

Adelaide smiled again, and this time her face was lascivious. "Isn't today a holiday?" Her slim fingers pulled her corsage down on her breast.

"It is a holiday," he agreed and caught her up in his arms. "Let's celebrate… for a long time."

ᔕ◆ᘓ

Lily spent the rest of the evening getting information about Virmans. Her source, the innkeeper, knew his subject well and was more than happy to sit with the Countess and tell her about his homeland. It pleased him that she had so many questions, and was interested in what he had to say. Virma was a little island where almost nothing grew. In bad years, they used up everything they had—even ground up fish heads—to feed their animals. Cows couldn't survive the harsh conditions, so they raised goats and sheep. The fleeces were then spun into extremely fine yarn that was used to knit beautiful wool shawls. But they couldn't feed themselves with shawl-making alone.

So, the Virmans were also pirates. Everyone knew it, but no one could do anything about that wasp's nest. Neighboring nations would have had to create a strong alliance to take on the Virmans, who had plenty of big ships and weren't afraid of a fight, or death.

There was no such alliance, so the other nations put up with piracy as an unavoidable fact of life. And the Virmans could be useful sometimes. Their ships circumnavigated the entire continent carrying cargo and engaging in trade. Virman warriors also offered their services to other kings as mercenaries. They were trusted because they took their promises very seriously. Everyone knew that a Virman had three things: his ax, his ship, and his word. If he lost his ship, he would earn it back with his ax and his word. If he lost his ax, he would earn back both with his good word alone. A Virman without his good word was no longer a Virman.

Lily sighed with relief. Then she wondered, Should I swallow my pride and go talk to the Virman about giving him a job? She hoped she wasn't getting in over her head. Pirates should be easier to do business with than peasants, right? They have a larger worldview, and those two obviously aren't idiots. But on the other hand, they may not respect me. They only respect strength. Do I have enough strength? Not yet. Should I jump out of the frying pan and into the fire?

The castle needed better defenses. Art said that the slave traders who had been buying young girls from Etor would be back in four to six weeks. She wanted to be prepared to greet them properly. There shouldn't be many losses on her side. *Losses...that meant people!* Her every step and thought affected human lives. Maimed bodies, mutilated futures; it was terrifying. She would have crawled under her bed if she thought that would help.

With the Virmans, Lily was contemplating setting a fox to guard the henhouse. She would tame and feed the fox and hope for the best. *I don't have a choice, do I?*

Her husband obviously didn't have the tiniest concern about her. Her father was indifferent, as well. "You're married now, so run along and have babies. If you have a son, I'll make a man of him."

So, what else can I do? Lie down and die? Like hell, I will! There was plenty of fight left in her. *I have plans for my estate in the middle of nowhere. And it's a good thing we're out in the middle of nowhere. That means fewer envious eyes and ears—fewer people to carry tales.*

Of course, it would be nice if the Virmans were honest people. But even if they weren't, she would try to buy their loyalty.

I have to at least give it a try. Good people are worth their weight in gold, and without people on my side, I'm nothing. A big zero.

ও◆ଔ

Leif Erkvig watched the shore gloomily.

He didn't get too close. The harbor was full of merchant ships. If a storm blew in, they would all be swinging on their anchors. He preferred to stay further away: thieves were less likely to bother him, and he was out of range of catapults. *Scratch that. They've got their catapults set up to cover the entire harbor. These Ativernese are no fools…*

He still stayed offshore. They could use the rowboats to go in as needed.

Leif knew he should set sail, but they had just arrived and still needed to buy supplies and fix one of the sails. And he had no idea where to go next. It was a crucial question. They could sail down the coast offering their services for hire, but they weren't alone. *Some of the men had wives with them, and children!* He didn't want to drag families from port to port.

Leif was fine with that kind of life, but he suspected that Ingrid and the other women wouldn't last. *So what am I to do? The sea takes care of Virmans.*

It's easy to seize and board a ship when you have your crew behind you, but not if you have defenseless women and children along who are depending on you. Anything could happen during a fight. That made it hard to look your beloved in the face.

Leif didn't consider himself a hero, but he knew what he had felt when Torsveg shot at Ingrid. And that could easily happen again. Enemies could shoot fire missiles at them—easy.

"You're unhappy." A warm shawl settled on his shoulders. Ingrid hadn't asked a question; she had made a statement.

Leif turned to her. He put his arm around her, pulling her onto his lap and covering her with half of the shawl. "No, sweet one. I'm just thinking."

"Where do we go now?"

Leif held her tightly. "You understand everything. I would feel safer if I could leave you on shore somewhere, but there is no place that your kin won't find us…or where strangers won't pursue us."

"That woman stood up for us today." Ingrid again seemed to read her husband's mind. Maybe she can. Fleina could give that gift and many others, but sometimes the price for her gifts was paid in blood.

"That was a random accident." Leif almost shuddered. For an instant, the cold seemed to penetrate under the warm shawl, sending an icy finger up his back. Things could have gone badly for them—very badly. It was just him and Dagry. Ingrid didn't count. He loved her, but she was no warrior and would be of no use in a fight.

Here in Ativerna, we are refugees without rights—people on the run. The Torsvegs were a tight clan. If he hadn't left, his family would have had to get involved. If anyone has a problem with me, they can take it up with me personally.

Those three rich boys were at home in their own town. They knew their rights, and they knew the city guards would protect them. Leif had seen the guards; there were six of them. That would have made nine men against him and Dagry. Even if the Ativernese swords were for show only, the Virmans would have been hard pressed. Leif had been in fights where the odds were worse. He would have fought his way out of the inn and retreated back to his ship, leaving wounded men in his wake. *But Ingrid…*

He was not afraid on his own account; he was afraid for her. She was his dear, his beloved, his only one. Leif knew how easy it was for innocent bystanders to be killed in a brawl. One accidental blow was all it took.

The fat woman in the dirty dress had saved them. Leif never forgot what he owed people.

"What if we try to talk to her?" Ingrid's voice was almost a whisper as if she was afraid of her own words.

Leif put his lips to her head. "The Countess of Earton?"

"Maybe she needs people?"

"Virmans? My dear, we aren't the best servants in the world. We are true to our word, but who would ever believe it?"

"What do we have to lose? We don't have anywhere to go."

Leif sighed. Ingrid was right. *But who would ever hire me?* His resume was written on his face in scars left by swords and knives.

"Don't forget that these people worship Aldonai."

"I thought she looked intelligent," Ingrid persisted. "Will we still be here tomorrow?"

Leif sighed again. "Yes. My dear, do you understand that we would have to trust her completely? And she is just the Countess. What about her husband? She was wearing a wedding bracelet."

"If her husband is intelligent, you will be able to reach an understanding with him."

"And if he's a fool?"

"Do you think a woman like that would marry a fool?" He could hear laughter in Ingrid's voice.

Leif smiled. "So, are you also an intelligent woman?"

"I love you."

"Do you have doubts about your husband's brains?" This was all new for Leif. He had never laughed and joked with a woman before. It was incredibly pleasant.

"How could I? You are my husband, my lord and master!" She pretended to be horrified.

"Madam, you may do as you like with me. I even allow you to touch my battle ax."

Ingrid laughed. Leif knew that he would go looking for Lilian Earton tomorrow. He couldn't waste the chance. To protect the woman he loved, he would do anything in his power—and even more. His pride wouldn't suffer. He would reach an agreement with it.

ಬಿ ♦ ෆ

Six men from Leif's Virman crew had been carousing in one of the port taverns. Olat, Gel, Elg, Torney, Illat, and Selt were all warriors who had seen more than one battle. That's why they were still alive.

Suddenly, the silhouettes of men with bows and spears appeared before them on the wharf.

"Put down your weapons!" a voice commanded.

"What's going on?" Olat asked. He was the soberest of the group.

"We have orders to take you to the magistrate."

"What for?"

The guard's voice was tired. "Boys, I'm not a free man. I just carry out orders. If you go for your axes, we'll lay you out. We have ten bowmen here, so the arrows will find you. You'll get a couple of my men, and they'll hang you for it later. Since you haven't done anything wrong yet, let's just go quietly. They'll probably let you go in the morning."

Olat thought for a moment. He knew they could take the guards, but he and his men were drunk. They had each drained at least two or three pitchers, so they were upright and able to talk, but the local wine would trip a man up when he least needed it. That evened out the odds. And it was always better to go up against archers in the daylight.

Also, he knew he would lose a couple of men in the process. He didn't know who it would be, but he knew most had wives and children. Gel, and Torney were still bachelors, but Olat had three children, Illat's wife just gave birth, Selt had two, and Elg was expecting a new baby any day now. *Which of those young children would lose a father tonight?*

Olat was not afraid to die, but he hated to leave his family facing the unknown. The gods would welcome him into their halls, but there would be no joy for him in the afterlife. He looked at his men. Gel and Torney were ready to attack, but the others were obviously thinking about their loved ones.

They hadn't done anything wrong. They could take the guards. But… He knew Leif would take care of his family, but he didn't want to waste his life on a stupid misunderstanding. And he really hadn't done anything wrong.

If they killed the guards, they would have to raise anchor tonight. Leif wouldn't be pleased.

He decided maybe they should just go along with the guards. They would spend the night in jail and get word to Leif in the morning. A Virman would never leave his friends in the lurch.

Olat raised his hands. "I don't have anything against you. Let's do it like this: I'll send someone to the boat to tell them where we are, and the rest of us will go with you without a fight."

The head of the guards wavered, and the youngest of Olat's men, Gel, decided to risk it. He made a giant leap for the water. He knocked into a guard, who shouted. Two bows twanged. There was a splashing sound.

The head of the guards was furious. "Put your weapons down, or I'll give the order to shoot!"

Olat cursed. He didn't think they had hit Gel. The young man would sober up on his swim back to the boat and tell Leif what had happened. Their captain would come to their aid.

"We won't give up our weapons. We will go with you and wait until the morning. But if those arrows hurt our friend, then…"

"Then it's his own fault. If he hadn't run for it, they wouldn't have shot at him," the head of the guards grumbled.

"If anything happens to Gel, I will find you," Olat promised.

"You won't have to look hard. Everyone knows where to find the city guards. Let's go."

Olat frowned. Was there any point in continuing to resist? It would be easier to wait until the morning. Once Leif knows where they are, he will clear things up.

But still, something didn't smell right.

The head of the guards didn't like the situation either, but an order was an order. *Maldonaya take all these Virmans!*

ༀ◆ༀ

Lily spent the night at the inn. She paid dearly for a room, but she ended up spending the better part of the night battling with bedbugs. In the end, she took the sheets and mattress off the bed and lay down on the wooden board. She figured her extra weight would cushion her. It didn't. By morning, her back and sides ached like nobody's business. Every inch of her hurt.

At least she could call for a hot bath, which she did at dawn. If she wasn't going to get any sleep, she could at least be clean. Then she headed out to the market with her trusty peasants. She wanted to look around first; it was too early to be buying.

Cattle were for sale outside the walls of the fort. Lily looked up and down. There had to be at least a million cows. The organizers of this medieval fair were apparently unaware that selling could be organized for the buyer's convenience, with all of the goats in one place and all of the cows in another place. Instead, all of the animals were herded into one long pen. Lily didn't like the looks of it.

There were goats milling around next to clay pitchers for sale, followed by chickens and a table of dried fish. Lily thought she was in hell. Everyone was yelling, bargaining, showing off their goods, and striking deals. The animals were bellowing, snorting, bleating, and stinking as if working against their owners to make it harder to sell them.

After ten minutes, Lily wanted one thing: to blow up the whole market and enjoy some peace and quiet in the shell crater. Thank the gods, she had sewed her gold into her nightshirt, petticoat, and drawers. She was already used to the extra weight, and it was a relief knowing that nobody would find anything in her pockets to pick. Accessing her cash would take time and require seam ripping.

Her peasants dragged her first in one direction and then another to show her the best goats, cows, and chickens. They wanted to buy the animals right away without bargaining. One of them ran Lily's hand over a sheep's white fleece to show her it was worth pure gold. They estimated the weight of the chickens. They asked how much milk the cows gave. They examined horns and udders…

Lily couldn't tell one breed from the next. As far as she was concerned, there were only two types of chicken: running around or on your plate. She felt pretty much the same about the other animals. She suspected she was a clinically diagnosed idiot. *Did I really think I could buy livestock at a medieval marketplace?*

By noon, she was ready to howl. People were shoving, animals were bleating, and someone always wanted something from her. *Lord give me patience! Or a half-gallon of nitroglycerine!*

To hell with all this!

Leif was trying to decide whether to look for Lilian Earton during the day or later in the evening. She probably wouldn't be at the inn during the day, and he wanted to avoid any chance meetings with the gang from yesterday. He decided evening would be better.

As always, reality intruded on well-laid plans. Something slapped up against his ship. He heard cursing, and about three minutes later, his men pulled Gel, wet but very much alive, onto the deck. Leif knew he was one of the crew who had gone to the fair. He thought they were still out drinking.

"The men are all at the magistrate's!"

"What?" Leif was furious.

"We were coming back to the ship when the guards stopped us on the wharf."

Leif spat out a string of curses. "What kind of guards?"

"They had longbows and crossbows. They were waiting for us on the wharf, behind the warehouses."

"Waiting for Virmans?"

"Yes!"

"I see you made it back."

"I was closest to the water. Olat distracted them with questions, and I just jumped in."

Leif sneered. According to the old saying, it was easier to catch a fish than a Virman. All Virmans were excellent swimmers. "And?"

"Our men didn't lay down their weapons, but when I turned back to look, the guards were leading them away. They said they were taking them to the magistrate."

"Why didn't they resist?"

"They would have if the guards had attacked. But it seemed like the guards didn't even know what was going on."

As a captain, Leif understood Olat's thinking. Earlier that day, he had tried to avoid conflict for Ingrid's sake. He wanted to curse but stopped himself because he was the commander. The ship's decking groaned under the weight of his hand. Things were not looking good.

He knew his men could end up in prison. And if he went to try and save them, he'd share their fate. He was only strong while he had Virma on his side. Now, he was alone outside the clan, with enemies working against him at home.

How can I find Lilian Earton without getting caught? Leif stared gloomily at the water. He didn't want to be dripping wet when he talked to the Countess, but he had no choice. *I hope they aren't waiting for me on the wharf…*

"No one leaves the ship," he ordered.

"But what if…"

"Say that your captain isn't here and that you are prepared to fight to the death." He headed to the rope ladder. It was beneath his dignity to jump.

₨◆ℓ

By noon, Lily was ready to blow a gasket. She gave up trying to make sense of the market and returned to the inn, where she ordered a pitcher of ale. She wanted to enjoy her drink and let her brain relax.

How stupid could you be? You can't just jump in and be an instant expert on livestock!

The cheese went well with her ale, but her mood remained dark. The peasants could sense her bad temper and kept their distance. Lily dismally concluded that she would never be a farmer.

"Countess."

The voice was familiar. She lifted her head. The Virman from yesterday was standing at her table. She searched her memory for his name. Leif. Leif Torvaldson of Erkvig. He was wet from head to foot.

"Sit down." Lily nodded at the pitcher of ale. She wouldn't push. She would let him tell his story.

Leif jumped into his tale. "My men have been arrested and taken to the magistrate."

Lily looked up. "You want me to help them."

Leif nodded. She was as smart as he thought. But her green eyes were cold and hard.

"Are they guilty of anything?"

"No. I think this is the work of the young men from yesterday."

"How do I know you won't be back with the same problem tomorrow?"

"I'll get them back on the boat, and we'll leave."

"What do I get for my assistance?" Lily was feeling him out. His blue eyes were clever and cautious. *Should I risk it or not? Hell if I know.*

"What do you want? Money?"

"I have money."

"We can work off our debt."

"I was told that if a Virman gives his word, he never goes back on it. Is that so?"

"We can be trusted." Leif said the words simply, but his tone added meaning.

Lily knew it was now or never. She couldn't tell about the other Virmans, but she felt she could indeed trust this one. She made up her mind. She would let this man feel like he had the power. She could have struck a hard bargain, but she needed people on her side. *Warriors, not servants!*

"Will you enter my service? I won't do you wrong."

Leif let his breath out. "In Earton?"

"Yes."

"Don't you have your own guards?"

It was Lily's turn to sigh. She would have to show him some of her cards, all in the name of mutual advantage. "My estate Comptroller was stealing. My husband doesn't care if the whole place burns down, so the Comptroller let all the guards go. Earton is almost entirely unprotected. Not entirely, but almost." She gave him a long look. "I know that Virmans keep their word. So do I. I want you to stay in Earton for three years. That's enough time for you to protect my lands from pirates and brigands while you train young men from our villages to take your place. I will give you a place to live and will pay you for your service. If you want, you can live on the estate, or we will build houses for you. Your pay will be generous."

Leif exhaled.

Lily had left herself open. She trusted him, and she hoped he wouldn't use what she'd told him against her.

"We will serve you for three years. Honorably. There will be a contract. I will choose the men, and I will make sure that they perform their duties admirably. But I have my own conditions."

"Which are?"

"Don't ask us to follow your religion."

Lily blinked. "I won't. You can build your own church and worship your own gods. Just don't make a lot of noise about it or the priest will get in my face. Although, he'll probably be up in my face anyway. But keep quiet just in case."

"I can promise that. We will be discreet. We can even come to your services sometimes. Is there anywhere to moor a ship in Earton?"

"There's no harbor. I don't know if your ship can get through."

"We'll see. I have a good river pilot. He can smell the reefs."

"Excellent. But let me warn you: I will not put up with bad behavior."

"And I will not put up with bad omens." Leif's eyes glinted. "I will answer for my men!" He seemed surprised when the woman nodded.

"If something doesn't sit right, you tell me. We'll talk it over and fix it. Don't argue with me in front of people."

Leif nodded. He understood. "We will discuss everything in private."

"That includes payment. How much do you want?"

Leif faltered, but not for long. "We are here with our families. We will need to live at Earton."

"You can stay in the castle until we get you set up. How many of you are there?"

"Around sixty people, including women and children."

"If your wives want to work, I can pay them, too," said Lily. "But we can talk about that later."

"Our women are not servants."

"That's not what I'm offering, I promise. The work I need would not be shameful for them."

Leif nodded again, letting her know he believed her. "Two gold coins a month for each warrior."

"Isn't that a little high?"

"We are worth it."

"And I pay your keep?"

"Yes."

"And all your wives and children? I offer three silver coins a month, plus bonuses if you earn them."

"Gold."

"Experienced warriors get one silver a month. I think you're asking too much."

After bargaining, they agreed on seven silver coins a month for each man. As commander, Leif would get double. They could make more through piracy, but the stability would be worth it.

It was a king's ransom, but Lily decided to go for it. Once she started implementing her ideas, the Virmans would be a goldmine. With their help, she would earn twenty times what she paid them.

People generate wealth. Forget about the money. I can always earn more of it.

"That works for me."

Leif seemed pleased. So far, she had agreed to all his terms. "The sea takes care of Virmans," he said.

"What does that mean? You want to go out sailing?" Lily burst out laughing. She gave him a mischievous grin. "To catch fish?"

"Exactly."

She saw that he had realized she was a woman who understood business. She had been told there were plenty of women like that in Virma. After all, they had to manage farms while their husbands were at sea for months at a time.

"Then I get a share of the catch." She grinned. "You'll be in my territory."

"One-twentieth?" Leif offered with a smile. He seemed to look forward to more bargaining.

She grinned back at him. "How much did you say? I want one-fifth. No less!"

"My Lady is joking. One-eighteenth!"

"You can't sell any fish without my permission. One-sixth!"

The haggling went on for about ten minutes and ended with both parties pleased. They agreed that the countess would take one-tenth of Leif's 'catch'.

All the ale and cheese were gone. Lily sighed. "Well, let's go get your men out of jail, shall we?"

"They're your men, now, Countess."

That's right. Now, I have to hold up my end of the bargain. "Should we all go down to the magistrate's office together?"

"I think that would be best."

Lily frowned. "Can you change clothes?"

"I can ask the innkeeper for something to wear."

"Do that. I'll pay." Leif understood what went unsaid. Lily turned to her peasants. "I want you back here, armed, in ten minutes. Get moving!"

Leif went off to talk to the innkeeper. Lily looked down at the empty pitcher.

So, this is how people become alcoholics. You start getting drunk because you want other people to solve your problems for you. But that never works. I wonder where the magistrate's office is?

ॐ◆ॐ

Lily was worried about getting back in the saddle. Her muscles had just started to relax. The good news was that the magistrate's office was only two streets away. The bad news was that she would have to ride. A

Countess shouldn't be seen walking. Leif led her horse by the reins, and her men followed along behind wearing white and green capes. Their marching left much to be desired, but it was the best they could do.

Lily had been surprised to learn that white and green were the colors of the Earls of Earton. *But I'm blonde here! I can't wear white!*

Green was the color of mourning in Ativerna, but she decided to have some green and white dresses made as soon as she had time. For now, she thanked the gods of both worlds that the former Comptroller hadn't managed to sell the guards' capes. She had found them collecting dust in one of the storerooms. Someone had sprinkled them with lavender to keep the moths away. Lily had debated about bringing them with her on the trip, but now she was glad to have them. The local city guards dressed similarly, each in his own clothes with capes and weapons issued by the magistrate.

She gloomily observed the medieval town as she rode down the middle of the street (to avoid the many things that could be tossed out of windows). This was the first opportunity she had had to study her whereabouts. The previous day, she had been distracted by the fight at the inn, and in the morning, she had been consumed by the market at the fair. So, she hadn't had time to stroll around town, and now that she saw it in the daylight, she didn't really want to.

The buildings were made of stone, but they were gray and boring. *Gothic architecture apparently isn't a thing yet...or paved roads.* Seeing her guards ankle-deep in mud, Lily decided she would ride her horse wherever she went. She had no desire to see if the mud came up to her knee or not.

She also noticed that the town stank. Its residents thought nothing of emptying their chamber pots out the window. Trash was collected in heaps in the inner courtyards, but sewage was everywhere. Lily began to feel sick from the smell and the motion of bumping up and down on a horse. None of the others seemed surprised by the filth. She swore that she would never let Earton get this bad, and she decided to build decent roads everywhere as soon as she had time.

That's a plan for the future. Right now, I need to decide what to say at the magistrate's office so I can spring these Virmans. I need them to protect my estate.

Still, she felt as defenseless as her holdings. There was no one to stop the Virmans from stealing everything she had, burning the place to the ground and sailing off to make mischief elsewhere.

But who will stop the pirates? And the slave traders? And the brigands?

It was enough to make a Countess scream.

"My Lady?"

While Lily had been lost in thought, they arrived at the magistrate's building.

Leif seemed very respectful as he helped her off her horse. *He'd better not be laughing behind his beard!*

ഇ ◆ യ

Lons had been on the brink of death at least twenty times, but Aldonai apparently had other plans for him. *Or is Maldonaya trifling with me?*

When he was taken from the coalman's hut, he figured he was about to be hung. And when the men brought him to a hunting cabin in the woods and presented him to the King's Jester, he assumed that the man wanted to kill him with his own hands.

But he was wrong.

The little man bored into him with his eyes. "Talk."

"About what?" Lons decided he wouldn't go down so easy. He was a nobleman, after all, and he didn't want to die a whining cur.

"About how you seduced the girl and convinced her to fornicate with you. I want to know what, when, where, and who else knows about it."

Lons spat at his feet. "Curse you!"

The Jester was unfazed. "If I walk out of here, the next person you see will be the hangman. The only reason I'm even talking to you is to avoid a scandal. I don't like blood, and I don't want to have to burn this cabin down. So, I'm making nice with you. Do you really think you can stand up to torture?"

Lons was terrified of pain, and he knew the Jester could see it on his face.

The man nodded—not at Lons, but at his own thoughts. "So talk. How old was she when you seduced her?"

Which of them had been the seducer was hard to say, but Lons was the man, so he answered, "Fourteen."

"Do the two of you have children?"

"No."

"Who else knows about your affair?"

"It isn't an affair. Anna is my wife in God's eyes."

"I'll talk to God later," the man sneered. "I just don't want mortal men to know about it. Where are the papers?"

"The priest had them," Lons snapped.

"Was he the only one who knew?"

Lons didn't even think about whether or not he should lie. *Of course, I should if I can.*

"Anna was afraid. Why would we go around telling people?"

The man didn't seem to believe him, his eyes cold and intelligent.

"Why didn't you hold on to proof?"

"I wanted to, but I didn't have time."

"Shall I call for the hangman? You're making me sorry that I didn't bring him in right away."

Lons broke down after another ten minutes of questioning. The Jester listened carefully as he explained where to find the papers. Then he gave orders to his followers and smiled sweetly at Lons. "We already destroyed the church records. And you? Once you're gone, the problem doesn't exist. You know the sentence for seducing a lady of noble blood is death."

"I suppose you want to do it yourself?" Lons hissed, but his anger left the Jester untouched.

"And dirty my hands on you?" He nodded to his followers. "Kill him and bury him so that no one ever finds him. Now."

The men grabbed Lons by the arms, and he prepared—yet again—to lose his life. The men dragged him from the room and put a bag over his head. As they led him away, they discussed what to do with him.

"Do we dump him in the swamp?"

"Oh, I bet he'd just love that."

"Or should we—you know?"

Lons pricked up his ears. What are they planning to do to me? Will I be buried alive? Anything but that!

"Do what?"

"How about we sell him to Farney?"

"To Farney?"

"Why not? Guys like him with an education and good looks fetch a high price in Darcom."

Lons gasped in horror. *Darcom!* He knew what they did to men like him in Darcom. They used them as eunuchs for the harem.

Run!

Before he could make a move, something struck him over the head, and he saw stars.

ಬಿ ◆ ಛ

The two men exchanged glances. They leaned the lifeless body against a tree. He was heavier knocked out.

It's a good idea. Why kill a strong young man if we can sell him? No one ever returns from Darcom, that's a fact.

Slavery was not widespread in Wellster, but it flourished in Darcom and the Vari Khanganat. The trade was supplied by crafty sea captains who sailed the coast and the river deltas looking to buy or steal humans for the slave markets. It was a risky profession, but the profits were enormous.

Farney was a slave trader who frequented Wellster, Ativerna, and Ivernea. He paid well and never went back on his word. The Jester's men had sold prisoners to him before, and they liked doing business with him.

"Is he around?"

"I heard he's getting ready to set sail. He can put this one in the hold, too. I bet we'd get three coins for him, what do you think?"

It wasn't every day a man could earn three gold coins. The other man thought for a moment and nodded. "Let's do it. He'll never escape from Farney to show his nose around here again."

Gold was a rarity in those parts. One of the Jester's men was trying to marry off a daughter and needed a dowry for her. The other was younger and had been in the Jester's service just a few months. He didn't know how the Jester handled disobedience. So, one motivated by greed and the other by ignorance, they decided to disregard their orders.

As for Lons, it wasn't much of a lucky break. They weren't going to kill him, but sitting in the hold of a slave ship wasn't much better.

೪♦೧

Darius turned red, then white, then green. He would have crawled in a hole in the ground if there had been one nearby. He usually got away with whatever devilry he caused in town, generally only against peasants and simple laborers, but this time his father was irate.

"Aldonai, how have I sinned that you gave me this idiot as a son? What am I guilty of in your eyes?" He turned to his son. "What are you looking at, you runt of the litter? Do you have any idea what you've done?"

Darius blinked. He had just been dragged out of bed. It wasn't his fault that the Virmans didn't show up at the wharf until it was almost dawn. He was sick of waiting for them, but the desire for revenge was stronger. If he had gone home, the guards wouldn't have dared tangle with them. As it was, one of the Virmans got away…

After sending the other five to jail, Darius returned home and went to bed. He slept until his father's servants ripped the covers off him. They let him answer the call of nature and put some clothes on before stuffing him in a carriage and driving him to the town hall, where his father, Baron Torius Avermal, raked him over the coals.

And all over what? A bunch of Virmans? This could have waited—let them stew in jail for a while so I could get some sleep. Still, it scared him to see his father red with fury, yelling so loud that the walls shook.

"Do you have any idea what you've done?"

"Maybe I don't!" Darius shouted. He was sincerely confused. "They're Virmans! Brigands and pirates! I did the right thing having them arrested. You should seize their ship and sell the pirates to work in the mines. Why not?"

The baron put his head in his hands. "Aldonai!"

"Father, what is the matter?" Darius truly believed he'd done the right thing.

143

"They have all of Virma behind them. You don't mess with Virmans!" Tired of yelling, the baron sat down in one of his armchairs. He looked up at his son. "We can't stop the rumor from spreading. People will tell, and others will carry the tale. The island of Virma will find out how we've treated their countrymen."

"So what?"

"Those men are still alive because they stand up for each other. They may be pirates, brigands, and scoundrels, but no Virman ever goes back on his word. If someone offends a Virman, the entire island will avenge his honor. It's one thing if a Virman is convicted in a fair court. But you just had them arrested for no reason!"

"You just said that they're pirates!"

"Did anyone complain about them?"

"I can find someone to complain if you want."

"Is that what you'll say when an entire Virman flotilla shows up in the harbor and wants to know who put their kin in jail?"

"Their kin?"

"Everyone on Virma is related to everyone else."

"But Father…"

The baron hissed something that Darius couldn't make out. Then he asked, "If I let them go, you haven't been up to any other mischief, have you?"

"Father!"

"On the other hand, they are Virmans."

ಬ◆ೞ

Suddenly, the door flew open and hit the wall hard enough to raise the ashes in the fireplace. The giant Virman from the day before stood in the doorway. Darius turned pale with anger, but before he could say anything, the Virman stepped forward, bowed politely and announced, "The Countess Lilian Elizabeth Mariella Earton!"

The fat lady from the inn sailed into the room. She was wearing a clean, expensively embroidered dress, with earrings jingling in her ears and an emerald bracelet glinting on her wrist. No one in the room doubted that she was a Countess; her bearing spoke for itself.

Darius shut his eyes and opened them again, seeming to hope it was a bad dream.

The vision in pink flashed him a predatory smile. "Good day. Is this the Baron of Altver I see before me?"

Baron Avermal stood up and bowed. "Baron Torius Avermal at your service, My Lady."

The vision spoke. "I'm pleased to meet you, Baron. I'm only sorry to be here for such unfortunate cause." When she glanced at Darius, her green eyes were openly gloating.

"Why unfortunate? My Lady, please have a seat. Let me call for some wine, and then we can discuss whatever has happened."

The baron was nervous. She was just a woman, but he knew that Jess Earton was a close favorite of the King. It mattered little that his wife was never at court. In any event, Jess Earton could cause him more trouble than he could load into a cart. The King loved him and listened to him, so that made his wife a force to be reckoned with.

As elegantly as she could manage, Lily lowered herself into the chair that Leif pulled out for her. He accidentally hit Darius' leg with the chair as he moved it, not hard, but the young man winced.

Lilian gave a cold smile. "Honorable Torius, please explain to me why my men were detained last night?"

"Your men, My Lady?" Torius stared at her in surprise. There were only the Virmans in the basement.

The Countess gave an even colder smile. "My Virman guards. You have detained five of my Virmans. I would simply like to know what they are charged with."

She had underestimated Baron Avermal. He quickly collected his wits. "Darius, go order wine and sweets for the lady."

Lily smiled at him. This was no time to mention her diet. The brat left, and the baron turned his full attention to Lily.

"My Lady, you say the men in question serve you?"

Lily's voice was cold and hard. "They are my guards, Honorable Torius. It matters nothing that they are Virmans. I value their loyalty."

"I have no doubt of their loyalty, My Lady."

"Then what are they accused of?"

The baron smiled. "It was a simple mistake."

The door creaked. A servant woman brought in a tray with a silver jug, silver cups, and a dish of sugared fruits. She bowed and set the tray on the table. The Baron poured Lily a cup of wine and offered her a plum.

Lily pretended to take a sip of wine. She accepted the plum and held it in her fingers, which soon became sticky, further igniting her righteous anger.

"Is that so? And whose mistake was it?" Her eyes were icy, but the Baron held firm.

"My Lady, the guards made an error."

"I see." Lily went heavy on the sarcasm. "A dozen of your guards decided it would be entertaining to take their longbows and crossbows and wait on the wharf to see if any Virmans happened by. Nobody ordered them to be there. Is that about the shape of it?"

The Baron shrugged. "I can order an inquiry if you like."

"So can I." She set her cup of wine down. "Honorable Torius, perhaps I should tell my husband how his men were treated here in Altver. Keep in mind, these are the men he entrusted with my safety. I think once he knows the facts, there will be a very thorough investigation, don't you agree?"

Torius winced as if something cold had touched a sore tooth. Lily sensed that she should press him.

"And why were you so upset with your son this morning? Perhaps it had something to do with the fact that I was so angry with him yesterday?"

Her instinct told her she was on the right track.

"My Lady?"

"Yesterday, your son rudely offended the wife of the commander of my guards. I was forced to intervene to prevent trouble before I had been in your town even five minutes. And this morning, I find my men have been put in jail."

Lily drilled into him with her eyes. Who cares that I'm a woman? Women can subdue tigers! This game is all about willpower, and that's something any doctor has plenty of. The Baron's face didn't change, but Lily felt him weaken for an instant.

"My Lady…"

"No, Honorable Torius, I understand. He is your son. I would defend my son, as well." Something like relief appeared on his face, but it didn't last long. "But you see, I cannot leave it like this. My husband will have to be told."

"My Lady, why worry him with such trivial matters?"

"Trivial?"

"You're all alive and well, no one was hurt."

"But your guards shot at one of my men and detained the rest of them for no reason whatsoever!"

"Perhaps we could compensate them for their trouble?"

Lilian almost smiled. "I suppose that would satisfy my husband. We don't want trouble, do we? I believe the nobility should always be able to find common ground."

"I agree with you wholeheartedly, My Lady. Is this your first visit to Altver? Can I make your stay here more pleasant?"

In other words, you want to know my price for keeping quiet about this. Lily lost her nerve for an instant. She needed to ask for something, but she didn't want to risk raising suspicions. It was Leif, with the instincts of a predator, who sensed her trouble. In just a few seconds, the baron would sense it, too. The situation was growing precarious.

Leif coughed quietly to draw her attention. "Lady Lilian, allow me to remind you…"

"Yes?"

"The men are still in jail."

The Baron jumped up. "I'll order their release and find out who is at fault here."

Lily smiled. "We will wait for you here. These fruits are lovely." She would have wiped the plum juice on her dress, but the price of the fabric stopped her.

As soon as the door closed, Leif turned to Lily. "Why did you lose your nerve, My Lady? There has to be something you could demand of him?"

ক◆ল

The Honorable Torius Avermal maintained a dignified pose as he left his office, but inside he was boiling over.

That woman is a snake! She guessed at everything. And his son was a burden sent by Maldonaya. I will have him whipped! The boy won't be able to sit for a year!

He found his firstborn leaning against the window in the hall, whispering something to a servant girl. That did nothing to improve his father's mood. *He's thinking with the wrong body part, as always!*

Torius grabbed his son by the ear. "Run on home, you ungrateful whelp! We'll talk when I get there. Do you understand me?"

Darius was afraid. He had never seen his father this angry before. "But Father…"

"Go home. Wait for me there. Run!"

Darius decided he had better obey if he wanted to keep his buttocks intact.

❧ ◆ ☙

"Come on in. Would you like a drink?" Jess Earton was glad to see his cousin.

"Red or white?"

"Red."

"Then just pour me a sip. Looks like we're leaving the day after tomorrow."

"Not looking forward to it?"

"Would you be excited about getting married?"

"Done it already. You know the whole story."

"Aldonai hasn't taken her yet?"

"Who knows? I haven't had a letter from Etor in a while. I sent my daughter down there, so I should get a letter from my head guard soon."

"It takes a long time for mail to reach Wellster."

"Good. The one person in this life I never worry about is my wife. You've met her."

149

Richard nodded. He had met Lilian once… at the wedding. He was grateful that his father had allowed him to choose his bride. He would meet both Anna Wellster and Lidia Ivernea and make his choice free of any interference.

"How are things with that doll you took up with?"

"Adele?"

"You're calling her Adele already?"

"Don't laugh, Richard. She's a good woman. She was a child when they married her off to that old goat, but she's in mourning for him anyway."

"I see. And she came to the capital to get some fresh air."

"Just look at her. She has no lovers. She lives very modestly."

"And she is always at court. I can tell she's gotten to you."

"Maybe a little."

"Have you…?"

"She's too chaste and virtuous."

"Even better. The more chaste she is, the fierier she'll be in bed."

"We haven't even kissed yet."

"Be careful, Jess. Otherwise, you'll end up with a pregnant mistress."

"I'll take care. I really like her. She's kind and intelligent, not like that *cow* I married."

ဆ ♦ beta

Lilian scowled at Leif.

"It's easy for you to say that I lost my nerve. I have to buy livestock here at the market and get them all back to the estate. I have to find a good blacksmith, a jeweler, some glass blowers, buy cloth, and sell a couple of things. You have no idea how much I have to accomplish on this trip. Lost my nerve! What do you know about it?"

The Virman showed no anger at her aggressive response. He understood her position. When he spoke next, it was not like a servant talking to his master or a Virman talking to an Ativernese Countess. He spoke to her as he would to a friend.

"You have good plans. We can find a blacksmith, a jeweler, and a glass blower. How much livestock were you planning to buy?"

"As much as I can afford. Leif, I don't know anything about farming, but I don't want any more children to die over the winter."

The Virman knew all about death. On Virma, they sometimes had years so bad that parents killed their newborn children because they had nothing to feed them. He didn't think Ativernese nobles generally worried about their peasants, but this woman was different. And since he was going to work for her for a number of years, their interests had to align. He would help her.

"I see. This is no place to talk."

Lily nodded. "You're right, but…"

"That ferret will be back any minute. Tell him that you will speak with him later about any compensation you deem necessary. That will give us time to think about what to ask for. Arrange to meet with him again this evening."

"Fine. Maybe I did lose my nerve. I appreciate the advice." She sighed in relief.

৪◆ଔ

Anna danced her way down the hall. Life wasn't perfect yet, but it was moving in the right direction. She had a closet full of new dresses, and her father had given her a box of jewels fit for a queen. She had never seen such fine things in her life.

And Lons was gone.

That meant that Anna Wellster was officially a virginal maiden. There was just one problem: she knew what virginity meant, but she wasn't sure how fake it. *Maybe the prince won't know the difference. I'll have to get a vial of blood from somewhere.*

The King's Jester appeared out of nowhere. "Come with me. We have to talk."

Anna shuddered. She feared the Jester with a physical terror that lived somewhere in her bones. A few words from him and her father would send her to a convent…or worse.

Anna was a sensible girl. She knew that she was beautiful and smart, but she also knew that anyone could be replaced. Her sisters were growing up—in a couple of years, one of them could marry the prince. That would be the end for her. She remembered the thin, pale lips of the Brides of Aldonai, their mournful eyes, and pale, sack-like dresses. She would rather drown herself than become a nun.

So, she followed the Jester. He led her to a small alcove room and pointed to the bed. "Sit down and listen to me." She obeyed. If he had told her to lift her skirt and give herself to him on that same bed, she would have done it. That's how scared she was of him.

"You were never married. I have all the papers, but I won't destroy them yet. If you do so much as take a step without my permission, I'll give them to your father. Do you know what he'll do to you?"

Anna nodded. Her throat was paralyzed; she couldn't manage to say a word.

"You're not a virgin, and we have to fix that. I'll send someone to get you tonight. You follow him."

"Wh-where?"

"To a wise woman. She'll help you. Richard of Ativerna will never suspect a thing."

"If he chooses me, that is."

"Even if he doesn't, who will want you the way you are now?"

Anna shuddered. She would follow the Jester wherever he led her, as long as things worked out in the end. She wanted to live and love, dance at balls, order other people around, be a princess…and she would have sold her own mother to do it.

"I'll make him choose me."

"I'm sure you will. Go now. And remember our talk. He'll come tonight."

Anna nodded. She slipped out of the alcove and ran as fast as she could from that terrible man.

ᔆ◆ᘓ

Left alone, the King's Jester—Count Altres Lort—sat down on the bed and shook his head. She was such a fool. *A cowardly, grasping, jealous fool. Just like her mother.* He had tried and failed to talk Gardwig out of marrying that woman.

Anna had a nice face and big breasts, though. Richard might bite. He could always out her to her father, but he didn't want to upset his brother without a good reason. He would tell him when the time was right, when it was safe, and then the two of them would decide what to do.

If the King had been looking for nothing more than a political marriage, they could have gotten rid of Anna easily by sending her to a convent or quietly wringing her neck. Wellster had plenty of other princesses to choose from. They were still small girls, of course, but long engagements had their purpose.

The problem, thought the Jester, was that Edward of Ativerna was allowing his son to marry for love—well, more or less. Richard could choose between two princesses. Edward would benefit equally from ties to Ivernea and Wellster, but Wellster was in desperate need of a long peace bolstered by a royal wedding.

Aldonai willing, Gardwig may live another twenty years. But is he willing? What if he dies before another ten years is out? Gardwig's son was still a baby, and his wife was a quiet homebody. If anything happened, Wellster would be defenseless against its avaricious neighbors. The kingdom would be in a much stronger position if Anna married Richard. They could use her influence to get help from Ativerna. After all, it wouldn't be difficult for her to convince her husband to offer protection to her younger brother. If Richard married into the royal family of Ivernea, however, he might be tempted to bite off a chunk of Wellster.

Altres Lort most definitely wanted Anna and Richard to wed. He would do whatever it took to make it happen, and no one would get in his way.

ꙮ ◆ ℭℬ

When the Baron returned, Lily was absolutely calm.

"My Lady, your guards are waiting for you downstairs."

Lilian held herself as stiffly as she could. "Most Honorable Torius, I hope they are in good health? They haven't suffered, have they?"

"Of course not, My Lady. They were not harmed at all."

Lily dropped her lashes. "Wonderful. Leif, see to things for me. I want to get some rest if I can."

"Yes, My Lady."

"Honorable Torius, I will look in on you in the future if I need your assistance."

"Certainly, My Lady. I'm always at your service."

With those few words, they struck their bargain.

You owe me for roughing up my guards. I don't want anything right now, but if that changes, I'll whistle, and you'll come running. If you don't, Jess Earton will find out what you're up to. And you won't like that.

The Baron obviously understood her perfectly. He might have been cursing the day she was born, but on the surface, he was the picture of politeness. He showed Lily out and kissed her hand. She couldn't help firing a parting shot. "By the way, could you recommend a good jeweler?"

"The best jeweler in these parts is Helke Leitz, My Lady. He has a shop not far from town hall. Anyone can point the way."

Lilian nodded. "Thank you. I've enjoyed our conversation. It's only a shame that we met because of such unpleasantness."

As Leif helped her down the stairs, Lily sighed. *This trip has certainly worked wonders. I've lost at least ten pounds, and my dresses are starting to feel baggy. But I still have a long way to go…*

ଅ◆ଔ

The Virmans were waiting for her outside. Faces sullen, the five giants bowed in unison. Leif must have explained the situation to them. Lily responded with a slight incline of her head and clambered up onto her horse. She looked back at her escort. *Can I show up at the jeweler's like this? Oh, why not. I'd bet a gold crown that he's a world-class swindler.*

Leif sent the Virmans back to their ship and took her horse by its reins. Lily looked down at her dress. Either she would have to invent soap right away, or she was out one very expensive piece of silk. Wood ash and roots would never wash the horse sweat out of the delicate fabric.

I wonder if I still remember how to make plain washing soap? I think it takes an alkali and a fat…or soda and vegetable oil. Plus additives to make it smell better. Let's start with the alkali first…

Lily didn't know if she would be able to find sodium hydroxide and calcium hydroxide, but she was sure she could prepare a weak alkali. All it would take would be ash, lime, and a couple of days of waiting. *Ash is easy to come by in any century, and I can make the lime myself if I have to.* She would heat marble and chalk together. *Easy as pie.* Even an open fire should offer sufficient heat. If it didn't, she would put her ingredients on a metal sheet and stick them in the blacksmith's forge. When she was done, she would have soap that would remove grease and oil.

She thought back with gratitude to her applied chemistry class. It was an elective, but she had put a lot of effort into the class because it was so interesting. And she was glad to still have all that knowledge in her memory. Cosmetics, perfume, soaps, and cleaners—Lily could make anything. If she had to, she could even put together a batch of gunpowder or make dynamite out of nitroglycerine. She could cook up some glass and blow it into almost anything. She could turn clay into ceramic dishes.

Chemistry was a good thing to know in any century. The main thing was to know where to find the elements she needed and recognize them when she found them. *I know where to get marble, but I'll have to find chalk. I wonder if the periodic table is the same here? If not, they'll just have to learn the Lilian Earton Table.* She also couldn't wait to get back to practicing medicine. She would buy all the herbs and plants she needed at the market tomorrow. *Who knows when it will come in handy? I'll be like Louis Pasteur, only as a medieval herbalist!*

Leif roused her from her thoughts. "My Lady?"

"Yes?"

"Do you really want to go see that jeweler?"

"I do. Why do you ask?"

"Judging by his name, he's likely to be a crook. He's obviously one of the Eveers."

"Eveers?" Lily looked at him sharply, and Leif saw that he would have to explain.

"Eveers don't have a country, but they do have their own religion and their own system of writing. They believe that they are the only people who were created by the true God."

"What do they think about Aldonai?"

"He's just an assistant to their god."

Lily grimaced. "How does the Church look at that idea?" She couldn't hide her sarcasm and was relieved to see something similar on Leif's face.

"The Church disapproves most strenuously."

"How does it express its disapproval?" Can it be true? Have I really found a person I can talk to? We aren't equals—it's the Dark Ages, after all—but even so, we can have a conversation!

"It expresses its disapproval by levying higher taxes on their trading. Eveers are not allowed to wear green, they can't live closer to a church than three flights of an arrow." Lily quickly estimated that to be about half a mile "They can't be buried in church cemeteries, they can't openly worship their god…"

"Why do they put up with all of that?"

"You can put up with a lot when you don't have a choice."

Lily nodded. "So what kind of work do they do?"

"They're merchants, jewelers, and loan sharks, among other things. Their god tells them to be literate, even the women, and they always have jobs that involve money."

Universal literacy. Lily liked the sound of that. Maybe it was a lucky break that she had learned about these people. She knew that it takes a team to get anything done, no matter what year it was or what world you found yourself in. *One man in a field is no warrior.*

She had seen how people built teams in school. Students who wanted to live quietly made friends with other sheep. The ones who wanted to shine chose friends they didn't think could compete with them, and the ones who wanted to be leaders always found two or three classmates who were ready to be led. *That's how it worked in school, but here, I'm looking at needing to survive…and build a decent life for myself. And then?*

Lily was afraid to think any further than that, but deep in her mind, the question worried her—Jerrison, the Earl of Earton, her husband. According to local custom, she was his property. *What will I do if he shows up like the lord of the castle and tells me to get in bed with him?*

Lily saw three options: kill him and run, just run, or kill him and say it was an accident. She could come up with an explanation easily enough. *I was just sitting there cleaning under my nails with a knife. Better yet, with a sword. It's not my fault that he slipped thirty-two times and landed each time on the sword...with his neck.* She would have to get her defenses ready before her husband came for a visit. That meant having a team in place. She had the Virmans for muscle, and she would try her best to keep them interested in working for her. Leif was certainly no one's fool, but his Virman crew was not enough. *Success has three components—knowledge, strength, and money. I have knowledge, the Virmans are my strength, and the Eveers have money.*

Lily had a huge storehouse of knowledge in her head, and judging by what Leif had told her, the Eveers were just the people to help her monetize it. And the Virmans were armed to deal with anyone who didn't toe the line.

Lily was prepared to be as polite as humanly possible to the jeweler.

What about the Church? I'll deal with them. Earton only has one priest, and there are plenty of lonely swamps to go around.

Lilian Earton began to build her team.

ಐ◆ಆ

The jeweler's shop was impressive. It was a two-story stone building with three golden spheres hanging over the doorway. *The owner must live upstairs. He even has glass in the second-floor windows where boys passing by in the street can't break them. He's doing well now, but soon he'll be doing even better. The annual fair is the perfect place to advertise.*

Lily got off her horse with Leif's help and pushed the door open. Inside, the shop was dark, quiet, and smelled faintly of wax from burning candles. *What do they add to the wax to keep it from melting quickly? And what are the candles made of? Tallow or paraffin? I remember about the wicks... Emma Markovna in applied chemistry told us that they used to soak the wicks in a solution of saltpeter or boric acid to make candles burn brighter and give off less heat and soot. Otherwise, you get black streaks on the ceiling.*

As soon as she walked in, the young man at the shop counter guessed that she was a Countess (and immediately tallied up the price of her clothes and jewelry and the Virman behind her). He bowed so vigorously that Lily was afraid he would break his nose on the counter.

"Young man, are you Helke Leitz?"

"No, My Lady," he hiccupped.

"But this is his shop, isn't it?"

"Yes, My Lady."

"Then call Helke for me." It came out sounding very regal and imperious. The color drained from the young man's face, and he ducked behind a curtain. Lily looked around her as she waited. The furniture was heavy. Candles sputtered in carved candle holders, and the large ceiling beams hung low over her head. The ceiling was black with soot.

I'll introduce better living through chemistry! Saltpeter is easy enough to manufacture from manure, even if the process smells awful. There's an idea: I'll punish people by making them work at my saltpeter piles. If I start now, I should have results in about two years. That's a long time, but when you want something done, you have to do it yourself. It may be worth it to try and make some nitric acid, too.

"My Lady?" An old man interrupted her thoughts.

The man bowed and kissed her hand under Leif's watchful eye. She rewarded him with a nod and looked him over from under her lashes. He was doing the same, looking her over and evaluating her. There was no telling what he thought about her, but Lily decided that she was dealing with a serious businessman. At first glance, he was just a short, dark-haired man with bad posture, worn clothes, and an obsequious look on his face. A second glance, however, revealed more useful information. The wrinkles on his face were not from age, but from frowning. He was clean, instead of smelling like sweat and incense like most other people. And his clothes may have been old, but they were clean, too. Lily reflected that after her trip on horseback, she would have to bathe three times in bleach to get that clean. He didn't move like an old man, either. His hands didn't tremble, and his feet didn't shuffle. His every move was precise and measured. Lily could have sworn that he was a master of working with precious stones and gold.

She wanted a magnifying glass. If there were glass blowers in her new world, she could get it done. She had already made one back at home for her mother. But first... She would have to give the old man a couple of ideas for free.

I don't believe he's all that old, though. He's probably no more than forty-five. He just hunches over like that to make himself look more pitiful.

The jeweler bowed and expressed his pleasure at her visit. Lily's brain hummed with ideas. "I would like to see some jewelry. Show me some earrings." She flicked a finger against one ear to make its emerald sparkle. "I think mine are too small."

He bowed again. "If you would like to have a seat, My Lady, I'll bring you some things."

"Of course, Mr. Leitz. I'll wait here."

"Thank you, My Lady."

He showed her to a chair. Lily let herself down into it and sighed. It had been a long time since she had exercised. Travel was interfering with her resolution to lead a healthy lifestyle.

Leif took up his place behind her chair. Lily smiled at him. "Tell me, what's the name of your wife?"

"Her name is Ingrid, My Lady." A smile broke out on the Virman's normally serious face, and Lily felt a pang of envy. No one had ever looked at her that way. Even her fiancé, Alex, didn't smile like that when he saw her. But Leif's eyes shone. For Ingrid's sake, he was ready to sail any ocean, walk across hot coals, swallow a live snake, or pull the moon out of the sky. Nobody loved Lily that much.

"Will you bring her to meet me this evening? I'd like to have a woman to talk to."

Leif's eyebrows went up. "Countess…"

"I may be a Countess," Lilian smiled, "but even a Countess needs friends."

"We are Virmans."

"The Book of Aldonai says that all of us have souls."

"Are you a follower of the Book of Aldonai, My Lady?"

Lily grinned. "Certainly. Like everyone in this world." The words 'as long as it suits me' hung in the air, unspoken, but Leif heard them and smiled back at her.

"I will bring her."

ಬಂ◆ಣ

The curtain whispered as it opened. The jeweler was back. He put a small box on the table in front of Lilian and bowed low. Lily opened the lid and gasped in delight. *What beauty!* If only she had the money… The box contained two cabochon emeralds of the deepest shade of green. Lily took one out of its nest. She examined the earring and shook her head. "Sit down, honorable Helke."

"My Lady, I wouldn't dare to sit in your presence!"

"Sit down anyway. We need to talk."

"Yes, My Lady?" The man seemed to expect something unpleasant from her, but Lily disappointed him.

"Tell me, are all your earrings like these?" She didn't like the fact that the earrings had no clasp. The emeralds hung on a bent wire that went through the ear. That was fine for cheap jewelry, but how could she be expected to wear expensive stones that way?

"My Lady?"

"They are inconvenient to wear."

The jeweler's eyes grew sharp. "Everyone makes them this way, My Lady…"

"I know. Mine are the same way. I want you to fix them according to my instructions."

"How is that, My Lady?"

"Do you have something to write on?"

Helke nodded and brought out some parchment, a quill pen, and an inkwell. Lily looked slyly at the inkwell.

It isn't non-spill like the ones I designed.

She tried to remember if she had one of hers with her. I don't think I do. But that can wait. I won't show him all my cards at once.

Lily dipped the pen in the ink and neatly drew a simple earring with an English clasp. "This would be easy enough to make out of almost any metal."

The jeweler studied the drawing. He looked up. "My Lady, I have never seen anything like this before."

"So, look at it now. Try to make an inexpensive pair from my drawing. If you want to talk to me, you can find me at The Pig and Dog."

"My Lady…"

Lily slowly and regally stood up from her chair to show that her visit was over. "If you decide to talk to me again, I will be in town through the end of the fair. Perhaps, you will want to see other new things…"

She smiled and was gone before the jeweler had a chance to respond.

₨◆ℳ

After she left, Helke shut the door, hissed to his assistant that the shop was closed, and ran back into his workshop. As a jeweler, he realized how perfectly wonderful Lily's idea was. Earrings with a clasp would not fall off ladies' lovely (or not so lovely) ears and get lost. And if he was the only one with the idea…

Helke was an official member of the jewelers' guild. He could bring in the idea and receive a percentage of future sales. He picked up his tools and got to work.

ಬಿ ◆ ೞ

Lily spent the rest of the day asking questions at the inn. She had a friendly conversation with the innkeeper and learned something that made her happy: there were guilds in Ativerna! Guilds of jewelers, weavers, tailors, stone carvers, leather tanners, merchants…That went right along with her plans. The locals already understood that no new invention could be kept secret for long. If it was a new method for processing leather, there would be the expense of taking on apprentices and feeding them. But what if it was something simple, like a new way to cut a gem, something that would be easy to copy…

At some point in history, the Ativernese came up with the guild system. Each guild was led by a master craftsman, and the other members worked under his protection. They paid membership dues and something like a tax, but if a member died, the guild would support his widow and help his children learn the trade. If a member came up with a good idea, he shared it with the guild and earned a percentage of sales for five years (some guilds offered longer or shorter periods). The better the invention, the more the earnings. Lily thought this was fantastic. Nobody was forced to join a guild, but it was risky to go alone without protection. The benefits of membership far outweighed the cost of what the guild took for itself.

Lily knew she had plenty of good ideas to share with the local jewelers and other craftsmen. She recalled the Kikabidze song about "My Years are My Wealth" and reflected that her wealth was her knowledge. She would apply what she knew, even if she had to use Helke to make money. She didn't care if he was an Eveer, as long as he shared the profits fairly.

ಬಿ ◆ ೞ

Back on the ship, Leif caught Ingrid's worried glance. *She understands everything.*

The Virman whistled sharply to get everyone's attention. "All on deck! I have important news!"

Ten minutes later, all the Virmans, including women and children, were on deck to hear their captain. Soon, their faces broke into happy smiles. *He had found a place for them!* They were going to live in Earton. They would live at the castle for a while, but after that, they would have houses of their own if they wanted. They would serve the Countess of Earton for three years. She was an intelligent, serious woman. There were some strange things about her, but she would pay them well.

Leif answered their questions in detail. When the large group broke up into smaller groups to discuss their future, Leif went to Ingrid. He put his arm around her, and she buried her face in his shoulder.

"You were right, dear. She is an intelligent woman."

"I knew it. You are the best of husbands!"

Leif hugged her. "But you know something? She can be very odd at times."

"Really?" Ingrid was much more interested in the warm arm around her waist that in Lilian Earton's problems. "What makes her odd?"

"She talks to everyone the same way," Leif said, trying to explain what worried him.

"The same way?"

"I have heard her talking with her peasants. And with me. With the Baron. With an Eveer jeweler. I think she sees us as equals. She was respectful with everyone she spoke to."

"Even with the Eveer?" Virmans had nothing personal against Eveers, but they knew how the world at large viewed them.

"She didn't care. She just saw him as a person. And here's the other thing, I feel like she is a little bit frightened of everyone."

"That's strange."

"It is. Very strange. My dear, she wants to meet you."

"Me?"

"I told her that Virmans are not servants."

"What did she say to that?"

"She said that all of us have souls."

"True enough, but she is a Countess."

"I think you'll forget about that after talking to her for ten minutes. She can be very charming when she wants to be."

"Do you like her?"

Leif snorted. "My darling, there is only one woman in the world for me, and that is you. Lilian Earton is helping us. We will serve her and live in her home and eat her bread. Why shouldn't we try to maintain friendly relations with her?"

Ingrid nodded, but she didn't look convinced.

ༀ◆ༀ

His Majesty Edward VIII looked at his son. "Come in and sit down."

Richard showed his father a smile full of white teeth and sat down in a chair. "What is the matter, Father?"

"You are leaving for Wellster in a few days."

"I am. Did you know that Jess found room in the delegation for…"

"You can tell me about that later. Richard, I want to ask you not to make your choice hastily." Richard's eyebrows went up, and Edward continued, "Even if you like the girl, even if you lose your head over her, don't offer marriage right away. Promise me that."

His son shrugged. "I promise. But why?"

"Do you know how I met Jessie?"

"Yes. At your wedding."

"I don't want you to repeat my fate. Take a good look at both girls and choose the one you really want. If we have to, we can invite them to come here. That will give you more time."

"Why didn't we invite them here right away?"

"Because you can find out certain things about them by visiting their homes. Get a good look at them, and then we will invite them here. Where they don't know anyone."

"I see this is serious for you."

"Imogene was never a true wife to me. And once she realized that I didn't love her, she became my enemy. We managed to get through it without serious consequences. But you remember the death of your older brother and of Jyce…"

His father didn't call Edmund by name. That said a lot to Richard.

"You were very close to Jyce."

"He and Jessie were like one person, and I loved her. Jyce was like a brother to me, too. I hope you feel the same about Jerrison."

"I only wish he really was my brother by blood."

"Be satisfied with what you have," Edward said, waving a finger at his son.

It was a secret he would take to the grave. Jess would never know that he had royal blood in his veins. Neither would Richard. It was safer that way. Edward had no fear of Jess or Richard conspiring against each other. He just felt that secrets were safer when known to one person alone. If he told the boys, there was no telling where else the information would end up. And there were plenty of evil people around the court who wouldn't mind playing games with other people's lives.

Jess and Richard are just boys. If only Aldonai would give him another ten years to live. Just ten more years—Jessamine and Jyce were both waiting for him there, on the other side.

"Father, I promise to weigh my choice carefully." Richard slid to his knees by his father's chair. Edward ran his hand through the young man's curls, as he had when his son was a boy.

"Do not make the mistake I made, my son. Now, tell me what Jess has going on with that young widow."

"I think it's serious."

"That's bad."

"Father…"

"Have you forgotten that Jess is married? He needs an heir from Lilian."

"How could anyone forget that hysterical fool?"

"Hush. August's boatyards are the best in the country."

"I know that. A man can marry anyone to get his hands on property. But to conceive an heir with her?" He shivered.

"What about duty? I will speak with Jess. He must have an heir before he looks for enjoyment elsewhere. You know the law is strict on that point."

Richard understood. If Lilian were to die without giving Jess an heir, Jess would be allowed to keep her dowry. That was a lot of money, but it was just money. The boatyards, however, which were still being managed by August, would not be his.

"I will remind him, but I think he is in love."

"Talk him out of it. Now go, you rascal. I hope you aren't taking anyone with you on the delegation?"

Richard shook his head. His latest mistress was staying home, much to her disappointment. He was first and foremost the Prince of Ativerna before he was a man and a knight. And since his mistress could possibly hinder his finding a wife, she would have to stay at home. If she didn't like it, he could easily find another skirt to chase.

Edward smiled. "Fine. Go. And talk to Jess."

"Can't you do it?"

"I can talk to him here in my study, but you can do it over a tankard of ale. He is more likely to listen to you."

Richard shook his head. "Your Majesty is a master of intrigue."

"Live and learn, they say."

"I will follow your example." Richard bowed and left his father's study. Edward smiled at his back. Wellster. Ivernea. Both alliances were good ones. He just wanted his son to be happy.

Help him, Aldonai.

ജ♦ദ

Lons opened his eyes. It was pitch black. He choked on the stench that hit his nose. For an instant, he thought he had gone blind or even died, but there was a thick odor of unwashed bodies and excrement.

"Where am I?"

He didn't expect an answer, but he got one. "In the hold of the Star Gull. They dragged you in yesterday."

Yesterday… Lons remembered his conversation with the Jester. His head was splitting, but he recalled it all.

"Slave traders?"

"By all that's unholy…"

Lons groaned and leaned his forehead against the side of the hold. He felt the ship rock and heard the splash of the waves.

"What will they do with us?"

"They'll sail along the coast to the Khanganat, where they'll sell you. Unless you die first, that is."

This outlook did nothing to make the teacher feel better, but he had no choice in the matter. Heavy chains prevented him from trying to escape.

Anna, my poor girl! What will they do to you?

ॐ ◆ ଔ

Lily looked from Leif to Ingrid with pleasure. They were a wonderful pair, and they loved each other. She could read it in their faces. He was tall and powerfully built, like an oak tree. Next, to him, Ingrid was like a slim beech tree. It was a pretty picture.

"Good evening, Leif, Ingrid. Have a seat. And have something to eat and drink."

There was a pitcher of light wine and a platter of steamed vegetables on the table. Lily would have preferred juice, but the innkeeper only had wine.

"Thank you, My Lady."

Lily took the bull by the horns. "We need to discuss many things. You will be working for me. Actually, you are already in my service. Here is your advance."

A heavy leather wallet landed softly on the table. Inside, were five gold coins. Lily had decided not to advance him too much at once. She would pay the rest later…with interest.

Leif didn't move. "You paid the advance when you freed my men. What was it you wanted to buy at the market, My Lady?"

Lily looked at him. He wasn't wasting time. She liked that.

"I already found a jeweler. Now, I need a blacksmith. A good one. And a glass blower. That's just the first round."

"They will not be difficult to find. I believe there is only one glass blower in this town. It is not a common profession."

Lily nodded. "Good. I also need to buy some cows, sheep, goats, and pigs. My villages have been losing people to hunger in the winter. That is going to stop."

Lily briefly recounted the situation in Earton. When she was done, she looked down at the pitcher of wine on the table. If she was wrong about these two, she would let them go immediately. Otherwise, her plans would not work.

Ingrid, not Leif, was first to speak. She had been sitting as quietly as a mouse, but once she saw that Leif had no interest in Lilian other than as an employer, and that the Countess behaved with simplicity and kindness, she opened up. "My Lady, how will you feed them?"

"Who?"

"The cows."

Lily sighed. "I have no idea. I suppose we'll buy feed."

"But My Lady, why not just get goats instead of the cows? Back home in Virma, we all keep goats. They provide meat, wool, milk, and they are much cheaper to feed and easier to care for. And I'm sure it would be easier to get them back to your estate."

The trip home…

Lily sighed. That was the weak spot in her plan. One hundred cows—a whole herd. Insanity. Even fifty cows was a sizeable number. It would take a dozen headers to drive them back to Earton. And that was just to drive them. *What about security?* Earton was a long way away… Lily groaned. *What do I do?*

Leif's voice broke into her thoughts. "My Lady, do you think the peasants had no plans for surviving the winter without your help?"

She heard the irony in the Virman's voice. He was not making fun of her. He could tell that Lily didn't know much about agriculture, and he wanted to push her in the right direction.

Okay, so how did the peasants intend to survive? What if the old Lilian was still here?

She was pretty sure they didn't intend to lie down and die, and she wondered if they were simply using her because they could see she felt sorry for them. She made a decision. "I suppose I could just buy grain. It would be easier to transport."

Ingrid nodded with a smile. "Yes, it would. And you could distribute it to those who are especially needy over the winter."

Lilian thought about her childhood home. There were always sacks of potatoes, carrots, and beets in a corner of the kitchen. She remembered years when she and her parents ate nothing but army-issued tinned meat and whatever they could grow in their garden.

"Yes, I will buy grain and have the merchants deliver it in their ships." Lilian ticked off what she needed, "Rye, millet, buckwheat... Since you're already going to Earton, you can follow the merchants to make sure they don't sail off with my grain."

"Do you have a mill in Earton?" Ingrid asked.

Lily had no idea. She would have to think about that. If Earton didn't have a mill, she would have to have one built. Water- or wind-powered? Why, oh, why don't I know anything about how mills are built? I could have read up on so many useful things if I'd known I'd end up here! All I know is that there's a big wheel and a small wheel. I don't know the ratio between the two wheels or the speeds they turn at. I remember the fairytale about the devil who was a miller, but that's not exactly helpful, is it?

Lily sighed doubtfully. "There should be a mill. Do you want me to call for one of the village elders?"

Leif nodded. "Which one?"

Lily looked around. Art Virdas and Sherl Ferney had wandered off somewhere. Jean Corey was nearby, pushing his luck with an attractive waitress. *I bet they're discussing Eastern philosophy. It will just have to wait.*

Leif's eyes followed Lilian's. He nodded. The handle of his ax hit the floor like a bolt of lightning. The sound was deafening. Even the braided onions hanging on the walls jumped. Jean turned to see what the commotion was about. Leif gestured for him to come over. Lily blinked.

Jean turned out to be a good source of information. There was a mill in Earton, and it belonged to the Earl *big surprise there!* Anyone who wanted to use it had to pay. The Comptroller had always handled those things.

Lily thought to herself that, with the Comptroller gone, people were probably using the mill for free. That was fine with her…for now. And it would give her leverage if she needed it in the future.

Jean also said that there were a few cows in the villages, but they were poor milkers. When he started to complain about the cows, Ingrid interrupted him. "Fifteen liters a day is very little for a decent cow. But why in the world would you go out and buy new ones? Do you have anywhere to keep them? What will you feed them? How do you know that the pasture grazing is any good?"

Ingrid then asked him about goats, sheep, and chickens. She wanted details on how much milk they got from their sheep and goats, and what kind of yarn they spun from their coats. How many acres did they plant, and how many bushels of grain did they harvest per acre?

About halfway through this conversation, Lily completely lost track of what they were talking about. She was listening and trying to follow the thread, but Ingrid was head and shoulders above her in her knowledge of farming and animal husbandry.

Who cares how much milk a goat gives if they don't have enough goats to begin with?

Leif noticed that Lily was falling behind and whispered to her, so Jean wouldn't hear. "Ingrid was raised to manage a farm."

Lily nodded. So that's how the girl knew so much. She would make a good Comptroller. There was also Emma. If three intelligent women could work together, the estate would thrive. Lily sat quietly sipping her ale and smiled sweetly at Jeanw henever he seemed unwilling to give Ingrid a straight answer to a question.

ε⋄Ↄ

Ingrid finally finished her inquisition and nodded. She was deep in thought.

"My Lady, grain is a must. But do not distribute it right away. Only hand it out as needed."

"What about livestock?"

"Your pastures are no good—almost as bad as ours, but you have swampy ground while we have rock. Good livestock needs good feed. Animals can die in the wrong conditions. I would just buy two good bulls for sires and maybe ten cows."

Lily reflected on that. It would be cheaper, and she could afford to buy really good animals that way. The Virman woman knew what she was talking about. A handful of cows would be easier to transport. They could live in the stockyard at the castle. There was an old barn that could be insulated, and Lily would have her own dairy, with fresh milk, sour cream, and cheese.

We can use the new bulls to inseminate the villagers' cows. That's a good idea! But still, how do I get the animals home? Trying to get anything done without trains or decent roads is just ridiculous!

She was cautious. "I like the idea about bulls."

"And you could buy goats, too. Virman goats. They give good wool, and they are easy to care for."

"Can we buy them here?"

"We'll have to look around at the market."

Lily nodded. "If I buy them, Ingrid, then you and the other women on your ship will be the only ones who know what to do with their wool. Will you do the work for me?"

Ingrid's eyes widened. "Well, I'm not going to sit around doing nothing all winter!"

"Don't worry about that!" Lily grinned. "There's always plenty to do. But we'll profit by it in the end."

"We can at least try."

"Do you know how to make lace?"

After a minute, it became clear that the young Virman had never seen a crochet hook. In her own world, Aliya had crocheted and knitted and even made tatted lace.

"Lace? It's very expensive. Merchants bring strips of lace from Elvana. You wouldn't believe how much they cost."

Judging by the look on Leif's face, Lily felt certain he would head to the market in the morning in search of lace. If such finery existed, his wife should have it. Lily smiled.

"What about lace shawls and dresses?"

In high school, Aliya had crocheted her graduation dress out of rainbow-colored yarn and sewed a satin lining for it. There was no one else with anything like it.

Ingrid's eyes grew wider. "Do you know how to make such things, My Lady?"

Lily's smile grew even wider. "We can talk about that later—at home in Earton."

The Virman woman nodded. "Good. But there is one more thing I wanted to say. Fish will soon be heading up the river to spawn. We should put in cages and nets so that we'll have fish to salt and smoke. One fish can keep a family fed for several days. So, that's fish and grain. We could also buy some chickens. Better yet, three-month-old chicks. Or ducks and geese…"

As she listened to Ingrid, Lily reflected on how lucky she was. Ingrid was smart and capable of a lot. If all was well at his home, Leif could have left her in charge of a large farm and headed out to sea for months. His wife could manage anything that came her way.

Emma had the same personality, and Lily planned to do her best to keep up with them. They would survive the winter. And in the spring, they would begin to farm for real. *We'll need a ton of fertilizer. Since we're buying all these birds, we might as well put in a compost pile. That will improve soil fertility quickly. And then we'll plant cover crops and turn them in. We could also…What else was there? I can't remember! What would my biology professor say if she could see me now? I thought I was paying attention, but now that I need the information it's all gone!*

Calm down. If I learned it once, I can learn it again. If I just give my brain some time, all the things I memorized in medical school will come back to me.

Lily took a deep breath. She relaxed her shoulders and smiled. "Has Leif told you that you'll be living at the castle until we can get something else put up for you?"

"He has. My Lady, won't your husband object?"

Lily shrugged. "He is never there, so I won't worry about what he thinks."

∞◆೮

Jess Earton was preparing for a rendezvous. Adele was waiting for him.

Sweet, gentle, fragile Adele, so beautiful and so helpless. *Am I doing the right thing taking her with me on this trip?*

On the other hand, he wasn't sure he could leave her. Jess knew quite well that he and Adele could never marry—at least while Lilian was alive. He had no heir as of yet, and the church wouldn't allow more than four marriages in a row. *But is that any reason to deny myself the pleasure of a lovely woman?*

They hadn't done anything yet. Maybe in another month or so… Jess enjoyed the hunt. He just had a niggling doubt: *could the hunt turn into something more?*

Jess had seen how his Uncle Edward and Aunt Jessamine had looked at each other. No matter where they were, sparks flew. They didn't just have passion; they were tender and understanding and warm with each other. It was love in every sense of the word.

Jess didn't feel that way about Adele. Or do I just not feel that way yet? He couldn't answer that question. Let's see, flowers and jewelry. A modest gold and sapphire brooch, Adele will like it. It's simple and in good taste. He realized that he still hadn't seen a report from his estate Comptroller. Etor had never been late before. The Earl of Earton was not terribly concerned with the family estate since he earned his money elsewhere. He had inherited a fleet of merchant ships from his father, and with the help of his father-in-law and his shipyards, he intended to expand the business. He would send merchants as far away as the Khanganat. And if he managed to improve the design of his ships…but that was a project for the future.

Some landowners looked down their noses at a nobleman engaged in commerce, but Jess' father Jyce had always ignored them. "Let them envy me," he had said. "They have to squeeze every last penny out of their land, while I am able to free my peasants from taxes. I don't trade in livestock, after all, but pureblood horses, spices, gems and other rarities. Why shouldn't I turn a profit?"

With his shipping business flourishing, Jess' thoughts only rarely turned to Earton. The family estate was in the middle of nowhere, surrounded by swamps and forests. It was a fine place to go hunting, but he thought he'd lose his mind if he had to live there. The castle hadn't been touched in many years. His grandfather had sold off some of the land in order to ensure that his children made advantageous marriages. He had looked askance at the idea of engaging in trade. He also disapproved of his daughter living as the King's mistress.

While the old Earl was alive, Jyce and Jess avoided Earton. When he passed away, he was survived by his wife, a sweet little old lady who shared most of her late husband's opinions. Jess remembered his grandmother well. She had detested him, and the feeling was mutual. For some reason, she had a strange aversion to all of her grandchildren except those Jessie gave birth to when lawfully wed. Whenever any of her other grandchildren entered her field of vision, she couldn't stop herself from harping and criticizing.

Jyce Earton had found it necessary to make a home for himself and his wife away from Earton, so he bought a small estate near the capital. All the other Eartons, including Amalia and Jess, preferred to live in the city.

A quiet knock at the door interrupted Jess' memories. "My Lord, the Duchess of Ivernea is here to see you."

"Show her in," said Jess, and turned back to tying the bow on his shoulder.

The door opened, and a laughing voice asked, "How are you, little brother?"

"Wonderful. And you?"

Amalia shrugged. Her shawl fell open, revealing her round belly. "Soon you will have another nephew. Or niece."

"Another one?" Jess rolled his eyes theatrically. "You and Pete are heroes." Amalia raised her eyebrows and smiled. Jyce had wanted only the best for his children. The marriage he arranged for Jess did not end up a happy one, but Amalia was more fortunate. Her father had engaged her to the heir of the Duke of Ivernea when the two were still in their cradles.

Peter turned out to be a good match. He wasn't ugly, and he wasn't stupid, and he managed to win one out of every five arm wrestling matches with Jess, which wasn't bad at all. Better yet, he adored his wife. Amalia felt the same about him. Their love was so strong that Jess already had a nephew and two nieces to spoil.

"Are you going back to Ivernea?"

"Of course. I came to see you before we both leave."

"You came just in time. I was about to…"

"You were about to run off to your little hen."

"Don't call her that."

"Then what do I call her? Jess, you aren't in love with her, are you?"

Jess shrugged. "I don't know. Would that be such a bad thing?"

Amalia's voice was serious. "With this particular woman, it would be a very bad thing. Jess, I am not often at court, but…well, your Adele is not as simple as she may seem."

"Is that so?"

"It is. Do you know about her cousin?"

"I know her husband had a nephew. Is that what you mean?"

"Did you know that the two of them are, how do I put this, closer than necessary? And did you know that her husband was literally shocked to death when he found them in a compromising situation? The blow killed him."

Jess raised an eyebrow. "Where did you pick up this awful gossip?"

"One of my friends knew Adelaide's husband quite well."

"That old fool…"

"He was a decent man. And he was just fifty-two years older than his wife."

"Sure. Half a century is nothing."

"Jess, you know exactly what I mean." Amalia stomped her foot. Jess couldn't help but admire her. She was so tall and beautiful. She looked a great deal like their Aunt Jessamine.

"You look like a queen today."

Amalia melted and gave her brother a smile. "Yes, you and I were fortunate. We look like our father."

Jess recalled his mother and shuddered. No one in his right mind would want to look like that stuck-up dried fish.

"You were also lucky with your marriage."

Amalia went to her brother and wrapped her arms around his shoulders—at least as far as she could reach. Jess was almost six and a half feet tall. "Don't let it get to you, little brother. You were not as lucky in marriage, but I'm sure everything will turn out for the best."

Jess sighed and buried his face in his sister's hair while hugging her tightly. "It will. I know it will. But I'm not a boy anymore. I want a family, children, love. Everything you have with Pete."

"Speaking of family, why did you send your little girl away?"

"What else was I supposed to do with her?"

"You could have sent her to us!"

"You have enough on your hands already. And you'll be confined soon."

"Even so, do you really think Lilian will take better care of her than I would?"

Jess snorted. "Of course not. But have you forgotten that Miranda does not get along with your brood?"

"Sissy and Jess didn't mean to hurt her!" Amalia's face turned red. "You know that perfectly well. How many times did I box your ears when you were little?"

"Every other day. But I gave as good as I got."

"You were awful. I still remember the time you filled my favorite shoes with earthworms."

179

"Do you? Well, who put a laxative in my porridge?"

The two grinned at each other and broke out laughing. Then Jess became serious again. "Miranda didn't want to go to your house. She chose Earton, and I didn't dare cross her."

"But are you sure Lilian won't upset her?" Amalia had a poor opinion of her brother's wife. Jess shook his head.

"Lilian won't pay her a bit of attention. She is happy as long as the storerooms are full of food and the priest comes around to preach."

Amalia frowned. "Brother, your indifference surprises me. Have you ever tried to interest your wife in anything? Have you ever actually talked to her?"

Jess wrinkled his nose. "No. And I don't want to." He didn't like Lilian. He just didn't like her! His father had been straightforward with him: they needed August's shipyards. Jess was invested in the family business, so he went along with the marriage. He just hadn't expected Lilian to be so narrow-minded and boring. Yes, she was one of the largest women he had ever seen, but it was her completely empty mind that disappointed him. They had nothing in common. Lilian's prayers and hysterics distracted him from his business, so he sent her to live at Earton. The family estate was just sitting empty, anyway. It was sad and a little shameful, and he didn't want to talk about it, so he changed the subject.

"Would you like a glass of wine? Something not too strong?"

"Golden mead," Amalia said. "Pete knows I'm here, so I can stay a while."

"All night?"

"Maybe. Could you find room for me? We could sit up late like we did as kids."

Jess smiled. "I'll order the mead. And you want honey cakes to go with it, right?"

His sister's loving smile was his reward. "Little brother, you are a wonder."

ജ ♦ ଔ

Neither of them gave a thought to Adelaide. She sat up all night waiting for her lover, who never came. In a fit of early-morning anger, she broke three vases, slapped her maid, and tore a pair of gloves to shreds.

Chapter 7

Plans and Needles

Lilian woke up feeling blue. *Why?* She tried to remember. The evening before, she had sat up drinking wine with Leif and Ingrid. The three of them had finished two pitchers. That was nothing to Leif, but the drink sat heavily in Lilian's head. She knew how to drink, but she hadn't eaten enough the previous evening because she was still trying to lose weight. Her method was simple: eat less and run more.

Running more was the easy part. Eating less was hard. Lily gave it her best. She avoided bread, sweets, and fatty meats, especially after six in the evening. She packed her plate with steamed vegetables and rarely put butter on anything. She could already see results. She was down to two chins (from three), and her dresses were growing looser. Lily suspected that she would never be thin, but she could at least be healthy.

She noticed that her new world had different ideals about beauty anyway. Women were expected to be plump, with wide hips for giving birth to lots and lots of babies. Lily, however, was aiming to get back to 150-pounds. Since she was five-feet-six-inches-tall, that would put her right in the range of normal—not anorexic and not an opera singer.

From the point of view of a doctor (or of a final year medical student), the problem with extra weight was not how it made her look, but how it made her feel physically. Lily was exhausted by her extra pounds, and she knew that as the years went by, it would just get worse. She didn't want to spend her life dragging around the equivalent of a large sack of potatoes. So, she was trying to lose weight the best way she knew how: walking, horseback riding, and eating healthier food. Her willpower was holding out for now. That being said… *I should have at least eaten some cheese with that wine last night.*

Lily forced herself up out of bed. She opened the door to the hallway and called out for a servant to bring her hot water. Then she sat down to comb her hair. *While I'm at it, why not invent the hairbrush?*

She remembered hearing somewhere that people used to use boar bristles for brushes. She would have to take a close look at the pigs in the market.

ജ♦ଓ

Before the sun was much higher in the sky, Lily, Leif, Ingrid, and four other Virmans (she didn't know their names yet) were on their way to the market. Lily and Ingrid rode horses, and the Virman men walked alongside. When they got closer to the market, the women got down. One of the Virmans stayed behind to hold the horses, and the others entered the crowd. The four men boxed in the two women so that no one could shove them. Leif strode along in front of the group and called out in a commanding voice, "Make way for the Countess of Earton!"

Ingrid was wearing a fur wrap. Lily looked at it closely. The cut was very primitive. She wondered if people in her new world knew how to dye furs. She made a note to herself to find out and to suggest more flattering cuts.

And while I'm at it, I'll hire someone to make some plain old underwear. I'm sick of wearing pantaloons and nightshirts.

The market was pandemonium, as always, with animals bleating and people yelling, but Lily was no longer bothered by the noise. Ingrid stopped at every pen to look at the cows. She felt their horns and udders and asked about milk yield and pregnancies. Lily discovered that a cow with a proven track record of delivering healthy calves cost twice as much as other cows.

But what if we get them home and they stop getting pregnant? Or what if they do get pregnant and they have complications? So much to know… Lily was no veterinarian, but she had done a rotation in obstetrics and had seen her share of breech presentations. She wondered if cows gave birth like humans. It has to be similar, right?

They made their way down the entire length of the livestock pens and stepped to the side to talk about what they had seen. Ingrid was serious. "My Lady, I saw several good cows and bulls. I believe we can buy the animals we need for two gold coins. Maybe a little less."

Lily nodded. She was thinking that maybe she should have shaken Etor a little harder before letting him go. There was no knowing who had his money now, but she sure could have used it—not for herself, but for Earton.

"We'll spend the money. Good animals are worth it. But how do we get them back?"

Leif answered, "We will have to reach an agreement with some of the traveling merchants. I saw several scows in the harbor. If they take on the stock, we will provide security."

"What about while we are still here?"

"That is easy enough. I will speak to the innkeeper. If he doesn't have a stable, he will know someone who does, and who won't mind earning a few copper coins."

"Then let's go buy some animals. Will they at least drive them back to the inn for us?"

Leif shook his head. "No, but we will manage. Don't you have dogs in Earton, My Lady?"

"Of course we do."

"Are they trained to work cattle?"

"No…"

"Then we should buy some young pups while we're here. Sheepdogs. They are a large breed with long hair, and they are smart enough to earn their keep with the shepherds. That's how they got the name."

Lily nodded. "We'll see."

"Let's buy a few cows now. We can come back several times."

"Sounds good. I will leave the bargaining to you, Ingrid."

Ingrid gave a shy smile. "I can try. I know a little bit about cows."

"I didn't think you kept cows on Virma!" Lily burst out. After their talk the evening before, she went away thinking of Virma as a heap of rocks in the middle of the ocean. It didn't sound like a place a nice cow would want to live.

"Some people do keep them. You have to have a certain degree of wealth to have a cow because they are expensive to feed. We don't buy anything but the best—except for meat. And I learned a lot from my mother. She prepared me to handle a farm on my own while my husband was away at sea."

Leif glowed as he watched his wife speak. Lily sighed with envy. Alex never looked at her that way, even when she told him she'd been accepted to medical school. He was proud of her, for sure, but he was also annoyed with her for going to school so far away. She'd never seen him express such pure, unadulterated pride in her achievements. She wondered if Ingrid knew how lucky she was.

The group turned back to the inn. They hadn't gone very far when they heard a loud commotion.

What's with the crowd? Why is everyone screaming? This is insane!

"A bull broke loose! A bull!"

Using all her strength, Lily gripped Ingrid with one hand and one of the Virman men with the other. If either of them were dragged away from her, they would still have her fingers attached.

The Virmans followed Leif's barked orders and pulled the women out of the crowd. Lily felt something hard behind her back. They had put her in a sheep pen with Ingrid. The sheep were not happy to see her: they were bleating loudly and butting their heads against her dress, but at least they wouldn't trample her to death like the crowd on the other side of the fence. Her Virman guards stood along the fence, and for the first time, Lily saw what a true warrior was worth. They never reached for their weapons, but the heaving crowd broke against them like a wave against a rocky beach.

And then it appeared—the bull. To Lily's eyes, the bull was enormous. But it was angry. Its eyes were red, and its sharp horns shone in the sun. It seemed to be coming right at her. Shouting and shoving, the people in the crowd pushed to get away. One man tripped and fell to his knees. Before he could get up, the bull was on him. It lifted him on its horns and tossed him like a piece of trash.

Ingrid screamed and held on to Lilian, who grabbed her hand. Both women thought the bull was looking right at them. The Virman men were not worried in the least by the animal. Leif held his ax lightly as he stepped forward to meet it. The bull snorted and advanced. Leif coolly waited for it. Three yards. Two. One…

God no! Lily bit her lip until it bled. *Can he…*

The Virman stepped lightly out of range of the horns and, almost without effort, brought down the butt of his ax right between the bull's eyes. It was a direct hit. The bull dropped to its knees as if it had been shot.

Leif looked it over and said, "If he lives, I might buy him. Nice animal."

Lily relaxed her aching fingers from around Ingrid's arm, and the young woman rushed out of the pen to throw herself on her husband's neck. Lily sighed and looked around. She saw a man lying still in the dust. She quickly made her way to the injured man. The Virmans made no attempt to stop her, with two of them simply following along behind her. She got down on her knees and took a closer look. One of the man's legs was sticking out at an odd angle. She felt his neck for a pulse.

Excellent. His pulse is strong. Now. I need to see what's broken.

Her training told her to put him on a backboard and send him for x-rays, but she didn't have over a thousand years to wait…A superficial examination showed that the leg was broken. The man's spine seemed to be unharmed. Lily ran her hands over his arms and neck and then looked up at the Virmans. "Help me turn him over. Be careful."

They did as she asked. Lily gasped. *Game over.* The man's tunic was rapidly filling with blood.

"Give me a knife!"

She held out her hand. Her voice was so commanding that Olaf handed over his knife before he even realized what she needed it for. After slicing open the tunic, Lily sighed with relief. She couldn't have pulled off an operation with a dirty knife in the middle of the street, but it looked like she wouldn't have to. The man was born under a lucky star; the bull's horns had just left a flesh wound across his hefty stomach. There was a lot of blood, but it wasn't dangerous. She just needed to clean it, stitch it, and bandage him up.

Lily looked around. "Where can we take him? I need to treat his wounds."

Leif was still holding up Ingrid. He looked around and then nodded his head. "Over there."

His men didn't wait for orders. One took off his cape. Then they rolled the wounded man onto it and carefully lifted him off the ground. Lily walked alongside taking the man's pulse.

ဢ◆ဣ

"Over there" turned out to be a nice-looking tavern full of people noisily drinking and talking about their business at the market. The crowd fell silent when the Virmans appeared in the doorway. Leif nodded to his men, and they lowered the wounded man onto one of the tables.

Using the same knife, Lily cut his pants to the hip. She had been right. It was a closed fracture. This guy is incredibly lucky. The bone could have broken through, but it's all nice and clean. I can feel it right here, and there aren't any fragments. I just need to set it and make a splint. The wounded man was still unconscious. Lily made a mental list of what she needed.

"Hot water. Strong wine. Thread and needles. Hop to it!"

Leif repeated her orders in a voice that made the oil lamps along the walls shudder.

"And open the windows. I need more light! Bring me two small boards and some cloth!"

She leaned over the man's body and reflected that it was a good thing the fall knocked him out. She didn't have any anesthesia on hand—except perhaps Leif and his battle ax. *One blow and you're out like a light.*

What do we have here? A man who looks to be about sixty. That means he's just forty or fifty. People age faster here. He has a short, black beard and dark skin...

"Khangan," someone behind her said.

"Khangan?" That's right. He must be from the Vari Khanganate. I read about it.

The man's clothes seemed strange to Lily: wide pants, a tunic made of fine, colorfully embroidered fabric, and an obviously expensive robe. It was beautiful work. Or, at least, it had been beautiful until it met the bull's horns and the dusty road.

"What will you do to him, My Lady?"

"Heal him," Lily said, as she removed the last bit of fabric from the broken leg.

"You shouldn't do that, My Lady."

"What do you mean?" Lily shot the Virman an angry glance.

"You shouldn't heal him," said one of the older Virmans.

"Why ever not?"

"He'll be lame the rest of his life. The Khangans have a custom: when a man's body is broken they drive him from his home and take his property from him. If you heal him, he will be a pauper for the rest of his days."

Lily snorted. "He won't be lame. If you get me the things I need, and..."

Someone handed her several needles. Lily reached for one of her petticoats. "Look the other way!" The Virmans stood around her in a circle to shield her from curious eyes as she ripped a piece from her petticoat. *It's clean silk. I just need to pull out some threads and rinse them in the wine.*

It was a nice white wine and looked to have all of about ten percent alcohol content. "Don't you have anything stronger?"

"Only iced wine, My Lady."

"Then bring that."

Next, the hot water arrived. Lily ripped off another piece of her skirt, soaked it in the hot water and carefully cleaned the area where she would operate.

I've got to get the ends of the bone together correctly. It shouldn't be too hard, as long as there aren't any fragments I can't feel. Damn animal! I hope they turn that bull into sausage! It was a clean break, just like in the textbooks. She had practiced this procedure many times.

But this is right in the middle of the femur. How did this guy manage to fall so hard?

She reflected that a broken lower leg would have been worse because it would involve two separate bones, and she had no instruments to work with.

I'll have to use whatever is on hand!

The pitcher on the table smelled like cheap rotgut. She liked that because it would have a fairly high alcohol content. Lily wiped the booze all over her hands and the knife, needles, and thread. Then she rinsed a plate, filled it with the remaining rotgut and put the needles and thread in it to let them marinate until she needed them.

She cleaned the area again and tried to decide what to do first: set the leg bone or stitch up the abdominal flesh wound. She would start with the flesh wound. Bleeding never improved anyone's mood. At home, she would have had an IV in this patient already. She wondered how much blood he had already lost.

What if the wound gets infected? I'll have to start growing penicillin on bread mold. The Virmans watched in awe as the Countess made a strange

189

gesture in front of her face and whispered, "Lord, help me." It was just a force of habit learned from Aliya's mother, and she didn't realize what she had done.

Then she began to sew up the bloody wound in the Khangan's side. Leif and Ingrid watched as Lily methodically cleaned the dirt and blood clots from the wound and then started to stitch together muscles and skin. Her movements were confident and calm; she knew what she was doing, that much was obvious in every flash of the needle.

ಬ◆ಛ

Field trip to the morgue to dissect corpses? Aliya Skorolenok did the work for herself and for anyone else who didn't feel up to it. *Surgery rotation at the hospital?*

"Skorolenok, get out of the way! Oh, all right, come here and let me show you how we do it."

The third year, same hospital: "Skorolenok! Get into the operating room. We have a nurse out sick. You can take her place."

The fourth year: "Someone find Skorolenok! We need her in the operating room!"

Aliya didn't just enjoy medicine; she would have lived in the hospital if they had let her. The doctors all saw her dedication, and they worked hard to teach her everything they knew. By her fourth year, Aliya was doing simple operations unassisted. *And it's a good thing this one will be simple. If one of those horns had gone into his abdomen or punctured a lung, then he'd be out of luck!*

Lily understood that she would need an entirely different set of instruments if she ever hoped to do more complex operations. But for now, a dagger would have to do. The one she was holding was sharp enough to split a hair. There wasn't much to cut away, but it was hellishly difficult. The patient was overweight, and she didn't have any wound retractors…

Lily swore silently that she would go to the blacksmith the very next day and order a full set of medical instruments. *Cost be damned!* Saving lives was more important than saving money.

After she finished the last stitches on the abdominal wound, she washed the area again with wine and asked Leif to find some honey. *A layer of honey under the bandage as a natural antiseptic will heal that wound in no time.* Leif went to ask the tavern keeper for honey while Lily started on the man's leg.

Setting the bone will be harder than stitching him up. Normally, I wouldn't have to do this alone… Lily sighed and got started. She was starting to notice that being overweight had its advantages every now and then. Aliya Skorolenok would never have been able to set the leg bone by herself; she just didn't have the mass and the strength. Lilian Earton just grunted slightly, and the job was done. She nodded at one of the Virmans. "Hold it just like this." The pirate obeyed.

He and the other Virmans were starting to look at Lily with obvious respect. Not because she stopped to help a stranger, but because they saw that she could do extremely useful things with her hands. As warriors, they placed a high value on skilled healers, and she did her work with confidence and decisiveness.

Once the bone was set, bound, and braced, Lily ran her fingers over the man's leg as if she were listening for something. Aliya was good at her job. A doctor had once told her that her hands could see like an x-ray machine. She hoped she still had it. Her intuition was silent. Either she'd left it behind in her own body, or the leg was absolutely fine. She wished for a way to make a cast.

It can't be done. This brace will have to do the job. He can make a sling when he gets home. For now…

How glad Lily was that the patient was still unconscious. She periodically checked his pulse and his pupils.

ଏ◆ଔ

"We'll have to take him with us."

"Back to the ship, My Lady?"

Lily shot him a dirty look. It was no time for humor. "Back to the Pig and Dog."

"But why, My Lady?"

"If we leave him here, he'll be robbed for sure."

"Why do we care? He can die for all it will bother me."

"After all the effort I put into patching him up?"

"I see. So, you were practicing on him?"

Lily was ready to scream. "Leif, if you don't have your heroic warriors find a stretcher this very minute, I'll rip your big ugly head off. Do you understand me?"

She added a few words she'd picked up from her father before she could stop herself. It worked like magic. The Virmans blushed and began running around. There was no stretcher to be found, of course, so they tied the man to a table, covered him with a cape, and four of them lifted the table.

Leif carried Ingrid. Lily walked next to her patient so she could keep watch over him. She didn't look forward to meeting him when he came around. As they walked, she made a mental list of things to buy at the market the next day. *I'll need plenty of medicinal herbs. St. John's wort, oregano (if it grows here), plantain… The forest will have to be my pharmacy. And we'll be needing vitamins over the winter. Rose hips, hawthorn berries, cramp bark… I don't want to lose any teeth due to malnutrition. Lemons, sauerkraut…*

Lily looked up at Leif. Her whole body fought against it, but there was something she had to say…and do.

"Let's leave this man at our inn and go back to the market. I need to buy lots more things."

Leif shook his head. "There's no reason, My Lady. We can go in the morning when we buy more animals."

"I need more than livestock."

"What else is on your list?"

"Sauerkraut. Berries. Herbs."

"To use in healing, My Lady?"

"Yes. And I need to see the jeweler again."

"Helke Leitz, My Lady?"

The jeweler happened to be waiting for them back at the inn. When Lily walked in, he stood up from the table where he had been waiting and gave a low, respectful bow.

"My Lady…"

Lily wanted nothing but to lie down and sleep. Better yet, she wanted to take a bath, lie down, and sleep, but business was business. She gave him a friendly smile.

"Honorable Helke, wait here for me. I'll give some orders and change clothes and be back in five minutes."

He bowed again.

Lilian went to her room. She was not particularly worried about the injured man. Leif would find a servant girl to watch over him. She had more important things to do. She took out a new dress to change into and then remembered that she couldn't unlace the dress she was already wearing without help. It was enough to make anyone use strong language.

In the end, she had to peek out into the corridor and call for a servant. A young woman dropped what she was doing and ran in to help. Lily was fuming inside. She swore she would find a tailor, or a seamstress, or whatever they were called as soon as possible.

The pink silk dress was as big as a tank cover. Lily swam out of it and looked at herself. *Is it my imagination, or are these dresses getting much too big for me?*

As a medical student, Aliya had read up on metabolism issues and knew not to try to lose the extra pounds too quickly. She supposed Lilian Earton had started gaining weight as a young girl, so it made sense that it would take at least a few years to get it all off. She wouldn't stress her new body with a starvation diet. *Normal weight loss is just a couple of pounds a month. Losing weight too quickly can be a sign of serious illness. And diets are worthless because as soon as you let your guard down, all the weight comes right back.*

She would continue to avoid sweets and fried food and not eat anything after six in the evening. Instead, she would fill up on steamed vegetables and whole grains. Pasta and dessert were a thing of the past. And she would exercise.

In the end, however, she knew that weight is a highly individual issue, and there was no way of knowing what kind of metabolism Lilian Earton had. She was just glad to see that one of her chins had disappeared. *I'm rocking this new body!*

☙◆❧

Once dressed, Lily went to check on her patient. As it turned out, the Virmans had put him in the room next to hers. A handsome servant girl was doing her best to look busy by fixing his sheets and wiping the sweat from his brow. Just in case, Lily gave her a cold stare. "If even one coin from his purse goes missing, I'll have you skinned."

The girl's hands flew to her face. "My Lady! I have never…"

"And you won't start now. Back on Virma, they cut thieves hands off," she added. "Just sit here and wait for him to come around. When he does, give him some water and call for me. Understood?"

"Yes, My Lady."

Lily sighed. *Am I starting to feel a little too comfortable with my role as a feudal lady?*

ೞ◆ೞ

The Eveer bowed as she entered the room. "My Lady."

Lily nodded. "I'm pleased to see you. What brought you here?"

"I'm afraid that what brought me here was terrible audacity." He assured her in many words that he didn't want to offend Lily and that he had the greatest respect for her. She noticed that the look in his eyes was not exactly respectful. They were intelligent, clever eyes…and calculating. He was testing her reactions to see if he could do business with her. Lily smiled.

"Honorable Helke, I suggest that instead of flattering each other, we get down to brass tacks. Time is money, and silence is golden. What brought you here?"

"My Lady, such words could have come from the mouth of a wise man, not a lovely woman…"

Lily feared he was launching into another half-hour recitation of her remarkable qualities. She sighed. "Honorable Helke. Please tell me: what brought you here?" It had been a long day. The market, the bull, the operation… *And now I'm expected to stand here listening to empty chatter?* Lily was ready to roar.

"My Lady, I brought you this tiny gift as a sign of my respect."

Helke took a small box out of his pocket. He opened the lid. Something clicked in Lily's head. *I know how small locks for jewelry boxes are made. If I draw one for him, I bet his eyes would pop out of his head. We could really make some money…*

Then she looked down at the red velvet cushion in his hand and saw the earrings. They weren't much to look at, but to Lily, they were worth more than all the gold in the world. Two little pearl earrings…with perfect clasps.

Lily smiled. She tried one on. It locked perfectly.

"Honorable Helke, have you taken this idea to the guild?"

"But the idea was yours, My Lady."

"I will not object to having my ideas implemented by you," she said with a clever smile. "For consideration, of course."

"But My Lady, what can a poor old man give you?"

"You won't be poor if you reach an agreement with me."

Lily smiled again. It was time to negotiate. The Eveer seemed to understand and smiled back.

"My Lady, do you mean…"

"I will give you good ideas. You will carry them out. I will get a percentage of the profit."

Helke shook his head. "My Lady, are you sure that your ideas will be successful?"

Lily shrugged. "If you don't think women will want earrings like these, I can take my idea elsewhere."

The jeweler's eyes shone. "How much do you want?"

"I provide the ideas. You provide the materials, the workshop, and the work. I think that earns me fifty percent."

The man looked pained. "My Lady, you will bankrupt me!"

"Not so. I will make you rich!"

"But I am a poor old man. I cannot give you more than fifteen percent."

"A poor jeweler? Forty-five percent. And not a percent less!"

"What about guild dues? And taxes? My Lady, twenty percent is all I can do!"

"And what about the fees the guild will pay you as the inventor? If I wasn't such a nice person, I would ask for sixty percent."

"But I still have to pay heavy taxes."

"So do I."

Lily enjoyed horse trading. The Eveer was a strong opponent, but she had grown up in Russia and knew better than to give her money away to strangers. In the end, they agreed that Lily would get forty percent. She was satisfied. They would sign a contract at town hall. That reminded Lily that she still needed to shake down the Baron.

She and Helke would turn a profit, of that much she was certain. Helke would be paying for the work, the materials, the rent and his employees, as well as any costs to advertise and bring the goods to market. That meant that he would skim a little off the top—she didn't need a fortune teller to figure that out. But he wouldn't take too much. Once he realized that working with her was profitable, he would do anything to keep her loyalty. In time, she would audit him. That would be interesting.

Lily sat down in front of him and sketched a dip pen. Then she went to her room and brought back her non-spill inkwell. She poured some milk into it to demonstrate how it worked. She had discovered that Eveers never touched any drinks that affected the clarity of mind, so she and Helke had been toasting their arrangement with mugs of milk.

"You could sell three versions of this." Helke's eyebrows went up. Lily started her explanation. "Make plain copper ones for regular people. For merchants, you would have nicer ones made of silver, gold, or carved wood. And for aristocrats, you would have ink-wells made of gold or mahogany decorated with precious stones and packaged in beautiful little locking boxes…"

Helke thought for a moment. It looked like a promising idea.

"My Lady, what if we were to send a nice set like that to someone as a gift from you?"

Lily paused. *Who could I send a gift to?* She didn't want to think about her husband. There was always her father. Perhaps she could send the ink-well to him. *Why not? He might even send me something in return.*

Lily wished she could remember how fountain pens were made. She was prepared to try to make a ballpoint pen, but she would have to find out what the locals used for ink. If they were just mixing ash and water, then the ballpoint mechanism would get clogged. The Eveer was studying her drawing with hungry eyes.

Lily smiled graciously. "Honorable Helke, when can you show me a prototype??

"My Lady?"

"The first one you make."

"Of course, My Lady. As soon as I have something to show, I will find you right away!"

"I won't be here much longer, so…"

"My Lady, I will start working immediately."

"Wonderful. And Helke, I wish you would recommend a good dressmaker, a blacksmith, and a glass blower."

The jeweler looked surprised, but he didn't take long. "Fine ladies here have their dresses made by Marion Alcey. Her shop is two streets away. There is a fine blacksmith near City Hall. As for glass blowers, there is only one of them in town. His name is Barney Agribas. But I must warn you—he is a strange man, and I wouldn't want you to encounter any unpleasantness."

Lily shrugged. "I don't suppose I will, not when I have my Virman guards with me. Thank you for your concern, Honorable Helke. Come back at lunch tomorrow, and we will sign a contract. And now, I think you probably want to get busy working on what we've drawn out here?"

The jeweler very much wanted to get busy. He jumped up, bowed and flew out of the inn. Lily gestured to the innkeeper. "Cheese, greens, and a mug of ale."

It was an indulgence, but she felt she deserved it. She couldn't overdo it, though. It would be too easy to use alcohol to hide from the world, and Lily had things to accomplish.

She stuck a bunch of parsley in her mouth—it was bitter—and headed off to find her companions.

☎ ♦ ☙

Leif was nowhere to be found. The peasants were gone, too. She remembered that she had told them they could wander the fair. Then she ran into two of the Virmans who had been with her that morning. "Where is Leif?"

"He took Ingrid back to the ship. He said to tell you that he'll be back in the morning unless you need him sooner."

Lily shrugged. "I don't think I will need him before that. And you are?"

"Ivar Reinholm."

"Olaf Raivesson."

Lily nodded. "I need to visit the dressmaker. Will you come along?"

The Virmans glanced at each other. If they let her go out alone, Leif would skin them alive. "As you wish, My Lady."

Lily nodded and headed for the door.

☎ ♦ ☙

It was not difficult to find Marion Alcey's shop. The first person she asked pointed her in the right direction. She didn't like the looks of the place. From the outside, it was a two-story stone building like Helke's, only a little smaller. She opened the door and found herself in a small room full of bolts of fabric. Two young women were at work on some blue material. At the sound of the door, they looked up with frightened eyes. Their cheekbones stuck out, and they had dark circles under their eyes. *Don't they get anything to eat around here? I don't want to be that skinny!* Something about the place bothered Lily. *Is it the fearful look in the girls' eyes? Or is it the shop's owner?*

A bell above the door had rung when Lily opened it, and Marion Alcey slid out from a back room. Her face reminded Lily of a dried fish. She was wearing a plain, dark dress and had a tiny lace cap pinned to her hair. Her eyes were small, dark, and deep-set. *How did a woman that homely become a fashionable dressmaker? She must be really good at what she does. We'll see about that.*

Meanwhile, Marion was sizing up Lily's jewelry and the expensive silk of her dress. Her mouth stretched into a wide, gruesome smile. "I'm pleased to welcome you, My Lady."

"Countess Lilian Elizabeth Mariella Earton," Lily introduced herself.

"What an honor for my humble shop." Lily lowered her eyes. In her normal life, she never gave salespeople attitude, but something about this dressmaker was very off-putting. She held a long pause, forcing Marion to speak again. "May I help you with something, My Lady?"

"Yes, please. I want to order a dress."

"At your service, My Lady."

"Show me what you have." It came out in a tone that combined arrogance and a lack of interest. Lily was proud of herself. *I'm getting good at this.*

"Does My Lady prefer pink? That's a lovely color, and it suits your face."

Lily winced. "White and green."

"Then you must be in mourning?"

Lily cut her off. "I don't think that's any of your business, is it?

"Forgive me, My Lady. I have a wonderful piece of green velvet." She turned to the shop girls. "Get up, you good-for-nothing girls! Bring me the green velvet!"

The girls disappeared into the storeroom. A few minutes later, they returned carrying cloth samples in green and white. Lily liked the velvet. It was a handsome shade of spring green. The white batiste was also nice. She wanted a dress that could be altered easily as she lost weight.

"My Lady, shall we take your measurements?"

"Of course."

Marion never did that kind of work with her own hands. "Marcia, get in here!" A shy girl came out of the storeroom with her head bowed. "Yes, ma'am?"

"Take My Lady's measurements. Come on, get moving!"

The girl bowed to Lily. "May I?" Lily gave a slight nod. She was sorry for the girl, but for some reason, she felt she had to be arrogant in front of the frozen fish who owned the shop. "Raise your arms, if you will, My Lady." Lily complied with a sigh. She wondered how they would manage to make something to fit her without having her undress. Maybe they could just baste something together and then adjust it to fit. Apparently, women in her new world didn't go around taking their clothes off, even at the dressmaker.

The girl worked quickly. Lily noticed that her fingers were thin and bore the marks of pinpricks and that her arms were skin and bone.

This Marion woman must be a real skinflint. If I had a whip, I'd crack it!

"Now, we can talk about the style."

What Lily wanted was a plain wrap skirt that she could take in easily as she lost weight. Above it, she wanted a long vest that she could wear over a white blouse. She couldn't care less that she was going against local fashions. Earton wasn't exactly a social whirlwind. Her other desire was for a cape that would also go over a blouse and could be taken in as necessary. If this first order went well, she would talk to the dressmaker about underwear and perhaps other types of clothes. Lily had a lot of ideas.

But as soon as she described the skirt she had in mind, the dressmaker gasped. "My Lady!"

"What is it?"

"We don't make clothes like that!"

"So, you can start now." Lily couldn't understand why the woman was so upset. *Who cares about what everyone else is wearing?*

"My Lady, it would be shameful for me to make something like that…"

"Then, have one of your girls do it."

The sarcasm went over Marion's head. "The whole town will laugh at me. I sew clothes for very highly placed ladies."

"Is a Countess not highly placed enough for you?"

"Let me show you some of the season's best dresses."

Lily opened her eyes wide. "Marion, will you take my order or not? If not, I will buy the cloth from you and do it myself. If you will do it, then I want the finished goods in two days!"

"I'll do it," Marion hissed.

"And your price?"

"Six silver coins."

Lily wrinkled her nose. "Two. And even that's too high."

"But My Lady, what about the cost of the cloth and the workmanship?"

The velvet was very nice, but the price was close to what Lily was paying each Virman guard for a month's work. She wouldn't be fooled.

"I'm not asking you to make a fancy ball gown. Just do as I instructed you—a skirt and a vest."

She said nothing about a blouse. Marion had made such a negative impression on her that she wouldn't risk giving her any new ideas. She actually liked Helke. He wasn't particularly friendly, but he had a lively mind. The dressmaker, on the other hand…

"I will do as you wish, My Lady." The look on the dead fish's face was clear enough; if she had her way, she would chase Lily from her shop with a dirty broom…all because she wanted a type of skirt that had not been seen in those parts. Lily wondered sadly how many mistakes she made every day. This dressmaker was just the first person to react openly. She feared that everyone else was just being polite and drawing their own conclusions.

How long will it be before I start to attract attention from more important people who won't be put off by my title? It was a frightening thought.

She was comforted by the thought that she hadn't yet heard of anyone being burned at the stake here.

80 ◆ cs

Lily was in a bad mood when she got back to the inn. The Virmans sensed that she was upset and made themselves scarce. When she walked in, the innkeeper saw her and came over. "My Lady, your injured man has woken up."

Lily nodded and went to check on him. The man was staring blankly out the window next to his bed. Lily noticed that his eyes were big and black.

"Are you Lilian Earton?"

"Countess Lilian Elizabeth Mariella Earton," she announced and threw back his blanket without asking permission.

The patient's apathy instantly disappeared. "What are you doing?"

"I personally set your broken bone and stitched up your side. I don't see any reason why I can't examine the results of my work. Are you afraid that I am interested in you as a man?" Lily knew she shouldn't have said it, but she couldn't help herself.

The man's eyes sparkled with fire. "My Lady…"

"Good. Your wound looks clean, and your leg is fine. Can you stay in bed for several weeks?"

"What for?"

"To regain your health."

"My Lady, I know that my leg was broken. Even if I walk again, I will have a limp. Do you know the customs of my people?"

"Yes. You kill or drive away anyone with a disability."

"You should have left me there in the street."

"Maybe so. But you will not be an invalid."

"There are no miracles in this life, My Lady."

"But there are." Lily spoke slowly. "A broken leg is not that difficult to treat. You simply straighten the bone and put a brace on it. If you're careful to keep it stretched out—and that is why I had them tie your foot to the end of the bed—then in twenty or thirty days, it will be good as new."

"You mean it will be just like the other leg?"

"Yes. As long as you don't disturb it. The wound on your side poses no threat at all. I washed it and stitched it up. You will be fine. Is there anyone who can care for you at home?"

"My wives. And my servants."

Lily nodded. "Then I will explain to you and to them what needs to be done. I promise—you will be just fine."

"But how do you know that?"

"Consider it knowledge from heaven. The saints were capable of healing by just laying their hands on people. I am not holy enough for that, but I can sew up wounds with a needle and thread. Now, it's up to you. If you stay in bed like I told you, you won't have a limp. How old are you?"

"Forty-six."

"Can I ask you what your name is?"

The man bit his lip. "I beg your forgiveness, My Lady. I have been impolite. My name is Ali Akhmet din Tahirjian. I come from a long line of caravan route guards."

Lily thought back to her reading. She didn't remember anything about a caravan route. She wondered if its location was kept secret. The fact that he was a caravan route guard didn't tell her anything. *Does that mean he is the equivalent of a customs agent?* She decided not to ask.

Instead, she stood up and gave her best imitation of a bow. "It is an honor for me to make your acquaintance. I'm sorry it had to happen this way. Now get some sleep."

"I doubt that I will sleep. My leg hurts."

"Do you drink alcohol?"

"Our faith does not allow it."

Lily sighed. Pain medication… But where to find it? That's easy. I just need to find the right kind of poppy seeds, plant them and wait a year. Easy as pie.

"Could you think of alcohol as medicine in this particular case? It can be a sleep remedy."

The man winced. "Our healers tell us to use a strong weed for those purposes, but I have none with me."

Lily's ears pricked up. "Where could I find other people from your country?"

"On the ship."

Lily wondered if this was a job for the Virmans. "What is the name of the ship?"

"The Golden Wave. If you give me a pen and ink…"

Lily called for a servant. A young woman came running in and gave a low bow. She was soon sent to find a pen, ink, and some wax to seal the letter. There was no paper to be had, but the innkeeper gave up a piece of parchment. He also loaned the patient a pen. Lily brought out her inkwell. Ali Akhmet studied it in surprise.

"What an interesting item."

"It's a non-spill inkwell."

"What did you say?"

Instead of a reply, Lily knocked the inkwell onto his blanket. Ali Akhmet lunged for it. There wasn't a drop of ink on his bed. He shook his head. "Wonderful. This would be a useful thing to have on the ship."

"There is a jeweler here in town named Helke Leitz who makes them," Lily said, sensing an opportunity to advertise. "The idea was mine, and he makes them. Soon, he will have some very interesting new quill pens…"

Ali Akhmet wrote a quick note, folded it and handed it to Lily. She melted some wax and sealed the letter with it. Ali Akhmet pressed one of his rings to the wax. Then he lay back against his pillow looking weak.

"My assistant's name is Alim Omar din Rashaya."

Lily took the letter and went to find the Virmans. "I need you to take this letter to Alim Omar din Rashaya on the Golden Wave and wait for his response." One of the Virmans nodded and left to perform the task. Lily went back upstairs to check her patient's pulse and take his temperature. Since she had no thermometer, she pressed her lips to his forehead. "You will have a rough time of it for a couple of days. I cleaned your wound as best I could, but infection is hard to avoid."

"I know you did everything you could, My Lady, and I am grateful."

"The best way to thank me is to get better quickly," Lily said. She sent up a silent word of love and gratitude to her mother, whose life as an army medic had involved backbreaking labor without much backup. Whenever a soldier was injured at a remote base or during training in the taiga, Aliya's mother had relied on her own skills and the tools at hand. By the time she was ten years old, Aliya was helping her mother set broken bones. Tatiana saw that her daughter had a firm hand and a good eye, so she let her jump right in. By the time Aliya started medical school, she had enough experience to qualify as a paramedic. *All that experience is coming in handy now! But I won't let another day go by without ordering the instruments I need from a blacksmith.*

Lily knew her surgical instruments backwards and forwards. As a girl, she had played with scalpels, forceps, wound retractors, clamps and tongue depressors the way other children played with cars and blocks. She knew they wouldn't be hard to make, for a price.

She looked out the window. It was getting dark. She had eaten breakfast at dawn and skipped lunch. Food was a necessity. Her patient would need sustenance, too.

"I'll bring you some broth. Do you have any restrictions on what you eat?"

"We do not eat the meat of pigs because they are unclean animals. Anything else is fine."

"Then I'll get you some chicken broth."

She would make sure Ali Akhmet took in plenty of liquids. That would help him heal faster and might even keep his fever down a bit. "I want to repeat my promise: if you follow my orders and keep off that leg, you'll walk just like you always have. Your leg may ache when it rains, but otherwise, you'll be good as new."

"Rain in the desert is a blessing."

Lily nodded and left his room. *I'd give anything for some painkillers right now! I guess I'll just have to plant opium poppies. I wonder if they have laws about that here.*

"What could possibly go wrong there?"

Jerrison, the Earl of Earton, looked up at the Prince. Richard had finished the preparations for his journey two days ago. Now, he had come to hide out at his cousin's house from the busybodies at court. He was lying on the bed and eating a bowl of nuts as he watched Jess scratch out a letter to his estate Comptroller.

"I have no idea. But Etor has always sent me regular reports once every thirty or forty days. It's been almost sixty days now, and not a word from him. That concerns me."

"What is it that worries you? The estate or your wife?"

"The baby."

"That's right. She's with a child."

"I hope to finally have an heir."

"She isn't due for a while yet, is she?"

"True. But I still worry."

"Write a letter if you want, but you won't hear back for a long time."

Now the earl was concerned—not for his wife, but for his unborn child, his heir. He turned to the prince. "How long do you think this trip will take?"

"Eight moons at the very least."

"That means I won't be home when my son is born."

"Or daughter. It may take six tries before you get a son."

"Bite your tongue."

"You can always try again," Richard mocked him lightly. "You knew what you were getting into."

Jess narrowed his eyes. He wrote a few more words and then spread some sand on the page to soak up the excess ink.

"You think you've got it all figured out, don't you?"

"Always have. Write to your Comptroller. Have him write your father if the child is born before you get back. My uncle can name it."

"That's a good idea." Jess added a few words to the end of the letter. "I will speak to my uncle about it this evening." He looked up at Richard, "Try not to take too long when you pick your bride."

"Quite the opposite. I'll have to spend the rest of my life with her, so I intend to make the right choice. You know me. I'll always have someone on the side, but I'd like to find a wife I can love. Like my father and Jessie."

Jess nodded. "You're right."

"You should take a closer look at that doll of yours. See what she's really made of…"

Jess shrugged and placed the letter in a thick envelope. He would have a man carry the letter to Earton and wait there for Etor's response before bringing it to him. At that point, he would already be in Wellster. It was a slow means of communication, but he had no choice.

ೞ ♦ ೲ

An hour later, Lily had forgotten all about her drug problems, as even getting her hands on a plain bowl of chicken broth was proving to be a challenge. It took all her patience to explain to the cook that she didn't need to add wine, cream, or a saddle-bag full of spices to the broth. All Lily wanted was for her to boil a chicken and salt the broth a little. Spices were too expensive for daily use, and Lily doubted the cook knew how to use them with restraint.

After raising her voice and cursing a few times to get what she wanted, Lily reflected that she was getting used to a style of conversation that she called 'I'm the boss, you're the idiot'. She wondered if it was the social rules of her new world that forced her into the role of slave-driver.

At least they don't have actual slavery here. According to what I've read, peasants can leave their lords as long as they pay their taxes and have a place to go. So why haven't all my peasants left? It must be the taxes. They could never afford to pay off Etor. It also occurred to her that Earton was far enough from everywhere else to make the idea of leaving sound difficult. Most of the peasants probably thought that their best plan was to wait around and see if things got better.

Things will never get better unless you put in the effort. After all, the only thing that falls from heaven is bird poop.

In the end, feeding the broth to her patient was much less trouble than getting the broth had been. Ali Akhmet obediently ate a piece of chicken, drank the broth, and even thanked her for it, adding a couple of compliments about her beauty. Lily snorted. She wondered if all Khangans were appreciative of blondes with sizeable glutes.

The real trouble started when the patient's family and friends arrived. A crowd of six women in bright saris and robes burst into the room. They circled the bed and began making so much noise that Lily's first instinct was to kick them out, but she waited to see how Ali Akhmet reacted. They were followed by several Khangans in colorful robes and three Virmans. She supposed Leif had sent them in to keep an eye on her.

The women were shouting over each other and gesturing with bracelet-covered arms. They smelled of Oriental spices, horses, and sweat. Lily edged toward the window to get some fresh air and saw a heavy copper tray lying on the window sill. She picked it up.

Bam!

The sound of the tray hitting the window sill was like thunder. For an instant, everyone stopped talking and turned toward the source of the noise.

"All you women out! Men, help them find the door. Ali Akhmet is recovering and needs his rest."

The Virmans began elbowing people away from the bed. The women were about to start up again, but Lily banged the tray again, this time even louder.

"Silence. Everyone out!"

All six women and two of the men—obviously Ali Akhmet's bodyguards—were shown out of the room. Lily took a deep breath and looked at her patient. "You aren't strong enough for that kind of crowd yet. I can give you ten minutes to talk with your family, but no more. And not all of them at once. Ten minutes. I'll be right back."

As soon as she left the room, the women mobbed her with questions in a language she didn't understand. It was too much. "Silence!" The mob became more subdued, but they still wanted something from her. Lily looked around for a solution. One of Ali Akhmet's bodyguards stepped forward. "Of the wives, only Leisha knows some of your language. Let me interpret for you. Speak, My Lady."

Lily sighed. "Tell them that nothing is seriously wrong with their lord. He just had a run-in with a bull."

The bodyguard gave a long speech in Khangan, and the women gasped in unison.

"Be quiet! I told you that nothing is seriously wrong with him. He had a cut on his side and a broken leg. If you take care of him, in about fifty days, he'll be running races like a young man."

The women still looked upset. That was understandable. If Ali Akhmet was rejected by their society because of his injuries, his wives probably wouldn't fare too well. Lily wondered what, exactly, would happen to them in that case. They were handsome women, full-figured, with dark hair and eyes. They wore their hair in a mass of tiny braids, each one ending in a gold ring, precious stone, or tiny bell. Their wrists and ankles were covered with bracelets that jangled when they moved. Taken together, they were overwhelming, but Lily had to admit that they were beautiful.

"My Lady, how did our lord end up here?" asked the oldest of the young women, who looked to be twenty-five or thirty. Her lips were painted a deep red, and the palms of her hands were a strange color.

Henna?

Lily was excited by the thought. Henna wasn't just good for hair coloring and body art. It was also a strong disinfectant that could be used on ulcers and wounds. It could even be used as a sore throat remedy. She wondered if they had basma, as well. That came from the indigo plant.

I'll have to ask Ali Akhmet about that. The young woman's question hung in the air. Lily folded her arms. "I was at the market with my people. We saw a bull attack your lord. We brought him here and washed and dressed his wounds. I can tell you right away that he will not be lame. If he follows my orders and you take good care of him, he will soon be good as new."

All of the women were overjoyed, except for the youngest. Lily thought she saw a strange expression flicker across her face like a shadow.

I must have imagined it.

☙ ◆ ❧

Exactly ten minutes later, after giving the women detailed instructions on how to care for Ali Akhmet, Lily walked back into his room.

"Your time is up. He needs to rest."

Judging by the men's faces, the room had filled with despair while she was gone. Lily hated despair more than she hated even the Health Ministry. She couldn't stand it when a patient crossed his arms over his chest and prepared to die, mumbling something like "Why bother with treatment? It won't do any good anyway." And then the patient's family would lose hope, too. That made Lily furious. Now, however, she was a Countess, and she could say what she thought, as long as she was careful not to raise suspicions.

"Din Tahirjian, as your medicus I have to insist. Your family and friends have worn you out. From now on, no more than two people at a time can be in your room."

"Woman, can't you see he's an invalid?"

Lily stared at the man who had spoken. He was young, maybe seventeen years old. He hadn't shaved yet and was carefully growing out a goatee. His robe was embroidered in gold, and there were precious stones on the handle of his saber. Real weapons were never decorated—they spoke for themselves. This saber must be for show.

She pulled herself up to her full height. No one could speak to her that way. "Call your horse a woman if you know her that well. If you wish to address me, however, you will call me 'My Lady, Countess Lilian Elizabeth Mariella Earton.'" Lily was surprised at how haughty she could sound when necessary.

The young man cursed and raised his hand as if to strike her. Lily would have been fine—her plan was to kick him hard—but just then, the Virmans appeared out of nowhere, axes in hand.

"You will not touch her," one of them said quietly.

Lily looked over at her patient. "Din Tahirjian, out of respect for you, I will not have my guards kick this young dog down the stairs, but if he dares to speak to me that way again..."

She realized the young dog looked surprisingly like her patient. They must be father and son.

"My Lady," Ali Akhmet spoke, "please forgive my nephew for his rude behavior. He has never..."

"Never what? Met a woman who was smarter than him?" She raised one eyebrow.

Then she edged around the Virmans and went over to Ali Akhmet's bed to fix his pillows. "I will forgive the boy, but I do not want to see him again. Once you are back on your feet, you can work on improving his character."

One of the other men coughed to get her attention. "My Lady?"

Lily turned. "Yes?"

"My name is Alim Omar din Rashaya. I am Ali's assistant."

Lily nodded. She wondered that he called her patient by his first name. They must be close. *Is this his advisor?* "Countess Lilian Elizabeth Mariella Earton. Pleased to meet you. I wish the circumstances were happier."

"I agree. My Lady, please forgive me for any impoliteness on my part, I have no wish you offend you."

"Then don't."

"Is what you told my Lord the truth?"

Lily sighed. She felt like a broken record. "Let me explain one more time. Ali Akhmet here was thrown by a bull. He has a wound on his side and a broken leg. I washed, stitched up, and dressed the wound. It is not life-threatening. As for the leg, I know that in your country, it would cause him to be driven from his home."

Omar smiled. "That custom is not observed so strictly anymore. But still, a man whose body is injured cannot lead other men. The star mare will not carry an invalid; it would bring misfortune on all of us."

So that's what he's worried about.

"The broken leg will not leave him lame. Does no one treat broken bones in your country?"

"My Lady?"

"Or do you just let them heal how they will?" Judging by the look on the man's face, that was exactly what they did. "Our medical knowledge is more advanced. I stretched his leg, aligned the bone and braced it tightly. If he keeps it still, in about fifty days, he will be able to walk again without limping."

"Fifty days, My Lady?"

Lily nodded. "Your Lord must stay in bed. That is an order. You can carry him where you will, but you must prove to me that you can do it correctly. I will tell you how to care for him on the ship."

Omar looked like a heavy weight had fallen from his shoulders. "My Lady…"

Lily raised a hand. "I understand that you have trouble believing me, but you will see. The wound on his side will heal soon. And then his leg will heal. I give you my word. Your lord will be whole. His only memory of this will be an achy leg when it rains."

Omar bowed low with his arms folded over his chest. The other men standing in the room did the same, but the nephew shot her a look that was full of hate. *He can just grind those teeth at me until they fall out.*

৪ ◆ ଓ

When she got downstairs, she found Omar sitting at a table and holding a cup of something light-colored. He stood up and bowed again. The nephew was nowhere to be seen. The clutch of women was seated at another table working through a tray of sweets. Din Tahirjian's bodyguards were nearby.

Lily sat down at Omar's table. "Sir, am I correct that you are in charge while Ali Akhmet is recovering?"

"Yes, My Lady."

"Then let's talk. In about ten days, you'll be able to move him. He should stay here for now. Do you want to pay the innkeeper's servants to care for him, or will they do it?" She looked in the direction of the table of women.

Omar smiled. "They are his wives."

Lily frowned. "But…"

"My lord has three official wives: Leisha, Zalvia, and Suleima. The other three—Lilaka, Talia, and Neelei—are his concubines, but he loves them very much."

"Then I suggest you organize them. Have them work in pairs over eight-hour shifts. They won't have to do much more than bring him water to drink and entertain him with conversation."

"I will do that, My Lady. And his bodyguards?"

"They can stay if you think he needs them. Make sure they understand that I am allowed in his room any time of the day or night."

"Even at night, My Lady?"

Lily squinted. She had made a mistake. It would have to be fixed right away. "He may take a turn for the worse at night. Do his wives have enough experience to react quickly?"

The man nodded slowly. "I will warn them, My Lady."

"Fine. Do you have a medicus on the ship?"

"Our bosun has some knowledge of healing. He can handle small problems."

"Does he have anything he can give your lord for pain?"

"He does."

"Have him send some here as soon as possible. I haven't had time to buy what I need at the market, and your lord may be in pain for several days."

Omar gave a condescending smile. "Pain is nothing to a man."

Lily paused. She couldn't stand it when men pretended not to be bothered by pain. She also knew that untreated pain could cause negative outcomes—even a heart attack. "My friend," she said coldly, "I know that a real man is supposed to laugh everything off, even a dagger to the gut. But I am also aware that severe pain can slow down the recovery process. So, if you want to see your Lord healthy and happy, forget those old-fashioned ideas."

Omar's eyes flashed. "I'd like to know who taught you the healing arts?"

Lily shrugged. "My mother was my first teacher. Other teachers were hired for me later. Most knowledge can be had for money."

"You are very confident in your skills, My Lady."

"Your Lord is not the first person whose leg I have fixed. All of my patients have gone on to walk—and run—just fine."

In the end, Omar left the two oldest wives and one bodyguard and, promising to send more people, took the rest of the wives back to the ship. Lily saw the nephew scowl at her as he turned to leave. She couldn't have cared less.

I have to check on my patient one last time and go to bed. First thing in the morning, I need to go back to the market, and then I'll find a regular blacksmith and the glass blower. When that's all done, I'll pay another visit to the Baron. So much to do! This job requires two people!

Chapter 8

Potions and Plantains

Anna of Wellster was walking through the forest.

There were two bodyguards following her, but she was terrified nonetheless. A third guard strode ahead to show her the way. She had a bag of coins tied to the belt of her dress. It was an old dress, and now it was stained with grass, mud, and dew. Her wet petticoats stuck to her clammy legs. Her shoes were soaked, and her feet felt like two blocks of ice. *I bet I come down with something after a night like this.*

They reached a clearing, and Anna saw a small cottage. She did not know her father's lands well, even in the daytime, so she had no idea that there was a village not far away. It was dark, and the trees seemed to grab at her with long, rough arms. She was sure that each of those arms concealed a terrible wild animal or a band of brigands. Or worse…

She began to shake.

The guards left her to go through the gate alone. Timidly, she scratched at the door of the old cottage. The door slowly opened, like the jaws of a hungry beast. If Anna had been alone, she would have turned and run away as fast as she could. But the Jester's guards were just beyond the gate, and the jester was more terrifying than any witch. So, she stood and waited.

Finally, a voice from inside the dark cottage said, "Come in, whoever you are."

The witch was an old woman in a simple, dark dress. She looked like a regular peasant woman, but her eyes were cold and intelligent. Something in them reminded Anna of the Jester. She took a step back.

The witch smiled. "I suppose you need to get rid of a competitor. And you want a love potion, as well. Am I right?"

"And some poison!" Anna spoke without meaning to.

The witch was surprised. "And what else?"

"I am not a maiden."

No further explanation was necessary. "Do you have a vial of blood?"

"Right now, I just need to get engaged."

"Good. If you had come at the last minute, I would not have been able to help you. There is still time. I will give you some powder. Mix one spoonful of it in a pitcher of water and wash yourself down there, where your man had his fun." She made a vulgar gesture to show where she meant. "In twenty days, you'll be as tight as a little girl. Any man will believe it. Especially if you smear blood on the sheet at the right time."

Anna nodded. "What about..?"

"I can't fix that. There's nothing in the world that will restore your maidenhead. But I can give you a potion that will prevent you from conceiving a child if you take two drops of it every evening."

Anna nodded again. "Give it to me."

"Do you have enough money, my girl?" Anna's hand shook as she removed the purse from her belt. The witch took it and shook the silver and copper coins into her palm. She nodded. "Good. Now don't confuse the potions I am giving you." The witch began putting together her powders and herbs.

An hour later, Anna left the cottage carrying the powder for use *down there.* The contraceptive was in the pocket of her cape. Most importantly, she had a tiny bottle hidden under her blouse. It was icy cold against her body. Two drops—just two drops of it would be enough to kill a person. Anna wasn't even sure why she asked for the poison, but she would keep it just in case.

ᛟ◆ᚳ

Adelaide's cousin, Alex, lay back on the bed and took a sip of wine. He smiled as he watched the candle flicker through the red liquid in his glass. It was a nice wine. The kind he couldn't have afforded to drink before.

Adele was smart. She didn't ask her Earl for money. She just waited for him to give her presents, which he did generously and often. She was constantly losing an earring or accidentally breaking the clasp on a brooch. "Oh my sweet Jess, I'm so clumsy!" she would say. Sweet Jess just smiled. Women tended to lose things. It didn't bother him. He was an aristocrat with plenty of money.

Adele certainly was smart, Alex reflected with a smile. His cousin was leaving the next day, so they were catching up on their sleep. She had been packing for days and needed a rest. Alex knew Adele saw Jess Earton as an object of pity saddled with an awful wife. She knew she would make a lovely Countess, and he knew she wouldn't forget about her cousin; as if Alex would allow himself to be forgotten.

ஐ◆ひ

By morning, Lily was exhausted. She had gotten up four times in the night to check on her patient. The bosun who supposedly knew something about medicine had shown up the previous evening and left some remedies for Ali Akhmet, but the only really useful item she found was willow bark for pain. There was also a lemon for scurvy and an assortment of powders the bosun claimed to have gotten from a medicus. She supposed most of them were laxatives. To be fair, Lily recognized that sick men didn't usually do much traveling, so a ship couldn't be expected to have a full medicine cabinet.

One of the laxatives was senna. She recognized it by its unpleasant odor. The bosun didn't know what it was, he just knew that it cleansed the bowels. *Good grief! They have all six of his wives on board and not a single doctor.* The stomach remedy smelled like licorice, and the powdered herb the bosun claimed was for the heart turned out to be digitalis. There were several other dried herbs she couldn't readily identify. It wasn't much of a medicine chest, but since the bosun looked to be worth one regular hospital orderly, she would just have to work with what she had. Lily set aside the pain remedy. Then she squeezed the lemon, boiled its peel and added to it the lemon juice. She gave the concoction to the two wives who had stayed behind and told them to have the patient drink it slowly. The vitamin C would do him good.

I'll have to find a fever reducer at the market as soon as it opens.

Her head pounded, but she washed her face in the icy cold water in her basin, pulled on a clean pink dress and got ready to go.

ഒ◆രൃ

Leif was waiting for her downstairs with five other Virmans. Ingrid approached her timidly. "My Lady?"

Lily smiled. If she had really been Lilian Earton, the young Virman woman's beauty would have upset her. But somewhere deep down, Aliya still felt attractive. She remembered her old body. It was strong and young and healthy. *Ingrid certainly is gorgeous, but who says I'm not? I'm just different.*

"How do you feel this morning?"

Ingrid grinned. "Much better. I was just scared for my husband yesterday."

"I was scared, too," Lily admitted. "Very scared."

"Leif told me how you healed the man. My Lady, can you teach me to sew up wounds like you do?"

Lily was surprised. She was about to ask why Ingrid wanted to learn surgery when she remembered that Leif was a warrior. Ingrid was probably worried that they would bring him home in pieces someday and wanted to be prepared.

"Didn't they teach you that at home?"

"No, My Lady."

"Do you know how to heal with herbs?"

"A little, My Lady."

"Then how about this: you teach me what you know about herbs, and I will teach you what I know about treating wounds."

Ingrid's face lit up. "My Lady, I hope there will be no more bulls on the loose at the market today."

Lily almost replied that there would be plenty of asses, but she held her tongue.

ৡ◆ଔ

A few hours later, she was convinced she had been right about the asses.

There were heaps of herbs for sale: chamomile, plantain, marjoram—they called it honey-herb—thyme, St. John's wort, fireweed with purple flowers, yarrow, and many others. The tables were loaded with plants she recognized, but as soon as she began picking up bundles, she realized they hadn't been dried properly and were almost useless to her. *I won't pay these prices for hay when I can cut it myself.*

Ingrid didn't like the look of the herbs, either.

Lily knew she had to stock up on herbs to last until she could prepare her own remedies in the fall. In the end, she bought a bag of rosehips, some hawthorn berries, and a giant aloe vera cactus growing in a bucket. Then she moved on to the last table in the row.

This last table was piled high with neat bunches of dried herbs in excellent condition. The boy behind the table looked hungry. He was about fifteen years old, she guessed, with pale hair that was cut unevenly but surprisingly clean. His clothes were also patched but clean.

"Do you have plantain?"

"Yes," he said, and then added, "My Lady." It was obviously an effort for him to be polite, but he did it.

"Show it to me."

He reached under the table and pulled out a neat bunch of plantain. Lily gently chafed one of the leaves between her fingers. It had been picked and dried properly. "How much are you asking?"

"One copper coin for three bunches."

Lily narrowed her eyes. "Show me what else you have." An hour later, Lily was completely satisfied. She had herbs to last her for the coming winter through to spring. Then she would prepare her own. She had even purchased a couple of herbs she had never seen before because the boy was able to give her detailed explanations about how they were used. She liked the boy. He was serious for his age. "You know herbs well," she praised him.

He bowed. "So do you, My Lady."

"If you find anything else of interest, let me know. I am the Countess of Earton." Lily smiled. "And I like how you prepare your wares."

"My granny taught me."

"I see."

"She died this spring. She was a fine herbal healer, My Lady. I do not know nearly as much as she did."

Lily sighed. A missed opportunity. "Well don't forget to find me if you come across anything good. I'm staying at the Pig and Dog."

"Yes, My Lady."

He bowed his head low, but his eyes sparkled with fire. They didn't look like the eyes of a peasant.

He's an interesting boy, but I don't have time to learn his story.

⁎◆⁏

Lily rented an extra room at the inn so that she and Ingrid would have space to sort and pack all the herbs she had bought. She wished she had a coffee grinder. Then she could have put the ground herbs in labeled jars. Without noticing it, she began to design a hand-operated mill.

I'll have to talk to the blacksmith about making something I can use to grind up all these dried herbs quickly.

But when Lily tried to explain her idea to Ingrid, the Virman woman did not react as she had expected. She looked thoughtful. "My Lady, the blacksmith will make this thing for you. And then what?"

Lily stopped laughing and did some quick thinking. Ingrid was right. Her rough design was lightweight and easy to use. She probably shouldn't go around showing it to just anyone.

But I doubt our blacksmith back in Earton can make what I need. What should I do?

"My Lady, I'm sure you know best, but…" Ingrid hesitated. For the millionth time, Lily reflected on how lucky she was to have found these Virmans.

"I suppose I could try to hire the blacksmith to go home with us," she said, thinking aloud.

Ingrid shook her head. "If he's a master, he won't go with you. He'll have a home here and a list of customers."

"But what about an apprentice?" Lily wondered.

"That's a possibility. An apprentice will be glad of a chance to become a master. They're always hungry, and they need to make money to pay the guild fees."

"I'll do my best," said Lily.

With that thought in mind, she went to see the blacksmith. His workshop was near the city wall. It was a stone building with a sizeable, clean yard. Lily liked the looks of it until she heard a man's voice from the forge. "You stupid son of a pig!"

A boy raced out into the yard, followed by a huge, muscular giant swinging a hefty stick.

Before Lily could react, her guards stepped forward and pulled out their axes. "Watch your manners in front of her ladyship," Leif warned in a cold voice.

The giant stopped on the spot. He blinked. Then he bowed low and begged her pardon. The boy took the opportunity to put some distance between his back and the hand of vengeance. He was obviously an apprentice. His arms were skinny but muscled from working the bellows and swinging a hammer. Lily wasn't sure what exactly a blacksmith did, but she was sure it involved hard physical labor. The giant before her had never seen a protein shake and was none the worse for it. He wasted no money on his apprentice, that much she could see. The boy's clothes were so torn and dirty that a beggar would have pitied him.

She interrupted the giant's attempt to beg her pardon. "I need a blacksmith. Is that you?"

He fell over himself working to convince her that he was the best blacksmith in the region. Lily had taken an instant dislike to him when she saw how he treated his apprentice, so she waved her hand to interrupt him again. "I need something made. If you can do it, I'll make it worth your while. If you can't, you won't be paid. Now, show me your best steel."

Half an hour later, Lily grudgingly admitted that the giant knew his business well. The knives he made shone icy blue and easily sliced through the sacking she held up.

Lily asked for a piece of birch bark and began to draw what she wanted: scalpels, clamps, wound retractors, forceps—both regular and cylindrical—and several other useful items. The blacksmith gaped over her shoulder as she sketched. When she handed him the piece of bark, he scratched his head.

"My Lady, how big are these things supposed to be?"

Lily sighed. She held out her hand and began to show him which things should be as long as her ring finger and which should be as long as her pinkie. *So much for standard sizes! I wonder how I can explain to people that they need units of measure… I don't even remember who developed the metric system. And good luck teaching them about meridians. The earth is flat, end of discussion. Any other opinion will get me beheaded.*

"My Lady, how soon do you need these tools?"

"When can you finish them?"

"In about ten days, if I hurry."

Lily nodded. "No sooner?"

"My Lady, I have other orders to sort out first."

Leif spoke up. "I see. You would rather make horseshoes for the local peasants than important tools for the Countess of Earton?" His voice was soft, but Lily got goosebumps down her spine listening to him.

"My Lady, in the name of Aldonai, I beg you!" the giant sank to his knees. "I'll have to buy more steel, but I'll do your order in eight days!"

Lily narrowed her eyes. "And how much will this cost me?"

The giant did some mental math. "Eight gold coins, My Lady, and three silver ones."

Lily laughed. "You must have knocked your head on the anvil in there. Your whole outfit isn't worth that. I'll give you two gold coins, but only because I'm in a hurry and the order is an unusual one."

"My Lady, I'll soon be a pauper if I do intricate work like this for such a price!"

"Such a price?" Lily lost what patience she had left. She hadn't slept well, which never improved her temper. Using the choicest phrases she had learned from warrant officer Sviridenko, she explained the blacksmith's business to him. In the end, she told him that if he didn't use the best steel for her tools, he would receive a visit from her friendly Virman guards.

₤◆₧

Leif watched her haggle with the blacksmith. He was curious about her motives and plans. She was an odd woman, but she was also very interesting. She did not know many simple things, and yet she had deep knowledge in other areas. She had calmly paid in silver for a cartload of dried herbs that morning, and yet she was fighting for each copper coin with the blacksmith. She could be equally generous and tight-fisted, and he had yet to understand why. It was strange but interesting. Leif was tied to the Countess by his curiosity, as well as by his perception that she would lay down her life for her people.

She haggled down to three gold and two silver coins. Her victory complete, they left the blacksmith moaning over her drawings and headed off to find the glass blower.

ೞ◆ೞ

There was just one glass blower in town, and his workshop was not far from the blacksmith's. When she found it, she saw that it was also a stone building with a sizeable yard, but she noticed that the windows had glass panes. Like the jeweler's windows, the panes were full of bubbles and had a greenish tint that made them hard to see through, but they were panes of real glass. She couldn't wait to get started improving the process. She already knew how to color glass with cobalt, nickel, lead, silver, and gold.

Leif hammered on the gate. "The Countess Lilian Elizabeth Mariella Earton wishes to see the master!"

A few minutes later, the gate was opened by a pale young boy dressed in rags.

It must be fashionable for all the artisans to keep their apprentices worse than their dogs.

When the apprentice ran off to find his master, Lily took a few copper coins out of her purse and handed them to Leif with whispered instructions. He nodded and sent one of his men on her errand. The idea was simple and worth trying; they would pay the blacksmith's apprentice to keep an eye on his master and let her know if any of the work wasn't done right. She would do the same with the glass blower's apprentice.

The glass blower took his sweet time coming out to meet her, and when he finally appeared, Lily realized she couldn't work with him. He looked her over with an arrogant expression and gave the slightest of bows, as if to say, "Aristocrats are thick on the ground, but there's only one glass blower here."

Lily straightened herself and got to business. "What is your name?"

He bowed again, ever so slightly. "Master Veldey, My Lady. Joannes Veldey."

Lily narrowed her eyes to slits. "They tell me you make things from glass. Is that so?"

"Yes, My Lady."

"I need some glass beads. Will you sell me some?"

She really did need beads for some lace she was planning to make. "Of course, My Lady. Please, come into my shop."

Lily followed him inside. She was soon disappointed. His beads were all the size of olives. Apparently, nobody had invented tiny seed-sized glass beads for thread lace yet. The muddy colors were also disappointing.

"Is this all you have?"

"I have several vases for sale, My Lady. Basins for washing the hands and face, cups, panes of glass for use in windows…" As he recounted everything he knew how to make, Lily looked around the shop and sighed. Even as a schoolgirl, she had done better glasswork.

I wonder if I could set up my own workshop. All I need is an oven and a metal tube. The glass she saw in the workshop was all at least a quarter of an inch thick, dark green and full of bubbles. *Completely useless.*

"My Lady?

Lily started. *Did I say my last thought out loud?* "Master Veldey, can you make glass in different colors? I want a green and white vase."

"My Lady, that would be very expensive…" The glass blower stalled.

Lily nodded. "I know. If I draw the things I need, will you make them for me?"

"My Lady…"

In the end, he said he would do custom work, but not for cheap.

"Is your glass fire-safe? Can I pour hot liquids in it?"

He admitted that his wares were not fire safe. Lily thought to herself that Master Veldey wouldn't have lasted long in a medieval glassworks in her own world. The Venetian masters might have taken him on as an apprentice, but even that was doubtful. She ordered a couple of glass coils in a range of diameters and left the workshop feeling despondent. If she wanted good glass, she would have to make it herself. *Why not?* She would need an oven. They didn't have muffles, of course, but any blacksmith could make the tubes she needed. Finding chemicals to color glass would be a problem, though.

Lily had never been strong in geology. *I know how to get potassium nitrate, but what about copper sulfate? Nickel compounds? Cobalt?* She remembered what they looked like and how they reacted with other elements, but she had no idea where to find them in nature.

"My Lady?"

It was Leif. He had watched as she halted her horse in front of the inn and sat staring into space, and he decided to interrupt her thoughts.

"I'm fine." Lily slid off her horse and went inside to eat. It was afternoon already, and she wanted to be sure to eat her largest meal during the day.

The boiled beef was as tender and juicy as shoe leather. Lily used her knife to cut it and poke the pieces into her mouth. She would ask the blacksmith to make her some forks with four tines instead of two, and she had a couple more ideas to discuss with Helke. She wondered if anyone in her new world knew how to make metal wire and if they had discovered the many uses of springs.

Leif and Ingrid wouldn't eat at her table—they felt they would be out of place—but they were sitting at a table nearby. She called them over and told them what she had in mind. Leif scratched his head, but Ingrid was overjoyed. "My Lady, what a wonderful idea! We have a blacksmith on the ship."

"You have your own blacksmith?"

"His name is Olaf," said Leif. "And he's not really a blacksmith."

Lily questioned him further and discovered that Olaf was, in fact, a blacksmith of sorts. He couldn't make chain mail or jewelry, but he could do basic work and repairs. She waved away Leif's doubts. "That doesn't matter. I'll tell him what I need."

Then she tried to explain to them about the chemicals she wanted to find. It was slow going, but once they understood that she needed colored crystals that dissolved in water, and liquids that burned everything they touched, their eyes lit up.

"My Lady, you will have to ask dyers or tanners for those things."

"Where do I find them?"

She discovered that dying and tanning were always done far outside the city walls because of the smell. Lily was amused. Nobody was worried about chemicals poisoning them, they just didn't like the smell. *How could anything smell worse than the human waste they toss out in the street?*

She made a mental list. Once she had the necessary chemicals, she would consider where to put her glassworks. Then she remembered that she needed to check on her patient.

ಬ◆ಛ

Ali Akhmet din Tahirjian was still in bed. His first wife was helping him sip a glass of milk. Lily had told them to give him as much milk as he would take. She had discovered they had decent cottage cheese and sour cream, but they hadn't heard of yogurt and didn't know how to whip cream for desserts.

When Lily walked in, the women jumped up. Lily smiled and approached the bed. "How do you feel?"

"Not so good." He said something in his native language, and the women all left the room. Lily took his pulse and then put her lips to his forehead.

"I thought it would be worse. You barely have a fever."

"Is that good?"

"It's excellent. You have a strong constitution. Are they giving you lots of milk to drink?"

"Yes. Why did you order that?"

"Because milk contains something that will help your bones heal faster." She didn't bother trying to explain about calcium. She wouldn't have told a rabbit about quantum physics, either.

"What is this thing in milk you speak of?"

"Bones are white, aren't they?"

"They are."

"And so is milk. That's how it makes your bones stronger."

"What about salt? Salt is also white."

Lily thought quickly. "But it isn't a liquid."

Ali Akhmet nodded, satisfied. Then Lily examined his leg. The splint was straight, and his leg was still stretched and tied to the end of the bed.

"I will tell your wives how to massage your leg in another ten days. Once you get out of bed, you won't even remember that it was broken."

"I will be in debt to you forever, My Lady."

Lily waved away his thanks. "Not for long, you won't. I have some items I would like to sell, but I can't do it myself. If you help me do the selling, you stand to make a fair profit."

"Do you mean the inkwells?"

"I do. Don't you think they will sell?"

"I'm sure they will. It's a lovely design."

Lily smiled. He couldn't even guess how many good ideas she had. In the meantime, she asked him if he had ever seen anything like the chemicals she would need for her glassworks. He admitted that he had not seen anything of the kind, but he went on to describe a strange substance he had recently encountered since she was interested.

"It is a liquid that burns all it touches, and its fire cannot be put out with water," he said.

Lily turned to him, excited. "What color is it? Does it shimmer like a rainbow when you pour it out? And does it have a terrible taste?"

"Yes, My Lady."

Lily was overjoyed. The liquid he was describing had to be oil. *Crude, unrefined oil, but oil nonetheless!*

"We value this liquid highly and use it for warfare now. It burns whatever it lands on, and can even burn in water."

"Where can I buy some?"

"I have several barrels of it on my ship. I will tell my men to bring one of them to you."

Ali Akhmet was rewarded by the look in the Countess' shining eyes. He realized that this woman had highly unusual interests. Lily took his temperature again and then went off to mix an herbal remedy.

Ali Akhmet called for his guards and sent one of the men back to the ship with a note for a barrel of oil to be delivered to him that same evening. That way, he could at least partially repay his debt to the Countess. He looked forward to making her happy.

๕◆๙

The two lovers met in secret, around the corner from the inn. "My love, this is our only chance. You can do it, can't you?"

"Of course I can."

"He has his own room. Those fools are in there with him most of the time, but I have a sleeping potion. They will sleep like the dead."

"And I will…"

"It's on the second floor. I'll open the window for you. In the morning, let everyone blame that fat woman who has been taking care of him."

"Why not? Sounds good to me."

"That's the only way we can ever be together!"

The man thought to himself that money was also an important consideration, but he saw no reason to disappoint his lover too soon. If she thought he planned to marry her, she would work harder to make the plot work. He could always get rid of her later before she started causing him trouble.

೮೦ ◆ ೞ

Lily had just sat down to work on her herbal remedy when Helke Leitz was announced. He would have come straight into her room if the Virmans hadn't stopped him.

"My Lady, I did it!" Lily took the package he handed her and felt his fingers tremble. She opened the package. It was a dip pen, just as she had drawn it, just like the ones she had played with as a child. "My Lady, I have already tested it. It writes beautifully!"

The pen was a simple silver tip mounted on a wooden stick, but it was an advance in technology for the time. Lily dipped it in her inkwell and wrote a few words on a piece of birch bark. The pen worked. *Now, I just need some real paper. I wonder if papyrus grows anywhere around here?*

Lily didn't want to make paper out of tree pulp. She hated the idea of wasting trees so that idiots could have their speeches printed in the thousands of copies. And she wasn't sure how the process worked, either.

She thought she might be able to use reed grass, however, if she could build large enough vats and get her hands on the right chemicals—and a press…and enough reed grass.

"My Lady?" Helke timidly interrupted her train of thought.

In the next instant, the jeweler got the shock of his life when the Countess jumped up and shouted, "Hurrah!" before kissing him on the cheek. "Helke, you did it! You are so clever!"

He felt his eyes tear up. "My Lady."

"You are a genius! You're wonderful!" Lily praised the jeweler for a good five minutes. He blushed, but accepted her praise with gratitude; he had earned it, after all, and it felt good. Lily knew that aristocrats generally ignored Eveers unless they needed money, so she understood his reaction to her praise, and she meant everything she said.

Finally, Lily calmed down and handed the jeweler a piece of birch bark. "Now, look at this. It's a hook-and-eye clasp."

"Hook and eye?"

Lily drew a bra and indicated where the hook and eye would go. Then she drew several other types of clasps and hairpins.

"These first ones work well on clothing. You can dress them up with precious stones if you want. These others are for pinning up hair. Now, look at one more thing…" It took her a while to explain curlers.

Helke thought for a moment. "Noblewomen may find that interesting," he said.

Rapidly she sketched out several more ideas, including a thimble and other handy sewing tools.

"My Lady, these are all fine ideas that will sell well."

"Of course, especially the curlers. I know that women are currently using hot irons to curl their hair." She was glad they weren't wearing wigs—that would be truly awful in the heat.

While she was on a roll, Lily sketched out a set of manicure tools. Helke studied the drawing and pronounced that no one would use such things. He wanted to start making curlers that he could sell to the women who offered hairstyling for noblewomen.

Almost without thinking, Lily delighted the Eveer with several designs for hairbrushes. She told him that they would be easy to make if he used boar bristles.

If we specialize in making beauty tools for hair and nails—I'll make the mirror glass, and Helke can make the frames—we will start to earn some serious money!

The jeweler's eyes shone with inspiration. He promised that he would neither eat nor sleep until he had made everything the countess had shown him.

◈

He left the dip pen with Lily, who took it to show Ali Akhmet.

The pen worked wonders on him, better than any herbal remedy. The merchant almost jumped out of bed when he saw it. Lily had to promise that she would bring Helke in to talk with him about orders, shipping charges, and payment. She was confident that the Eveer would strike a hard, fair bargain.

She left Ali Akhmet examining the dip pen and went back to her room to make some anti-inflammatory and fever-reducing mixtures for him. She was tired and would have enjoyed a glass of lemonade with mint, but decided against sharing her recipe with the innkeeper. Some good ideas she would keep to herself.

◈

The road from the capital city to Earton was long and difficult. Miranda Catherine continued to whine and cry, and the trip stretched on longer than it should have because her entourage had to stop for several days in each village to buy the things she wanted and relieve her temper.

The men in her entourage were furious. The only thing that kept them going was the thought that they would eventually reach Earton and turn over their charge. But they were also uneasy. They had heard enough about the Countess to know that she was a match for Miranda. *Will the castle stand up to two unpredictable, short-tempered crybabies?*

Only one person in the entourage was completely at peace. He had a job to do, and he had been paid generously in advance to do it. So, he had no worries… The child could be as naughty as she liked. With every day on the road, he was getting closer to his goal.

ᔥ◆Ც

When she went to bed that night, Lily couldn't help smiling. She was happy. The barrel of liquid Ali Akhmet's servants brought her was, indeed, crude oil. In time, she would figure out how to refine it. Thoughts of refineries reminded her that she wanted to talk to Helke about making a still. She was sure he would be enthusiastic. Her tired brain kept turning over plans for the future. Finally, after doing some exercises and checking on her patient one last time, Lily got into bed and closed her eyes.

I need a cat to help purr me to sleep. She had a startling thought: in all her travels she had yet to see a cat. *Do they even have cats in this new world? And how can I find out?* She imagined drawing a picture of a cat and asking people, "Have you ever seen one of these?"

At that, her brain finally shut off, and Lily fell into a deep sleep.

ᔥ◆Ც

The next day was just as hard. In the morning, Lily went back to the market, taking her peasants with her. They bought a dozen goats that Ingrid picked out for their soft fleeces. She said that they wouldn't stand a chance of surviving on Virma, but that Earton's milder climate would suit them fine.

They bought a bull. Judging by his size, Lily suspected he was the infamous bull from the other day, but she wasn't sure. And they bought six cows. Ingrid swore that the cows were in excellent shape, and she thought two of them might be pregnant. They decided against buying any horses and put off purchasing poultry until right before they left for home.

Lily sent the peasants back to the inn with the animals and went off with Ingrid, Leif, and five more Virmans to find a tanner. They could smell the tanner's workshop from half a mile away. The stench made their eyes water. Lily stopped and wet a large handkerchief and tied it around her face. Ingrid followed her example. The smell was a complicated blend of chemicals, leather, and manure, with sharp, burning overtones. Lily couldn't tell exactly what she was smelling, but she suspected that a gas chamber would smell nicer.

She kept going, despite the fact that her stomach was threatening revolt. She kept her mouth shut as they rode into the tanner's yard and Leif announced her. And she kept it shut while the master tanner bowed and introduced the other tanners. Lily deduced that several tanners used the workshop, which was surrounded by a number of small houses.

The visit went well. She had been hoping to find lime water, soda, potash, and sulfuric acid. The tanners were amenable and immediately promised to sell her a large supply of the substances she needed if she would bring her own containers. She gave them some earnest money and turned her horse to go back to the inn. Her plan was to go back to the glass blower's shop after lunch and buy the containers she needed, but upon returning to the inn, she discovered that three of the dressmaker's girls had been waiting for her for over an hour. They had brought her order. Lily looked them over. These were the girls the dressmaker had called "stupid and lazy." As a matter of fact, they looked hungry. She pulled the innkeeper aside. "Did they order anything to eat?"

"No, My Lady."

"Then set out a good lunch for them—without wine. I will pay."

The innkeeper did as she wished. He was prepared to do anything for a customer like Lilian Earton, who paid regularly for everything she and her people ate or used. Better yet, there had been no fights in the inn since the Countess took up residence. And the city guards had taken to drinking there in the evenings. With his dining room full and his customers drinking in peace, the innkeeper saw his profits slowly rise, copper coin after copper coin. He even liked having all the Virmans around—just the look of them discouraged drunks from causing trouble, and they had tossed a couple of troublesome alcoholics into the pig trough the previous week. So, the innkeeper wished nothing but continued health and wealth for the Countess of Earton.

When Lilian came back downstairs, the girls were in a much merrier mood after getting enough to eat for the first time in a long while. When a person has been near starvation for years, finally eating a full meal can make one act almost drunk.

Lily shook her head. "Follow me, girls." They obeyed. Lily took them to her room, shut the door and posed a question, "Do you know that you have to follow my orders?"

"Yes, My Lady."

"I am a Countess, and my wishes take precedence over those of your employer. Do you understand that?"

"Yes, My Lady."

"Then listen to this, I order you to lie down and get some rest. We can try the clothes on when I come back. I will tell my people not to bother you. Now, rest."

"But My Lady, what will Marion say?"

"You'll just tell her that I was very demanding, and it took a long time to finish the fitting. If I have to, I'll pay for the extra time. Now lie down, all three of you. I'll tell the innkeeper's wife to send up milk and buns."

Judging by the girls' faces, they thought they were in heaven. Lily went out and closed the door. After ordering the milk and buns, she called for her Virman guards. It was time to return to the glass blower.

It took her an hour to get there and an hour to get back, but only about twenty minutes to tell the master exactly what she needed. He was extremely unpleasant to her the entire time, but she ignored his contempt. She simply didn't have time to think about it, aside from wondering if he hated all aristocrats or all people in general.

He can go hang himself, as long as he makes my containers first.

When she got back to the inn, Lily ate a bowl of soup and went upstairs to look in on Ali Akhmet. She noticed that the two wives had been replaced by two younger wives who didn't understand a thing she said. Ali Akhmet sent them out of the room while he talked to the Countess.

Lily examined his leg and his abdominal wound. The honey had done its work, and in another few days, she would be able to take out the stitches. Ali Akhmet looked good, but the best doctors Lily had ever known were superstitious individuals who had taught her not to drop her guard until the patient was completely out of the woods.

Chapter 9

Plots and Priests

The dressmaker's girls bowed low when Lily walked into her room. She sat down in the only chair and waved for them to relax. "Calm down. Let me sit here for a few minutes, and then we can do the fitting."

She closed her eyes for a minute. Exhaustion weighed down every limb.

"My Lady."

Her eyes opened. The skinniest of the girls—the one called Marcia—handed her a cup.

"Drink this, My Lady. You are tired."

Lily took the cup and drank. It was milk, cold and delicious.

"Thank you."

"My Lady, we did everything as you asked. The colors and designs are as you wished."

"Can the clothes be taken in later?" That was Lily's main concern. She didn't want to keep buying new clothes as the shape of her body changed.

"Yes, My Lady. May I show you?"

Lily stood like a post for the next ten minutes while the girls took off everything but her undershirt and dressed her in a white long-sleeve shirt that went down to mid-thigh. Then they took out her new skirt. At first, it looked like a plain strip of fabric. On closer inspection, Lily realized how cleverly they had done their work. The skirt tied around her waist and had a line of buttons from waist to hem. Opposite each button was a neatly hidden loop that could be used to hold in the skirt. As she lost weight, she could simply move the buttons to narrow the whole skirt. The vest was just as well-made: green velvet tastefully embroidered with black silk thread. The girls knew their work.

"Which of you did the embroidery?

"I did," said the second girl. She was a little taller than Marcia and had blonde hair and blue eyes.

"Good job, girls. This is wonderful work!" Lily beamed at them. The clothes fit perfectly and could be taken in as needed. *What else did a woman need?*

"How much do I owe you?"

The third girl suddenly burst out, "My Lady, please take us to work for you."

Lily fell back in her chair. "What about Marion?"

"You just pay her for this order, and we will leave."

"Don't you owe her anything?" Their faces betrayed them; they were in debt to their employer. "How much?"

"Six silver and fourteen copper coins," Marcia whispered.

Lily sighed. She could tell they had never seen that much money in their whole lives. She took out her purse. "I will give you the money. In return, you will work for me for one year, starting today. I will pay you one silver coin each month. If you do your work well, I will pay more."

The girls stared at her, eyes blinking. "My Lady, are you serious?"

"Yes, I am very serious."

"My Lady!"

All three girls fell on their knees.

Lily sighed. "Let's think this through. One of you can go back to the shop, pay Marion and collect your things. I'll send one of my guards with you as a witness. Have her give you a receipt for the money. Is that clear?"

"Yes, My Lady."

"Which of you will go?"

The girls glanced at each other. "My Lady," Marcia took a step forward. "I will go."

Lily nodded. "Fine. Here is the money." Then she paused. "Wait. I have another question. What exactly is your relationship with your employer?"

"We're her apprentices."

Lily bit her lip. She wasn't sure where apprentices fell in the grand scheme of things, and she didn't know for a fact that they even had the right to leave their master. "Who sets the terms of your apprenticeship?" They might think her question was odd, but she didn't care. Lily needed to buy a ton of different things, and she suspected the guilds would refuse to sell to her if she helped Marion's apprentices escape the service they were bound to.

The girls fell over each other explaining that they were apprentices and that in order to become master dressmakers, they needed to pay off their debt and pass an examination held by the head of the dressmakers' guild in that town.

"Who heads the guild?"

"Marion."

"I suppose she won't want to let you go."

Judging by their faces, she was right. If they paid their debt and left without taking the examination, they would lose the right to join another guild for three years, even at the level of apprentices. But if Lily hired them, that wouldn't matter.

"What if you pass the examination? What steps would you need to take to join the guild if it was headed by someone else?"

They told her they would need to pay their debts, announce their intentions, and present their handiwork for the guild to judge.

"Handiwork?"

"Yes, My Lady. A dress or a man's suit. Whatever the guild asks for."

Lily nodded. That made sense. "Fine. Let's say you do that. Then what?" If their work passed scrutiny, each girl would have to pay a fee of five silver coins and hold a feast for the entire guild. "Let's think, girls. Can you make whatever they ask you to make?" The girls all nodded. Lily gave them a hard look. "I will give you the money for Marion, and for the guild, and even for the feast."

"But My Lady, we will never be able to pay you back!"

"You will. You know how to sew."

"Anyone can sew."

"But not just anyone can make the things I need made."

"Like what?"

Lily pulled out yet another piece of birch bark and started to draw. Her sketches were clumsy, but she explained to them in words what she couldn't draw. Two hours later, the girls had decided to return to Marion for a few more days, where they could sew whatever she needed very quickly.

"Tell her that I want you to alter some other dresses for me."

Marcia shook her head. "My Lady, you should come tell her yourself."

"Fine. I'll stop by tomorrow morning."

"But My Lady, won't you be going to the service tomorrow?"

Lily blinked. What service are they talking about?

"Tomorrow is the fifth day. The Temple of Aldonai will be holding a service."

Lily almost cursed out loud. A religious service. *Do I go or skip it?* It was a stupid question. Of course, she had to go. *I already stick out here. I'd better toe the line on religion, or at least look like I do.* "Yes, I'll be at the service tomorrow and talk to Marion afterward."

Marcia, Lidia, and Irene nodded like three bobbleheads. Marcia reached out to hand her money back to her, but Lily shook her head. "No, girls. You hold on to it. I trust you."

"We will be in trouble if Marion finds it, My Lady."

"And we have to come back and do more fittings with you, anyway."

"But don't you need to buy fabric?" Lily asked

Marcia kept one silver coin and several coppers, which she tied into a knot in her petticoat.

"This will be enough, My Lady."

"You'll need to make your handiwork for the examination. If they ask you to make dresses, make them to fit me. And yourselves, as well. I won't have my servants wearing rags. Make three dresses for me and two each for yourselves."

The bobbleheads nodded again. "Will you have them be pink, My Lady?"

Lily almost choked. "The colors of Earton are green and white. Use those colors for my dresses and any other colors you like for your own."

When they finally left, Lily shut the door behind them and lay down on her bed. She was absolutely exhausted.

৪৩◆ଓ

Lady Adelaide Wells stood on the ship's deck, where the breeze tossed her dark curls. She heard footsteps but did not turn around; she knew how well she looked in profile. Someone kissed her on the neck. She almost purred with pleasure but stopped herself in time.

"That was impudent, My Lord!"

"You looked so wonderful standing there that I couldn't help myself." Jess didn't look the least bit guilty.

"I'm an honest woman!"

"Have I asked you to lie about anything?"

She shook her handkerchief at him. "When you make free like that, you put my reputation at risk!"

"Nobody can see us."

"What about the sea? And the sun? And the wind?" Adelaide was flirting. *Why not? I don't want to be too strict with him. And...* Adelaide was used to regular intimacy. Alex was far away, and she wouldn't see him again soon. She thought she might lead Jess around by the nose for another month or so, and then she would give in. She would most definitely give in.

"How about I kidnap you?"

Adelaide laughed. "And take me where?"

"To my cabin. It's a comfortable one."

"No, My Lord. I could never do that. You're just toying with me. I won't let myself be ruined."

"Adele, my dear," Jess crooned in a velvety voice, "you're much more than just a game for me."

"You're married, My Lord."

"I would have married you, but my father never asked my opinion."

"Then don't break my heart."

"Adele, my dear, I could never..."

Her answer was a sultry glance from under her eyelashes. She was enjoying this game. She knew that the sun was hitting her hair just so, and she reached up to touch the necklace that rested on her breast.

You'll end up in my nets, Jess Earton. You'll come right to me and bring all that money with you. I'm an intelligent woman, and I know how to train a man like you.

ஐ◆ርߞ

The bottle of sleeping potion was pleasingly heavy in the woman's pocket. She knew that the large, fair-haired woman would check on his Lordship one more time that night, and she was ready. When her husband told her to leave his room, she would have time to pour some of her potion into the pitcher of wine that the guards drank from. Then, she would pour the rest into two more pitchers—one for the Countess and one for her Virmans. Her lover had brought the pitchers to the inn earlier that day.

She could do it. She knew she could. She was sick of the old pig who had bought her. Sick of his snorting in bed, his sweat, his beard… She hated her husband enough to poison him, but she couldn't get away with it. A harem offers no place to hide, and his other wives would certainly find out.

They would kill her, and she wanted to live. That was a new feeling. Before she met Chika, she had just been existing, but Ali's nephew was young and handsome and brought her joy she had never known before. *How I want to be his wife!* She would wash his feet every evening. The only thing stopping her was the old merchant.

The woman had thought for a long time about how to get rid of him. She couldn't get her hands on poison. It was just by accident that she had managed to steal the sleeping potion. She would use it now.

A pitcher for Ali. A pitcher for the guards. One for the Virmans, and one for the fair-haired cow. If she had any left over, she would add it to the food in the kitchen.

Everyone would sleep soundly. She would, too. In the morning, she would cry the loudest.

ஐ◆ርߞ

Lily was extremely pleased with the innkeeper. A mere mention of the next day's church service had sent him off on a very informative monologue.

She learned that the temple was beautiful and that the glass panes for the windows had cost a fortune, and the priest was an excellent speaker. His name was Father Leider, and he had come all the way from the capitol.

Lily hinted that she would like to attend the service along with everyone else for safety and to avoid getting lost. The innkeeper thought that was odd but agreed.

Then Lily went upstairs, where she checked Ali's wounds before heading to bed.

There was a pitcher of wine on her bedside table. At first, she thought it was juice, but when she poured herself a glass and sniffed it, she winced. It smelled terrible.

Who brought this in here?

She pulled on a nightgown and stretched it tight around her waist. She tried to judge how much weight she had lost. A mirror would help. All she needed was a piece of glass that she could paint black and then silver.

As a small child, she had broken her mother's mirror and been surprised to find the layers of paint behind the glass. It was worth trying. She wondered if she would be able to find silver paint or metal powder. There were artists in her new world—someone had painted the murals in the Baron's office, after all. That would be a good place to start. *Or should I use a silver sheet as the base for my mirror?* Silver and nitric acid shouldn't be too hard to come by. It was worth a try. Lily made a mental note to find out the price of silver.

She sighed. She still had rolls of skin on her stomach, and her thighs would have sent a top model running for cover. But there was definite improvement. Her waist was smaller, and she could already manage to do fifty squats in a row when even one squat had been impossible not that long ago. Her aching joints worried her. Lilian Earton was just twenty-two years old—too young to have creaky joints. Then she remembered that women in her new world got married at the tender age of fourteen to sixteen.

From talking to her nanny, she had learned that her father had married her off when she was eighteen, almost nineteen. *Three years of married life, and still no children. But that's no surprise.* Anger started to rise whenever she thought about her husband. Lily was used to the feeling. *He sent his wife to live in the middle of nowhere and visits once a quarter; of course, they don't have children! It takes more than holding hands to get a woman pregnant. What a pig!*

Then she reflected that, in all honesty, she was no prize herself. She wondered why in the world the Earl had agreed to marry an overweight girl with a temper. *Was it her dowry? How much did he get? Could she get her hands on any of it? Why not try?*

Lily vowed to go through all the paperwork she could find at the castle and then write to her father. She was his only child, after all. If he thought her request for money was strange, she would remind him that she had recently taken a tumble down the stairs and had a miscarriage. *Or I'll tell him it was a miracle that healed me of my bad attitude.*

But first, she would have to find out what the law said. Sooner or later, her dear husband would pay another visit to Earton, if only to try once more for an heir. *What will I do then?*

Troubled by that frightening thought, Lily finally fell into an exhausted sleep.

⁚♦⁝

Everything was ready. The whole inn was asleep. The woman held a candle to the window to show that the coast was clear. All he had to do was climb over the fence and do his job. A dog barked. He tossed it a piece of meat that had been marinated in the same sleeping potion.

Eat it, you stupid animal!

He was over the fence in one movement.

⁚♦⁝

Lily woke in the middle of the night because she needed to go to the bathroom. Only instead of a bathroom, the inn had an outhouse in the yard. Her Virman guards always accompanied her when she visited it. The only other option was to use the chamber pot, which would stink the rest of the night unless she tossed the contents out the window. Lily found both options repellent, so she got up to go outside.

She wrapped a cape around her shoulders, lifted the latch, and pushed the door open. What she saw in the hall stunned her: her Virman guards were asleep on the floor up and down the hall.

What the hell?

Lily had grown accustomed to being guarded day and night. She nudged one of the men with the toe of her shoe. Nothing. She nudged another one. *They've been drugged. And I recognize that pitcher. There's one just like it in my room on the bedside table. Who would want to drug my guards?*

Lily cursed under her breath. Obviously, someone had tried to drug her, as well. That was bad. But why? Hell if I know. I'll go wake Ali and ask if I can borrow one of his guards. Or better yet, I'll just spend the night on a cot in his room. His wives are there with him so no one will gossip.

Lily laughed at herself. She was past caring about gossip. She'd rather be talked about than be dead. She walked down to the end of the hall and cursed for the second time. Ali's guards were laid out on the floor, sleeping like the dead. Lily burst into her patient's room, thinking nothing of the potential danger.

What if he's been poisoned? He's too weak to survive an attempt on his life!

Ali was lying in bed asleep. She could hear him snoring. His wives were asleep on mattresses on the floor. The shutters were open, and a candle was burning on the sill.

Lily frowned. I'll put that out before it causes a fire… Oh, hell!

She thought she heard a noise outside the window. *What was that?* There was no time to think about whether she or Ali was the intended victim. She grabbed Ali's chamber pot and ran to stand beside the window.

Whoever climbs in this window better watch out! This doctor doesn't give up her patients without a fight!

ඬ ◆ ര

Chika drove his dagger into the wall and used it to pull himself up to the second-floor window. It wasn't hard for a man in his condition. The shutters opened noiselessly. He looked in. Everyone was asleep. His uncle's belly rose and fell under his expensive silk blanket. His wives were snoring on the floor next to him.

He leaned into the room and listened to the soft breathing of the sleepers. Suddenly, out of nowhere, something crashed into his head. He fell off the sill, his head covered with clay and other things. Chamber pots are almost as good as a multi-tool if you have the right inspiration. Lily didn't have time to stick her head out the window to see what happened to her would-be attacker, because a screaming, scratching beast landed on her back.

Normally, her weight would have given Lily an enormous advantage over most people, but she was out of shape. Even so, two hundred and seventy pounds can be an effective weapon if you sit down heavily on top of your opponent. Lily did just that. Underneath her, something whimpered. *That's what you get for pulling a Countess by the hair! I come from a long line of warriors! Well, I don't know about the Countess, but I do!*

Lily gave the whimpering creature under her a sharp blow with her elbow. Something cracked. She judged by the sounds the creature was making that it wouldn't attempt to get up. She got off it and looked down to see who had taken such a dislike to the Countess.

It was Neelei, writhing on the floor in pain. *How interesting.*

"What do you have against me?" Lily asked.

Judging by the other woman's furious black eyes, they wouldn't be having a heart-to-heart talk anytime soon. Lily kicked her and pointed toward the door. She had no intention of leaving her helpless patient alone with this piece of trash.

Neelei shook her head. Lily kicked her harder. Then she took the candle from the windowsill and went back to Neelei, who was still hurting from Lily's wrestling moves. She kicked her again and pointed toward the door. The young woman shook her head and hissed something that sounded angry.

Fine. Have it your way.

Hot wax burns like hell, especially on the sensitive skin of the neck and face. Neelei jumped up and dashed at Lily, but Lily was ready for her. She used her free left hand to grab the young woman's black braid and pulled it with all her might. Neelei howled like an animal. Neelei shut her mouth when she saw the candle flame flickering an inch from her face. All of a sudden, she decided that it would be best to hold still if she didn't want to smell like fried concubine.

Lily would have fried her but decided to leave that for tomorrow. She dragged Neelei downstairs and thanked her lucky stars when she found that one of the servant girls was awake. The girl couldn't understand what the Countess was trying to explain to her, so she went and woke her master. The innkeeper crawled out of bed and listened to Lily's explanation. Then he helped her lock Neelei in the cellar. They went out into the yard and found the man who had come through the window. He ended up in the cellar, as well. *We'll sort him out in the morning. Now, maybe I can get some sleep.* Lily assumed the service in praise of Aldonai would be held early in the morning, so she resigned herself to lying down on her bed for a little bit.

ॐ◆ॐ

In the morning, Lily put on her new green and white outfit, and headed off to the church feeling cheerful that at least women didn't have to cover their heads in her new world. Since almost everyone was still asleep, Lily's companion was the innkeeper's family: his wife, two daughters, and three sons. The oldest girl was fifteen, and the youngest boy didn't look to be a day over five. Lily's peasants got up in time for church, too. She noticed that they were looking at her differently as if she was doing something right, something they found to be logical.

That's strange. I don't believe they go to church often back home in Earton. Ha! Here I am calling Earton home already.

Maybe it was her home. Lily sighed. She didn't want to think of Earton as home, but there was no other word for it. And where church was concerned, she would need to avoid problems. She couldn't go around showing off her knowledge of medicine and other dark arts without attracting attention. She had read enough historical romances to know that she was in danger of being tortured and executed if anyone so much as suspected she might be a witch. No, she would just have to go to church and pray, or at least pretend to. She could handle it.

Before leaving for church, Lily sent Tres Mattie to run back to the ship and tell Leif what had happened that night. Someone had drugged her guards and made an attempt on Ali's life. The young man's eyes flashed with fire as he listened to her story. When she was done, he ran off as if dogs were chasing him.

ଐ◆ଔ

To Lily's surprise, the church was an attractive, even comfortable building. The high ceiling and walls were painted blue and white, and the floor was green. There were no icons anywhere to be seen. Instead, she saw a painting of the sun with a white bird in front of it. *Is that a dove?*

Best of all, there were benches for the worshipers to sit on. Lily was used to Orthodox churches where you had to stand through the entire service, so it was with gratitude that she plunked herself down on a padded bench.

The smell of incense in the air combined with the odor of unwashed bodies.

"My Lady?"

"Honorable Torius." She didn't have to turn around to recognize that ingratiating voice.

"I am pleased to see you enjoying the service in our humble church."

"Don't be so modest. It's a very nice church," Lily replied. Torius was still standing. "My Lady, allow me to invite you to share my bench since you do not have one of your own here. I assume you do not want to sit among the peasants and tradespeople."

Lily bowed her head regally. She reflected that having a little extra weight gave her gravitas and a noble bearing that she wouldn't otherwise have. *I have to lose weight if I don't want to die young of a heart attack, but for now, these extra pounds are coming in handy.*

The Baron gave her his hand and smiled. Lily sat down on the carved mahogany bench and straightened her back.

A retired ballerina once said that good posture can turn a cow into a queen…or vice versa.

"My Lady, people have told me that you have dealings of some sort with the jeweler Helke Leitz."

"That is true."

To hell with the small town rumor mill! I can't let him see my annoyance.

"I have to say I was surprised that a highly placed noblewoman like yourself isn't averse to dealing with an Eveer. They are heathens, you know."

In her mind, Lily made the sign of the cross. She didn't believe in God, but she needed all the help she could get. If the dressmaker's girls hadn't told her about this service, she would have slept right through it and hurt her reputation.

"Honorable Torius, money does not smell. Helke has fine ideas, and as Countess of Earton, I am pleased to help him in any way I can. He makes the most wonderful earrings; you should see them."

"He has not shown them to me."

Lily took off an earring and placed it in Torius' palm. He gazed down at the pearl and the special new clasp and whistled quietly. "This would sell well in the capital."

"It would sell well anywhere, Honorable Torius. So, I suggest that you pay attention to Helke and make sure he has everything he needs to be successful. His success is your success, of course."

"What do I get out of it? Am I the Baron or a dog's tail?"

"We'll give you a cut, but only if you help us."

"Is that so? I could teach you a lesson!"

"And I could write to my husband. Am I a Countess or a dog's tail?"

For a few seconds, the two sets of eyes waged such war that the church seemed to fill with sparks. Then Lily smiled and looked down.

The Baron is nobody's fool. He'll come for his cut of the money, but he knows I won't give him much.

Just then, the priest, dressed in a green robe, appeared in front of the painting of the sun and began to sing. His voice was quiet, and Lily couldn't understand the words, but she liked the singing anyway. He had a pleasant baritone. The congregation sat quietly as the priest sang his greeting of the dawn. Lily listened as long as she could, and then she began to doze. It was a warm, familiar feeling.

ಬಿ ◆ ೦೪

A new wave of memories broke over her… She was small. Not Aliya, but Lilian Broklend. She knew she was small because she was looking up at her father.

"Papa, are we going to the temple today?"

"Yes, my little one. How beautiful you look today."

Lily looked down at her pink dress. *More pink. Someone must have told little Lily that she looked good in pink.* She could barely remember the dark streets, but she could still hear the priest's voice and the taste of something harsh in her mouth…

She liked sitting in church. Lilian Broklend had always liked it, and present-day Lily could remember those feelings. Her mind was her own, but Lilian's deepest memories were still there somehow, like reflexes.

The service did not last long, no more than about forty minutes. Then the priest walked along the benches and made the sign of the sun over each member of the congregation and put something in their mouths using a long spoon.

Lily cursed silently. She would have to do the same. I'll survive. Back in my old world, people used to kiss icons without getting sick. I think. And I'm in the first row, so not that many people have licked the spoon before me. I'll be extra careful.

But when he got to Lily, the priest looked surprised. "My child, I have not seen you here before." She wasn't sure what to say. "Stay after the service, please."

Great. Just great!

Lily nodded obediently and, barely touching the spoon with her lips, took a taste of the white substance on it. It reminded her of cottage cheese. *Do I have any money with me? I think I do. The dressmakers wouldn't take the pay I offered, so I put it back in my purse. But this priest won't get more than two silver coins out of me, and that's a fact!*

∽◆◌

Father Leider was an interesting man, tall, with dark hair and a face that reminded her of paintings of Cardinal Richelieu. He was even somewhat attractive. Aliya had never liked men that were too good looking, but Lilian Broklend was a different story. For an instant, Lily relaxed. She gave a stupid smile, and her body made the familiar sign of Aldonai.

"Bless me, Holy One."

"May Aldonai take you under his wing."

Lily bowed her head, and the official part of her private meeting with the priest was over. She hoped their business dealings wouldn't take too long since the innkeeper and his family were waiting for her outside. Lily had asked him to wait, and he had been happy to oblige, or perhaps he was just afraid of what her Virman guards would say if he left her.

On second look, Lily decided she didn't like the priest. But that's no big deal. I don't have to eat him for lunch. I just have to talk to him.

"My child, why haven't I seen you here before?"

"I only recently arrived and will be leaving soon," she kept it brief.

"I would remember such a charming woman."

Lily almost sat down on the floor. Charming, was she? He must be angling for a new roof on the church.

"I just came to town for the fair and the market. I didn't want to put my soul in danger by missing the cleansing rites," she said, batting her eyelashes.

"My Lady…"

"Countess Lilian Elizabeth Mariella Earton."

"Very pleased to meet you. I am Father Simon Leider." Lily gave a slight nod. He took it as permission to continue. "How long will we have the pleasure of seeing you in our town?"

"Not long."

"But I hope you will attend our daily services?" Lily smiled and said nothing. "Piety is an important virtue in a woman." He went on for another five minutes about how he hoped to gain Lily's support and how pleased he was to see such a lovely woman sitting in the front row.

Lily kept her mouth shut while he talked, but when the priest tried to take her hand, she cautiously withdrew it from his viselike fingers.

Really?

Then she remembered what she had read about the church. Priests were not required to take a vow of celibacy until they reached the level of Aldon.[x] Until then, they could do what they liked with whomever they fancied, and no one raised an eyebrow. *I bet he'd like to be known as the spiritual advisor for the Countess of Earton. That's more important than just the priest of a small town people visit for the market each year.*

Lily smiled sweetly. "Of course, I'll be coming to services. My husband highly values piety." It was just a slight hint. If he didn't catch it, she would hint again with something heavier.

The specter of Jess Earton made the priest visibly nervous. It would take a much braver man than Father Leider to make a cuckold out of the Earl. Lily listened politely to his assurances of devotion, took a moment to feel sorry for Anne of Austria, and took her leave, telling the priest that she had important affairs to handle for her husband. "Our estate Comptroller is incompetent, so I have to handle many things on my own, you see."

The peasants and the Baron were waiting for her outside.

"My Lady…"

Lily stopped him. "Honorable Torius, I would be happy to see you at Helke's workshop at noon. I hope you do not object?"

He did not object, so Lily headed back to the inn. She wanted to talk to Ali and Leif before she went to Helke's workshop. They had not had their agreement stamped by the Baron's office, and she felt it would be a good idea to do so.

I'll buy off the Baron, and I think I've put Marion in her place. The priest doesn't look like he'll cause me any trouble.

She found herself longing to go home to Earton, where there was peace and quiet, and they had just recently cleaned everything.

Leif was mad as a devil when Lily got back to the inn. His men had fallen asleep on the job and put the Countess in danger. It didn't matter that the attacker was after Ali, Lily could have been hurt or killed. And then they let her go off to church in the morning without any protection. Two of his men were dripping with water when she walked in, and Lily guessed that Leif had dunked them in the rain barrel outside. She didn't feel too bad for them. Instead, she gave Leif a brief account of the night's adventures and went upstairs to see Ali.

Things were no better in her patient's room. Lilaka was sniveling in the corner like a dog that had been kicked. Ali Omar, looking furious, stood over his nephew and Neelei, who were tied up tightly and sitting on the floor. Ali spat out something in their language, and it didn't sound friendly. When he saw Lily, his face changed, and he overwhelmed her with his gratitude in a mix of Khangan and the language of Ativerna.

Lily waved away his thanks and sat down to take her patient's temperature and pulse.

"All that sleep did you good. Let me see your wound."

The wound looked much better, and Lily decided she would remove the stitches the next day. He would be all healed up in no time.

"My Lady, how can I ever thank you?"

She smiled. "The best way to thank me is to get better. I've put so much work into you, you at least owe me that!" Gratitude was better than money.

Ali understood her perfectly and smiled back. "I'm forever in your debt, My Lady. You helped me discover a viper in my home."

"Two vipers."

Omar's eyes flashed. Lily preferred not to ask what would happen to the two people tied up on the floor, but she could easily guess. The ocean was deep, and there were plenty of stones to be had in the area. *They did the crime so they can take the punishment.*

Downstairs, Leif told her he would go with her to the jeweler's workshop. As they rode, he tried to apologize for his men falling asleep on the job. Lily told him that she wasn't angry in the least. He could discipline the men however he saw fit, but she didn't want to hear any more about it. She also suggested that they be warned about taking wine from attractive young women. Judging by the look on Leif's face, she suspected his men would be introduced to the concept of dry law.

The jeweler gave a big grin when he saw Lily and immediately presented her with the hair clips and hook-and-eye closures he had made. When she informed him of the Baron's planned visit, he cursed quietly. There was no way around it. Mayors and governors in every universe expect kickbacks, and Helke knew that.

He just hoped the Baron wouldn't get in their way.

ಬ◆ಛ

The Honorable Torius Avermal was quite taken with Helke's achievements. He nodded, gasped in surprise, and in the next breath asked them to make him a partner at thirty percent. Lily kept a straight face as she reminded him that Helke could always follow her back to Earton, where she would be happy to set up a fine workshop for him. Then the Baron would get nothing.

The jeweler was delighted to find that, in addition to being a lovely woman with interesting ideas, the Countess could bargain like a true Eveer. He would never have dared speak to the Baron that way in fear of getting whipped, but the Countess calmly brought the Baron down to ten percent in return for his protection and assistance building more workshops. Then she put in a condition of her own.

She was heading home with a large quantity of livestock and asked the Baron to take charge of delivering the animals to Earton. She took it for granted that his men would divert some of the livestock for official purposes, but while they were at it, they could build pigeon coops along the way to house the carrier pigeons that she would use to communicate with Helke. Her home was too far for her to visit often in person.

That condition agreed to, she put forth one more: she wanted the Baron to keep the guilds from interfering in her plans. If she hired an apprentice, that person should be allowed to take the examination for guild membership. She knew Torius could do it.

Helke shook his head in admiration.

Lily's plan was to wait for the dressmakers to pass their examinations. Then she would hire them and a couple of other apprentices and head home. By that time, Ali should be back on his feet.

ဢ◆ఆ

The next three days passed relatively peacefully.

She went back to the market with the Virmans to buy the extra livestock the Baron would want for himself. The Virmans put marks on the animals so that they could be identified later.

Then she removed Ali's stitches and replaced the splints she had made in a hurry with better splints she had ordered from a local carpenter. Lily saw that the bone was healing properly. Ali saw the same thing, and his eyes filled with wonder whenever he looked at her. Lily suspected that if she hadn't already been married, he would have offered her a place in his harem. She could possibly have had her choice of harems; Omar's eyes went soft whenever Ali wasn't looking.

It's nice to know I have options. If my husband is the pig I think he is, then he can fall off his horse, and I can go live in the Khanganat. The Khangans won't extradite me, and they're good to do business with.

Ali didn't look like much, but Lily had never cared what people looked like. Her mother had taught her never to judge a candy by its wrapper— you have to actually unwrap it to know what you've got.

Why is it that women always fall for the good-looking men? Her father had never been handsome. As a girl, Aliya had always thought he looked like a fairytale gnome, but her mother had loved him powerfully.

It's the candy, not the wrapper that matters. And it's the person you live with, not their good looks.

The glass blower was just as terrible as she had suspected. He had made her a glass coil, but it was crooked and almost useless. *When I was twelve years old, my teacher would have given me a C for work like that!* She was even madder when he told her the price.

In retribution, she managed to steal away his apprentice, not by promising the lad sacks of gold, but by offering to share the secret of colored glass with him. She had bought the chemicals she needed from the tanners. The apprentice was eager to move to Earton and make colored glass. Lily never found out how the Baron handled the glass blower, but three days later, the young man showed up at the inn and informed her that he was now a master glass blower and could practice his trade wherever he chose, and the blacksmith's former apprentice decided to go to Earton with Lily, as well.

The dressmaker's girls brought her several dresses they had altered for her. They had pulled off all the lace and pink bows and added white and yellow trim, so now Lily could look at the dresses without her stomach churning. With Marcia's help, she sold some of her dresses for cash. The girl was smart, and it was no wonder the other two let her do all the talking. She then used the money to buy velvet, satin, and silk to make new dresses that were not pink at all. It was an expensive outlay, but Lily felt it necessary.

Her purchases were finally loaded onto the Virmans' ship. Leif allowed it, but he grumbled. Lily took the edge off his annoyance by suggesting that he take the opportunity to buy any new weapons he and his men needed. It was another expense, but a necessary one.

Helke had been working day and night. Lily met with his cousin, who was what they called a hair artisan, and showed him several ideas for hairstyles and explained the principles behind curlers. The man immediately made plans to expand his business in Altver and then move to the capitol. He promised to stay in touch with the amiable Countess, mainly because he hoped to pick up a few more good ideas from her.

Marcia, Lidia, and Irene finally became master dressmakers, costing Lily a couple of gold coins in the process. They were terribly grateful to her and went to work right away altering her dresses. Lily showed them a number of things they had never seen before, including buttons, pockets, and darts. The girls were so overjoyed by every crumb of new knowledge that it was a pleasure to share with them.

While all these other things were going on, Lily and Helke put together their first still. It was a failure—it leaked in several places and didn't capture the cooled vapor like it should—but it was a start.

ဆ◆ဗ

One day, Lily looked up from her work and saw the young boy she had bought dried herbs from. She raised her eyebrows. "Do you have something more to sell me?"

"No, My Lady. I want to go with you."

"Why do you think I'll take you?"

"You've hired many other young people. Why can't you take me, too?"

Lily looked even more surprised. "But what do I need you for?"

"I'll work it off, My Lady."

"But how? And why would I take a person I know nothing about into my home?"

"You don't have to take me into your home."

"Maybe not, but what's chasing you away from Altver?"

The boy wavered for a minute, but in the end, he told her his story.

Lily discovered that the boy's grandmother had been considered a witch, but in fact, she was descended from a long line of herbal healers. The gods did not give her a granddaughter, so she taught her grandson everything she knew. The boy's mother was also an herbal healer, but his father was a minor noble. The boy didn't know his father's name, but he had started to notice that the priest gave him dirty looks in church and other people avoided him. He was worried that people might drive him out of town, or worse. He was more than ready to leave town with this Countess who was always running around and knew quite a bit about plants. She seemed kind, and that was enough for him.

Something about the story didn't add up. Lily had a low opinion of the priest, but she certainly didn't think he was a frightening figure. When she voiced her doubts, the boy confessed the rest of his story. There was a girl he liked. He wanted to marry her, but he was too young, and nobody knew who his father was. And so, in order to stay out of trouble, he wanted to go to Earton.

That sounded closer to the truth.

Lily suspected there were other reasons, but after thinking for a minute, she sent the boy to get his things together. She would ask Leif to see what he could find out. Her Virman guard later returned with good news. He had been unable to find out anything that would change her mind about taking the boy. He was not a thief or a murderer or a practitioner of black magic. He would do fine. Lily was glad to have him since she didn't know all the local herbs and would need an instructor.

There was barely time to think, much less be bored. Preparations for the journey home were moving along quickly. Each day, she found she was tying her skirt a little tighter. Whenever it looked like she might be ready to leave, she found more things that needed doing, buying, or explaining.

Helke was knocked off his feet by their first batch of vodka. Pure alcohol shocked him speechless when Lily showed him how it could be set on fire. She wanted to try distilling some of the crude oil Ali had given her, but she was afraid it would spoil her not-very-good glass coil, and it was the only one she had. The glass blower was vindictive and had refused to make her another one. *To hell with him!*

Lily was keeping a mental list of all the things she could do for herself. It was a long list, and it got even longer when the blacksmith's apprentice agreed to return to Earton with her. With the Earton village blacksmith, this new apprentice, and Leif's wandering Virman semi-blacksmith working for her, she stood a good chance of getting some useful things made.

I wish I knew how to make a blast furnace, but I don't. Ignorance was frustrating. Lily could have kicked herself for all the things she didn't know, but it wouldn't have helped, so she didn't bother. Instead, she tried to be grateful for the things she did know.

൰◆ඤ

A week passed like a whirlwind, and suddenly, Lily realized that it really was time to go home. They would be sailing, at Leif's insistence.

She was no longer concerned about Ali. He was in fine shape to be carried to his ship. She had taught his wives some basic massage to improve the circulation in his leg. They were appreciative all around. When she went back to his room, Ali threatened to sail to Earton when he was well and present Lily with a trunk of gold jewelry.

She told him that wouldn't be a good idea.

The merchant had to be satisfied with expressing his undying gratitude and hinting that he might, after all, show up in Earton someday with gifts. Lily thanked him and hinted that he would do well to talk to Helke about finding new markets for his inventions. The Eveer had already given her a year's supply of all sorts of clasps and closures.

The chemicals she had acquired from the tanners were very carefully loaded onto the Virmans' ship. While she was overseeing their stowage, Lily discovered what it meant to be violently seasick. As soon as she got into Leif's rowboat for the short trip to the ship, she realized she might not be able to hold onto her lunch. It occurred to her that a long sea voyage would be a good way to lose weight, but she decided not to risk it.

The Baron stopped by to see her several more times before she left. He invited her to a ball he was hosting. Lily inquired about the details, and when he told her the ball was in celebration of the end of the market season, she decided to attend. Three more days wouldn't change much. If the peasants back in Earton wanted to rob her blind while she was gone, they had probably already done it. Advertising was another consideration; if she went to the ball, she could show off her new dress, hairstyle, and earrings in order to help Helke's sales. If she hurried, she could even get him to make her a fan in time for the ball.

Helke jumped on the idea of a lady's fan and got busy making one. His first prototype was a simple wooden frame around a piece of parchment. Lily tried to decorate the parchment with some paints she had bought. It came out pretty bad—more avant-garde than elegant—but she was satisfied that she would make an impression. And it looked perfect against the background of her new green and white dress.

Lily was so busy that she skipped every other church service. She made sure to be at special services, but she didn't have the time or energy to sit through the daily attendance. When she went, she tried to pretend that she was at a fancy concert. She sat and listened to the music, entertained herself with her own thoughts and wished that she could use the time to take a nap.

∞ ◆ ∞

It was almost the day of the ball. Lily turned her attention to her appearance. Helke's cousin had given her an attractive hairstyle with bangs in front and curls in the back. Her nails were clean and shaped. The girls had made her a gorgeous white silk dress with green trim using the money they got from selling her old pink tents. Lily felt like a queen.

Strangely enough, she wasn't nervous about meeting the local elites. She had done a good deal of listening during her time in Altver and had learned that the highest-ranked person in Altver was probably a Baron. Everyone else at the ball would be merchants and wealthy craftsmen, with a few landless minor nobles thrown in for good measure. That explained why no one had tried to make her acquaintance. She was simply too important, so locals didn't expect to be noticed by her. That suited Lily fine. She was too busy for social calls. If she had time, she would meet with the local shoemaker and show him some ideas for long-lasting soles and maybe for high heels, too. *And wedges, and platform shoes!* There were too many opportunities to count, especially if Helke could figure out how to make the right buckles and clasps. Lily reflected that she shouldn't overload Helke—he had enough to work on.

By the day of the ball, Lily was as weary as an old horse. She didn't want to talk to anyone, much less dance. Her only wish was to lie down on her bed and sleep for twenty-four hours straight, but she had promised to go.

The Baron sent a carriage for her with his son as escort. Apparently, it wouldn't do for her to arrive alone, and Torius' son was one of the highest-ranking young men in town. Lily didn't object. *Honestly, I'd rather ride in a dark carriage with a little brat than with that priest. I don't like the way he looks at me during services.* The priest obviously hadn't given up his secret hope of moving to Earton to serve as Lily's spiritual advisor.

But she was too busy to pay attention to him, and it wasn't in her nature to waste time on an affair. The one bright spot in her preparations came when she picked up her surgical instruments from the blacksmith. She was gratified to find that everything was as she had ordered. *Treasures, all of them!*

In her reading, Lily had learned that doctors in her new world knew nothing of surgery. In fact, as far as she could tell, metal instruments were never used on the human body. Anatomy was another mystery, and one the church was likely to frown on. So, doctors treated their patients with herbs. If that didn't work, they practiced bloodletting. Amputations were occasionally performed, but no other operations were ever done because they had no way to keep wounds sterile.

That makes sense. Why bother operating on a patient if he's just going to die of infection?

Without the benefit of microscopes, people in Lily's new world knew nothing about bacteria and other microflora. They talked about bad blood and good blood. A doctor's toolkit contained pliers for pulling teeth, a saw for amputating arms and legs, and herbs that caused diarrhea to "cleanse the insides."

Darius interrupted her train of thought when he leaned over and tried to say something gallant. Lily nodded and then turned back to look out the window. She was ready to shine at the ball, but she didn't want to shine too brightly. Her dress buttoned up the back with buttons made by Helke, but it didn't have pockets. She would let the dressmaker's girls be the first to wear pockets. A wide, elegant shawl over her shoulders was just the thing, but she had used a plain straight pin to pin it. It was too soon to show off everything she knew.

There was a small golden box of fragrant herbs tied to the waist of her dress. Helke had recommended that she wear it, and Lily had agreed. Her new fan was tied to her wrist with a silk ribbon. Her hair was arranged in a crown of curls around her head that showed off her earrings. Helke had taken her emerald earrings and reworked them with the new clasps. The Eveer was already planning to expand his business. Lily's dip pen and inkwell were a success, and merchants were lined up around the block to buy them from him. He had hired four more people to try to keep up with demand, but he made sure that every set bore his craftsman's mark.

Lily could tell Helke adored her, and he promised to visit her in Earton every month. Lily reminded him that if he did that, he wouldn't have time to work. They agreed that Helke's nephew would visit her. Since Aldonai had not given the jeweler children of his own, his nephew, Simon Leitz, was his heir.

Lily approved of the nephew. He was intelligent and practical and even looked a little bit like a hobbit—short, with dark, curly hair, and bright eyes. Whenever he talked to the Countess, he was respectful and businesslike. Lily expected he would skim a little off the top for himself, but as long as he did his job, she wouldn't mind.

"My Lady?" Lily turned to the young man with impatience. *What on Earth does he want from me?* "My Lady, I wanted to apologize most sincerely again for the misunderstanding with your guards."

Lily put up a hand. "Your father and I have reached an understanding. You don't have to keep apologizing."

ﶈ ◆ ﶉ

Darius Avermal could have howled in anger.

Look at her just sitting there without a care in the world! Daughter of Maldonaya! Lily was queenly in her indifference to Darius, and that hurt his pride. She looked very different from the sweaty, angry woman who had confronted him in the inn. Back then, she had been a fat lady in a ridiculous pink dress. Now, as he looked at her, he saw a woman who was large, but well-proportioned. He noticed for the first time that she had green eyes and gorgeous golden hair and a calm, clear smile. He knew she was clever since his father had given him a lengthy lecture about the folly of angering an intelligent woman.

It must be that new dress. She doesn't look bad at all.

Darius frowned. The Countess was undoubtedly a servant of Maldonaya. There was no other way to explain the shape-shifting changes in her. He thought about sharing his concerns with the priest, but his father had told him that Father Leider was very fond of the Countess and couldn't stop talking about her mental energy. *And yet she did business with Eveers and hired those godless Virmans to work for her. Surely the priest will want to know about that?*

ଡ଼◆ଔ

Lily was so deep in her own thoughts that she never noticed Darius' hostile demeanor, and she almost missed their arrival. However, she came back to the present moment just in time to elegantly descend from the carriage holding up her skirt with one hand.

If I can get out of an army jeep without jumping or falling in the mud, I can get out of a carriage without looking ridiculous.

She took her escort's arm and walked with him to the front door of the town hall. A man dressed in red bowed, opened the door, and announced, "Her ladyship the Countess Lilian Elizabeth Mariella Earton."

Lily stood elegantly in the doorway and gave Altver's high society a chance to look her over. She studied them, too.

Wonderful!

She counted about three dozen gentlemen and the same number of ladies. Some of the men were obviously there with their wives and children. Lily squinted with pleasure. She was ready to advertise some of her best products. *They don't have television or top models, so I'll just have to do it myself!*

As Lily sailed into the room, she hoped she looked more like a southern belle than a cowbell. Baron Avermal boosted her self-esteem when he hurried to her side and said, "Countess, you look wonderful!" He took her hand and bowed, pronouncing compliments all the time, and then led her off to introduce her to high society.

For the next hour, Lily was much in demand. She felt like a rock star at a small-town diner. Altver's best and brightest were tripping over each other to make her acquaintance. The town's leading craftsmen and merchants had heard rumors about her work with Helke and the local carpenter, and each of them wanted to make sure she remembered his name. Their wives wanted to meet her, as well, so they could look over her hair, jewelry, and dress.

Lily had been careful to wear several new and interesting items. Her fan was the hit of the evening, especially after Lily demonstrated its usefulness as a screen for gossiping or drawing attention to one's low-cut dress or face. The ladies in the room were insanely jealous. Lily was confident that Helke would soon be overwhelmed with orders.

We'll need to have more than one type of fan, all made of different materials. Nobody has ever seen one before, so we have to take advantage of the demand!

The guild had given Helke a five-year monopoly on ladies' fans. He and Lily had already agreed that he would put his mark—a letter H surrounded by flowers—on all the new goods. When he had suggested that they add the Earton crest, Lily was taken aback. She was already worried about what her husband would think about her business interests, and she didn't want to get caught using the family crest. She could just imagine his surprise if he walked into a store and saw his family crest on a fan or a hairbrush. He would naturally make inquiries and discover that, instead of dying along with their stillborn child, his dear wife was alive and well and turning a profit. As far as Lily could tell from her reading, wives (and their property) belonged to their husbands. So, her husband could quite reasonably expect to confiscate any money she made, and if she complained, he would just remind her that Aldonai had willed it.

After much thought, she had told Helke to make her symbol a red cross, the international symbol of doctors and medicine. Lily alone would know that it was a silent testament to her old life and her parents. Her new world did not use the cross as a symbol of anything, so Lily felt free to do so. Helke promised to put her cross on everything he made using her designs. She told him to make the crosses out of carnelian—her favorite stone. He also promised to make sure that her name and her connection with Earton were never mentioned, and she took him at his word. She knew that the jeweler saw her as a valuable source of ideas and that he would take great pains to keep her happy. Thankfully, she wasn't worried about running out of innovations anytime soon.

They had not yet tried to sell any of the vodka she had taught him to distill, but Lily expected it would do well. She suggested that Helke flavor the vodka with berries and herbs and sell it in fancy bottles.

When he asked her for help naming the different flavors, she thought back to the bottles lined up on shelves in her own world. They would call their straight vodka "White Nights." The vodka infused with walnuts would be called "Nutcracker." Berry vodkas would be called "Cranberry" or "Currant."

Helke would make the classic, double-distilled vodka with the help of his second and third cousins, nieces and nephews and other members of his clan. Lily saw that the Eveers stuck together, both at home and in business. *That makes sense. They're outsiders, so they have to watch out for each other.*

৪୬◆ଓୡ

The evening's program was simple: a party, followed by dinner, and then dancing. Lily felt that the party went well, but she wasn't looking forward to the dinner. She didn't like to eat late at night. At the table, she enjoyed a plate of beef stewed in red wine, tossed back a glass of the local sour wine, and even tried a baked sugared apple. It wasn't much, but it was more than she usually ate after six in the evening.

Then came the dancing…

Lily whispered to the Baron that her husband didn't like for her to dance. He nodded in sympathy and made sure that no one pressed her to join the dancing. *I would die of shame if anyone found out I just don't know how!*

Lilian was a good dancer, but Aliya had two left feet.

"My Lady…" The priest had snuck up on her like a bad case of appendicitis.

Lily bowed her head with a smile and asked for the priest's blessing, which she immediately received.

"I see you are not dancing."

"I promised my husband I wouldn't."

At the mention of her husband, the priest winced. Then he recovered and turned on his charm. Lily reflected that Lilian Broklend would have been easy prey for a handsome, smooth-talking priest, but she herself was harder to impress. The dorm at her medical school was no monastery, but Aliya had always been faithful to her fiancé Alex because he was the smartest, kindest and most handsome man she knew. She realized that it was her love that assigned him all those good qualities, but that made no difference. She loved him, end of story. And when she died, her love died, as well. So, Lily gazed at the priest with cool indifference.

"Then can I persuade you to take a walk in the garden, My Lady?"

Lily shook her head. "My reputation…"

"Will not suffer in the least. I am your spiritual advisor."

Interesting! Where did he get that idea from? Lily decided not to contradict him just yet. She would wait and see what he really wanted. "No, I won't take a walk in the garden with you. But if you need to speak with me privately, I noticed a bench in a quiet corner on that end of the room."

She indicated the corner she had in mind. The priest grimaced but realized it was the best he could hope for.

Lily sat down on the bench, and the priest started his speech. "My dear girl…"

Once all of his metaphors, similes, and hyperboles were brushed aside, what was left was the naked fact that the priest had fallen madly in love with the Countess of Earton. As soon as she walked into his church, she was as lovely as a rose blooming in the snow, and he lost himself in the light of her green eyes. He was prepared to risk everything for her.

Lily translated his poetics back into reality. The result was depressing. The priest needed something, and he needed it so badly that he was prepared to sleep with her to get it. The answer was not long in coming. While Lily stared at him, the priest told her that he couldn't bear the thought of never seeing her again and asked for permission to accompany the most remarkable Countess back to Earton. That way, he could see his goddess at least once a week at services.

Lily thought for a moment. Her husband was not presently at Earton, and she had never actually laid eyes on him. Still, she plowed ahead. In a few short words, Lily managed to describe Jess as more bloodthirsty than a man-eating tiger. According to her depiction, he ate men for breakfast if they looked at his wife. Lunch consisted of men who dared pay her compliments, and dinner was the stewed meat of those who were foolish enough not to learn from the ones who were eaten for breakfast and lunch.

The priest listened attentively. When Lily paused, he said, "My child, he wouldn't dare raise his hand against a man of the church."

Lily looked down into her lap, thinking frantically. Finally, she said, "I cannot do anything without my husband's consent. Write to him. If he tells me to invite you, I will be happy to do so."

"I see. But how can you live without the light of true faith?"

Lily blinked. "Have you forgotten? We have our own priest. I go to church regularly and frequently converse with him about the teachings of Aldonai. Father Vopler is a very intelligent man."

Take that!

She reflected that she would have to find out where the church was when she got home.

Father Leider sighed. Lily had left him no options. "Can I at least visit you from time to time?"

"I suppose so if you are careful. Our roads are not passable in the winter, and the forest is full of wolves and brigands. I would hate for something to happen to you."

The priest sighed again. Lily smiled. You're used to having your own way. Not today!

She bid the priest a friendly farewell and went to find Torius. I've had enough of this! I've shown off my fancy new things, and I want to go home! First to the inn, and then back to Earton.

Chapter 10

Hearth and Home

The way home took eleven days. Lily was aggravated, but there was no way around it. Their caravan consisted of several wagons heavily laden with goods and a company of Virmans who had never ridden horses before. Naturally, the pace was slow.

Leif had forced her to take several guards with her. He would have gone with her, but he couldn't send his ship to Earton without its captain. Before they left, he had explained in a few short words what he would do to the guards if anything happened to Lily. As a result, Lily couldn't even pay a visit to the bushes on the side of the trail without three guards standing around her.

Her entourage also included the glass blower's apprentice, the blacksmith's apprentice, and the young herbalist, who demanded that she provide a separate wagon for his bundles, bags, and jars. Then there were the three young dressmakers, who were not happy unless they were riding next to Lily. Marcia asked permission to be Lily's Lady in Waiting when they reached Earton, and nothing Lily told her about the amount of work involved would dissuade her. The Countess needed a Lady in Waiting and Marcia needed to express her gratitude before it overwhelmed her. Lily insisted that she would soon be busy enough.

Around the campfire in the evenings, she taught the girls to line their eyes with kohl, pluck their eyebrows, and arrange a variety of hairstyles. Helke had given her a lot of hair clips to use, so they practiced on each other and were extremely pleased with the results.

Lily noticed that some of the unmarried Virmans were more than a little interested in the three girls. She had no objection, but she had a quiet word with the commander of the guards, a man named Ivar, and told him to keep an eye on his men. If any of them got one of her girls pregnant, he would have to marry her or get the hell out of Earton.

She only had a few cows with her on the trail. The rest would be delivered within a few months by men the Baron would hire. Lily was extremely satisfied with the terms of that agreement. The delay would give her time to fix up barns and coops for the rest of the livestock and poultry before they arrived.

The long road home gave Lily plenty of time to think about how she would organize life at Earton. At the moment, she was leaning toward the idea of a collective farm with one boss—her. She wanted to control how the farming was done and how the crops were distributed. On the other hand, she remembered what happened on Russia's collective farms. Some people were hard workers, but most were idle freeloaders who sat around waiting for handouts. *When you give someone a handout, they come back to ask for seconds. And if you don't give them thirds, things get ugly. I don't want that.*

By the time the caravan reached Earton, Lily was feeling dejected. On top of everything else she had to worry about, her menstrual cycle had begun again, and she was experiencing physical discomfort. *Next items on the list: normal underwear and decent menstrual pads.* When she rode in, Earton was all quiet—and clean. The lawn around the castle was neatly trimmed, and the porch had been freshly washed. Emma came out to greet her wearing a new dress and a white apron.

"My Lady!" she smiled and held out a hand.

Just then, someone came running down the stairs. "My little girl!" Martha refrained from throwing herself on Lily, but her eyes shone like diamonds. Lily couldn't stop herself from giving her old nanny a bear hug.

"Nanny, dear!"

Martha's self-control gave way, and she burst out in tears. After a minute or two, Lily motioned for Marcia to come over and take charge. The girl nodded and led Martha away for a cup of tea so that Lily could look around her domain, which was exactly what she was longing to do.

Rest and put my feet up? I'll do that when I'm in the grave. Lily marched around the castle with four Virmans behind her. The stable was filthy. After a brief but frightening interview with Lily and some knocking around by Ivar and Gel, the three grooms found a new enthusiasm for their work and began shoveling manure at a rapid pace.

Lily checked the stable off her list and headed out to inspect the rest of the estate. What she saw did not make her happy. It was obvious that there was no Comptroller to keep things in hand. Emma was clearly no estate Comptroller, and the peasants simply ignored her when Lily was not around. The castle was also far from clean. When Lily found a small pile of human waste in one of the out-of-the-way corners, she finally lost her temper. Once again those ancient walls echoed with the direct speech of an army officer. The servant girls were upbraided and fined half a month's wages. Lily then instructed them to go clean everything they laid eyes on, starting with her room. Then they were to prepare accommodations for the Virmans and Lily's new hires.

In short order, she gave the village elders the task of bringing in thirty strong women from their villages to clean the castle top to bottom. The Countess of Earton had no intention of living in a pigsty, and she wouldn't let anyone else live that way, either!

You already washed that floor? Then washing it a second time will be even easier!

Those orders given, Lily called Emma into her study and peppered her with questions. The answers revealed that the peasants had taken advantage of her absence. The harvest was suspiciously small, the mill had been used without payment, and few fish had been caught. Emma explained that she had done her best, but she wasn't a Countess or a Comptroller, and had little authority over the village peasants.

Lily understood, but she had no intention of giving up. The ship with the Virmans should be arriving soon. Leif had expected Lily to beat him to Earton by about five days because of the unfamiliar river channel and the heavy load he was carrying. Once Ingrid was there, Lily would turn over management of the estate to her and leave Emma to oversee the castle. The older woman was fully capable of controlling the servants, especially when Lily was at home. Leif would be in charge of guarding the estate and surrounding villages, building fortifications, and organizing watches to keep out brigands and other strangers who would do harm. Ingrid would spend her first weeks in her new home visiting the villages and evaluating what needed to be done. Lily planned to go with her. She would watch and listen and take notes.

At the market, she had purchased several sacks of seed potatoes and a few more sacks for food. As far as she could tell, potatoes were not a staple in the local diet. *I'll fix that! Once they try my fried potatoes, I'll have to set guards to watch the potato fields. Eventually, I'll grow enough to hand out sacks of potatoes for work well done.* Then her thoughts turned to tomatoes and eggplants. She couldn't wait for spring to come so she could start planting. She looked out the window on the Earl's large garden, an area that was worked by all the peasants in turn. Without noticing it, she leaned against the sill. Her body was tired.

More than anything, Lily wanted peace and quiet, a warm, comfortable place where she could work on strengthening mind and body without constant pestering from the servants. *That isn't likely to happen!*

Her to-do list washed over her and pulled at her like a strong tide. She needed to write to Helke and Torius. The estate needed to be put in order. She wanted to start producing her inventions. No, she wouldn't be building factories any time soon—that just wasn't realistic. But she knew she could make glass, even colored glass, and she knew the secret of making glazed clay dishes. She believed that she could learn to do anything if she set her mind to it.

She would make quality dyes out of St. John's wort, onion skins, and other natural ingredients. She had bought fabric for making batik (she couldn't draw worth a damn, but she'd find someone who could). The dressmakers would need to be taught to sew the kind of clothes she wanted (with pockets), and even to play with different styles.

Then she would introduce knitting, crochet, and even lace tatting, which was a completely unknown art form in her new world. To get started, she just needed carved wooden shuttles and a little stuffed cushion. Making knots was easy, and she was confident she could teach anyone the simple hand motions needed to make airy lace. She would teach crochet lace, too. Lily had seen very little lace, and even that was poorly done, so she was eager to organize a workshop where the village girls could make lace of all kinds. Helke, she was sure, would be interested in selling fine lace to the ladies of Altver. *And we'll make beaded lace! They'll stampede Helke's store!*

Lily was an expert at making things with her hands. Growing up in a small army town during Russia's economic shock of the nineties had taught her the lessons of making it yourself, making do, or doing without. She had plenty of business ideas to discuss with Helke. Instead of email, they would use carrier pigeons to exchange messages. Lily had brought back pigeons and a trained boy to look after them. *I wonder how the birds know where to go? I suppose the boy will handle that. All I have to do is provide a place for him to build a coop.*

She wondered what the Earl would say when he found out about her commercial interests.

Stop ruminating! It took all Lily's willpower to turn her thoughts away from the earl. She would worry about how to behave with her husband if he ever showed up. For now, she would write to her father. There were enough memories left for her to feel sure that he loved his daughter. He had certainly tried his best to find a good match for her. And if he didn't visit, that was probably her own fault; Lilian was tiresome and rude and not the best of company, even on a good day.

Her plan was to send her father a letter with a humble gift—a pen and inkwell set made of pure gold and encrusted with precious stones. Helke was a master jeweler, and Lily was confident that her father would be pleased. He might even come to see her.

Good Lord, how will I talk to him if he does come? Just to be on the safe side, Lily would search through all her old letters. She couldn't believe that father and daughter hadn't met or even written since her marriage. *I'll dig through all my papers and see what I can find. If there isn't anything, I'll just have to cross that bridge when I come to it.*

Her most immediate problem was the Earton Estate. Before the Virmans arrived, she wanted to meet with the priest and tame him so that he would keep his nose out of her affairs. *I want him to know he can do as he likes, as long as he stays on my good side. Otherwise, I'll hand him his head on a gold plate.*

She believed that people knew where their interests lay and the only thing that prevented them from putting more butter on their bread was laziness. *Thank goodness I don't have that problem. So, in order: Earton, my old letters, the priest, and my manufacturing projects. I'll deal with the Earl if and when he makes an appearance.*

℣◆∞

She heard voices in the courtyard and frowned. *Who could that be?*

She found out five minutes later when Mary burst into the room as if a dragon was after her.

"My Lady! She's here! Lady Miranda!"

Lily stared at her. "Who?"

"Lady Miranda, your stepdaughter!"

Wonderful. Her list of problems got longer.

"Is she alone?"

"No, My Lady. She is with her entourage."

Lily let out a sigh. No Earl. That was good. *I can handle a child, can't I?*

"Fine. Get them settled in their usual rooms. Dinner is in two hours. I want Lady Miranda to be there."

Lilian's memory churned up some information, and Lily remembered that her husband had a daughter from a previous marriage. She had no idea how old the girl was or anything else about her. *I can handle this, too.*

℣◆∞

"How are you?"

Jess looked up at Richard, who was glowing with pleasure from the sea voyage. "Wonderful. Couldn't be better."

279

"You don't look it. What's wrong?"

"How long is this trip going to take?"

"Well, we have to spend the winter with Gardwig, no way around it. In the spring, when the roads dry out, we leave for Ivernea. If we go by sea, we can leave a little sooner. I haven't decided yet."

"We could take the Limmayer, couldn't we?"

"I suppose. We would have to sail through Avesterra, but there's nothing wrong with that. Imogene was my mother, after all."

"Do you ever think about her?"

"No. She wasn't a good woman. She yelled a lot. And fought with father. You know, if anything, I remember Jessie taking care of me more. I loved her."

"Imogene was probably unhappy."

"That's no reason to make other people unhappy."

"I'm sure she didn't mean to."

"What made you think about Imogene?"

"I don't know."

Rick studied his cousin for a moment. "Tell me what's going on. Is something not right with Adele?"

"No. I'm very happy with her, but I'm married. I can't give her anything. I'm not the King, so being my mistress isn't exactly an honorable title."

"You knew how it worked when you got married."

"I didn't know how hard it would be to spend my life tied to a woman I couldn't love."

"I hate to hear that, but you know that divorces are only allowed in extreme cases."

"Or if she dies."

"Don't even think of helping her along. August is a tough old bird. If anything happens to his little girl, he'll make you answer for it."

"I can't believe you would think that about me. She can live as long as she wants. I just…"

"Don't bother. I understand. Want a drink?"

Jess looked at the pitcher of wine. He reached for it, but then he pulled his hand back and shook his head.

"No. I don't want to drown my problems in wine. I'll go stand on the deck for a while."

"I'll go with you. There's a nice sunset."

The two men looked into each other's eyes. One of them had already been pulled into a marriage of convenience; the other was facing the same fate. Neither of them liked it.

ೞ◆ೋ

Anna Wellster was almost ready to receive her eagerly awaited guests. She washed her face and hair and took an herbal bath, carefully following the instructions the witch had given her.

She had only seen her father a few times since the conversation that had changed her life. Whenever he encountered her, he looked her over, nodded in approval and sent her on her way. There hadn't been any balls of late. The Lion of Wellster was tightfisted with his treasury; winter was coming, and Richard of Ativerna was coming to Wellster with a large entourage.

Anna studied her dark hair, olive skin, and shining eyes in the mirror. She was beautiful, very beautiful. She knew she could captivate any man. *But can I turn Richard's head?* She had heard that Richard was good looking and that he had had more than his share of successes with women. *What if I don't measure up?*

Anna had no burning desire to get married, but every now and then, she caught the Jester watching her, and that reminded her that things could go badly with her if she didn't manage to do what he wanted. She rarely thought about the husband who had been taken from her, and when she did think of him, it was with annoyance. He was dead, but she was still alive and in all kinds of trouble because of that idiot.

Anna had conveniently forgotten that she was the one who seduced Lons, along with several other awkward things, like the fact that she had loved him passionately. None of that mattered to her anymore. All that mattered was Richard. She had to enchant him.

She would do her best.

ॐ ◆ ૪

Altres Lort, personal jester to Gardwig II and his boyhood friend, sat listening to reports from his men. On the whole, he was pleased. Richard was approaching the borders of Wellster. The kingdom was quiet, and Altres could easily ensure his safety. Only the report by Gardwig's physician disturbed him. According to the healer, his brother had no more than ten years left to live. His blood was full of bile, and he had ulcers on his legs that wouldn't heal.

Altres was not particularly interested in the medical details. What worried him was who would take the throne if the King suddenly died. His son was still too young to be of use. *Gardwig had been crowned at fifteen and had managed to hang on to his throne, but at what price?*

Altres would never tell how he had counseled the young Lion of Wellster in those early months. The country was coming apart at the seams, and political opponents made at least six attempts on Gard's life in his first two months as King. It was a miracle that he survived.

What would happen if a small boy was made King?

Gardwig had long ago dealt with the men who had gone against him, but his son would still need a strong mother in order to hold on to power. Mila was kind, but had led a sheltered life and would need protecting if Gard was gone. She still hid in her room when Gardwig carried out executions. There was no way she could act as regent.

Altres wanted to have a candidate ready. He couldn't do it himself. Too many of the court nobles disliked him. His best chance was to sign a mutual assistance treaty with Edward of Ativerna. The boy king would then have the support of a neighboring kingdom. That would help.

He didn't think Richard would attempt to gain the throne of Wellster for himself. Ativerna was big enough for him and his two sisters.

A marriage between Ativerna and Wellster would give Altres stability, so he needed Anna for the moment. Otherwise, he would have tripped her in a dark forest weeks ago. He didn't like whores, especially when they held power.

ଯ ◆ ଓ

Edward VIII was in a foul mood. Jess' sister Amalia was insistent that she needed to see him. Edward had always allowed Amalia, Jess, and Jyce to see him at a moment's notice. He adored Amalia. She was an exact copy of Jessie, even if she did have a few features that resembled her father's. Her stubborn chin and full lips were Jessie's, while her eyebrows and the way she held her head reminded Edward of himself as a boy. Her eyes, though—those were definitely her mother's, bright and blue...

"What is the matter, dear?"

"Uncle Edward!"

"Yes?" He stood up from his desk and embraced her. Then he sat her down opposite him. "Tell me what happened, my dear. I thought you and Pete were already at your country house. The city is no place for a woman expecting a child."

"That was our plan, but..."

"But what?"

"Uncle, I'm afraid Jess is in serious trouble."

"Is that so?" Edward was surprised. He loved his eldest son and cared deeply about all his affairs.

"My doctor is the same one Jess sent to Earton when he found out Lilian was with child."

"And?"

"She had a miscarriage."

Edward sighed. *One more blow for Jess.* "Is she alive?"

Amalia nodded. "Yes, but she is behaving very strangely."

"How do you mean?"

"Craybey—that's the doctor—says that she literally threw him out of the castle."

"But whatever for?"

"After she recovered, she asked Craybey how he had treated her. When he told her, she told him to leave and never let her see him again."

"What's surprising about that?"

"But Uncle…"

"I believe Lilian has always been strange."

"True. And I've only seen her twice."

"I have seen her no more than you have. But I believe that such behavior is quite normal for her. Lilian has always been mentally unbalanced."

"Perhaps. But Craybey says that she also fired the estate Comptroller for stealing from her."

Edward frowned. That was more serious, but he hesitated to worry. *So what if she fired the* Comptroller? "I don't believe she's in any danger of perishing without an estate Comptroller. It's too late to travel to Earton this winter. In the spring, I will ask August to visit her."

"That's good. What if she's lost her mind?"

"Then Jess will have a hard time of it." Edward sighed. Insanity was not considered grounds for divorce. If a man's wife was insane, he was expected to bear it as a punishment from Aldonai. He knew that Jess was unlikely to see it that way.

"I will send someone in the spring. Now, I want you to pack your bags and go to your country house. This is no time for you to be concerned about others' problems."

"Yes, Uncle." Amalia kissed him on the cheek and went out.

Edward shrugged his shoulders and turned to his desk. If Lilian really was insane, he would have to do something. I hesitate to send a ship for what could turn out to be nothing. I could send runners, but they will not return for many weeks. Perhaps I should send someone, just in case. Then another thought came to the King. It was an ugly thought, but he examined it closely. He was the King, and he was accustomed to facing unpleasant tasks.

If something was truly wrong with Lilian Earton, he would not have her killed, but he could make sure she was cut off from all assistance. Stuck in the middle of nowhere without supplies, she would surely die. It would be nobody's fault, and Jess would be free.

His Majesty only wanted his son to be happy.

The End

Read the whole series…

The ball winds tighter, pulling in threads from around the land…

A ship full of Virmans is headed to Earton, and so is a slave trader's ship.

Ali Akhmet remembers Lily as the woman who saved his life, and Father Leider remembers her as the woman who spurned his advances.

Baron Torius Avermal counts his profits, while his son dreams of seeing Lilian Earton dead in the ground.

Intrigue simmers quietly at the courts of the kings…

Adelaide dreams of a wealthy husband, and her cousin dreams of the same thing. Those dreams do not bode well for Lilian.

Alicia Earton has plans of her own, while her "daughter" Amalia is concerned for her brother, the Earl of Earton.

Meanwhile, Earton is humming with activity, both seen and unseen, but that makes life no less dangerous…

And that is just the beginning.

Book Recommendations

Thank you for reading First Lessons.

If you enjoyed this book then please like my page for Lina J Potter. Also you can get a 20% sample of our books on the LitHunters website.

I would like to draw your attention to some other great works from LitHunters.

The gripping and head-turning love tale of a man and a woman that sign a perilous contract for two months and three days

« Presented as the Russian Fifty Shades in Russia. In reality, more than the very black-and-white moral universe of Fifty Shades trilogy. » – Julie A. Cassiday, language and literature specialist at Williams College (USA)

Two Months and Three Days by Tatiana Vedenska is available for order now.

An ordinary young boy finds himself in a life and death struggle as he must adapt to his new environment. In order to survive after accidentally falling through a portal to another world, Andy must undergo an ancient ritual to become a Dragon. Read this exciting adventure now by the best-selling author Alex Sapegin.

[i] A tennight is ten days, and a month is forty days. A year has nine months and three extra days, the length of which depends on the phase of the moon. New Year's is celebrated during those three days.

[ii] Radiant Ones are similar to angels in the local religion.

[iii] Edematous fever was an old name for mumps.

[iv] Wool sock—local slang for an old maid

[v] A local variation of chess.

[vi] Green is the color of mourning in Ativerna. Pastors also wear green to remind people that life is short.

[vii] Something similar happened at the Vatican in the Middle Ages, when a papal conclave was asked to decide whether women were humans or animals

[viii] There were several types of aristocratic titles. Hereditary titles, such as duke, count or baron, added the name of the family's estate to the person's name. For example: Lilian Earton, Amadeo Troquer. Lons Avels was a chevalier. This title came with no estate, but it was hereditary. If he had managed to acquire an estate, he would have taken the name of the estate. Without an estate, he used his parents' last name. Non-hereditary titles were assigned for feats of bravery and service to the king, or they could be purchased. If three generations of a family receive a non-hereditary title, it became hereditary and the family could own land. Otherwise, this avenue was shut off to them. Without a title, no one was allowed to own an estate.

[ix] A shield facing outward signaled that the boat was ready for battle, while a shield facing inward signified peace, negotiation and trade. Virmans often painted their signal shields red, the color of blood and battle, or black, the color of earth and trade.

[x] The church system ranked its servants as follows: Father, Father Superior, and Aldon. There were only 12 Aldons, and they all took a vow of celibacy. The Aldons were the leaders of the church, like the College of Cardinals without the pope.

47342303R00174

Made in the USA
Columbia, SC
01 January 2019